CAPITOL VENTURE

★ ★ ★ ★

BARBARA MIKULSKI AND MARYLOUISE OATES

A SIGNET BOOK

SIGNET
Published by New American Library, a division of
Penguin Putnam Inc., 375 Hudson Street,
New York, New York 10014, U.S.A.
Penguin Books Ltd, 27 Wrights Lane,
London W8 5TZ, England
Penguin Books Australia Ltd,
Ringwood, Victoria, Australia
Penguin Books Canada Ltd, 10 Alcorn Avenue,
Toronto, Ontario, Canada M4V 3B2
Penguin Books (N.Z.) Ltd, 182–190 Wairau Road,
Auckland 10, New Zealand

Penguin Books Ltd, Registered Offices:
Harmondsworth, Middlesex, England

Published by Signet, an imprint of New American Library, a division of
Penguin Putnam Inc.
Previously published in a Dutton edition.

First Signet Printing, September 1999
10 9 8 7 6 5 4 3 2 1

 REGISTERED TRADEMARK—MARCA REGISTRADA

Printed in the United States of America

PUBLISHER'S NOTE
This is a work of fiction. Names, characters, places, and incidents either are
the product of the author's imagination or are used fictitiously, and any
resemblance to actual persons, living or dead, events, or locales is entirely
coincidental.

BOOKS ARE AVAILABLE AT QUANTITY DISCOUNTS WHEN USED TO
PROMOTE PRODUCTS OR SERVICES. FOR INFORMATION PLEASE
WRITE TO PREMIUM MARKETING DIVISION, PENGUIN PUTNAM INC.,
375 HUDSON STREET, NEW YORK, NEW YORK 10014.

HARRISBURG—Sen. Eleanor Gorzack was nominated Tuesday for the U.S. Senate at the party's state convention held here.

The nomination ends weeks of backroom bickering, as Governor Hartung—faced both with Gorzack's name recognition and a shortened campaign season—finally bowed out.

A newcomer to politics, Gorzack had been appointed by the governor to fill the Senate vacancy after the death of Sen. Michael Gannon. In her first months in office, Gorzack was instrumental in returning to American soil the remains of what are now numbered at more than three dozen American MIAs, including those of her late husband, Navy pilot Jack Gorzack.

She went, as one insider put it, from "the candidate who couldn't win to the candidate to beat to the only candidate in town. At least in our party."

But Hartung's indecision about entering the race has left Gorzack severely handicapped by the calendar, with less than five months remaining before the November special election. The race promises to be high profile and hotly contested. Gorzack's opponent—criminal justice expert Henry "Hank" Dugdale, the author of "Imprisoning America"—is seen as being far ahead in organization and fund-raising.

Promising to run what she called "a fair campaign, based on the issues and needs of Pennsylvania," Gorzack said she would be hiring her campaign staff in the next week.

CHAPTER I

I was making risotto—with porcini mushrooms and a little fontina cheese—when the President of the United States called me on the phone.

I knew what the call was about.

For more than forty-eight hours, heavy rains had clobbered northeastern Pennsylvania, a disastrous end to what morning-show weathermen had been saying was the hottest Memorial Day weekend in a century. The battering rain had pushed already swollen rivers and lakes to flood stage, and old-timers were recalling Hurricane Agnes and the 1972 deluge.

My office had been on alert since the first flood report early that morning. The phones had never stopped—whether it was our calls to state officials, to the White House, to the Federal Emergency Management Administration, or calls from mayors and county officials asking for emergency assistance.

So I was half expecting the President's call. But don't get me wrong. I *am* a U.S. senator, but it's not like when I'm hanging around my kitchen and the phone rings I wonder if it's the commander in chief on the line—or my mother.

"Okay, Senator," the President announced. He always takes me off guard. Everything he says sounds like a proclamation, so he's exactly the same on the phone as he is on television. "Okay. We're going to declare a big chunk of your state—hold on, let me get a number . . ." I could hear him quizzing somebody, "Okay. We're going to declare nine counties in northeastern Pennsylvania a federal disaster area. And, I might add, we're going to throw in a slice of southern New York State and the upper third of New Jersey. Unless Jersey floats out to sea with all this rain. Wonder how many electoral votes that would cost me?"

I figured out that the last sentence was a joke. Sometimes with the President it wasn't so easy making that joke/no joke classification.

"My staff tells me that this thing is finally moving east, and we'll be able to head up tomorrow morning. We'll leave Andrews about eight a.m. if the weather holds. Do several flyovers, then land in Jericho. Probably work best if I just bombed the flooded areas with checks. Threw the federal dollars out the plane's windows. Right?"

"Yes," I answered. "I guess that's certainly the idea. Bomb the damage. Bring the bacon home." He'd led me into a labyrinth of mixed metaphors. But the good thing about the President, I had discovered, was that it didn't matter much what you said. His definition of conversation was him talking, you listening and, of course, agreeing. I did even better with him in person because I had such a clear, direct, and forceful nod.

"Anything else? No. Good. See you in the a.m."

I hung up, nodded at my sadly crusting risotto, suddenly as outmoded as the last decade's weapons system.

"Yes. Yes. Yes," I shouted as I dialed a private number on Capitol Hill. Milton Gant, my administrative assistant, had said he was heading home as I left the office, but we both knew it was a lie.

"Yes, Senator." Milton's cranky rasp was as predictable as the fact that he was still there.

"The President called. Hold on while I stick my risotto pan in the sink."

"What? Senator! What are you talking about? The *Toto Plan*? What Toto Plan? Is this like the doggy in *The Wizard of Oz*? So what's up? After the rain, then the tornado?"

Milton was obviously operating under a lot of strain himself. Our recently discovered friendship, which had replaced our short-term employee–employer animosity, was fragile enough to get bent under the heavy touch of his sense of humor.

"No. No Toto. This isn't Kansas, Milton. *Risotto pan.*

I was cooking when the President called. We're going to Pennsylvania tomorrow. We're leaving early in the a.m.—that's what he said—to tour the flood sites and promise federal help."

"How much time is he spending with us, compared with New York or New Jersey?"

"I don't know. Is that important?"

"Senator, you're not running for election in any state except Pennsylvania, so it doesn't do you any good to be handing out goodies somewhere in Jersey. Anyway, I'll call over to the White House, I'll pull things together, and I'll be by your apartment sometime around, ah, four a.m., 'cause they'll probably send a car to pick you up around six."

"Milton, it's almost midnight! What about some sleep?"

"Don't worry about me, Senator. I'll be fine."

He hung up before I could tell him the sleep I was worrying about was my own. Anyway, in less than twenty-four hours, a good night's sleep would be the least of my worries.

I was going on *Air Force One*—one of the two sleek customized 747s that are on presidential service. I'd been on board once before, with the vice president, when he came to bring me and the remains of sixteen MIAs back from Vietnam. I tried not to think about that other trip, now only a few months in the past, and instead tried to focus on the day ahead.

My years in public health and in public service had

taken me from one end of Pennsylvania to the other—from the urban denseness of Philadelphia where I grew up, to the lush farms around Gettysburg, to the hills of western Pennsylvania and the frosty north-western tip that edged Lake Erie.

But I had spent only occasional days in the Pocono Mountain areas, which was, the ads in area magazines reminded, America's most romantic honeymoon des-tination, with dozens of hotels where heart-shaped hot tubs and three-day lovers' specials were always on tap.

I was worried about the economic storm that would hit this tourist-dependent area, and was glad that I'd have the chance to talk to the Member who repre-sented Jericho County, Congressman Bob Bercolini, who was right behind me crossing the tarmac. We went through the established procedure—we had checked in at the gate to the base, we were being checked in at the stairs, and we would check in again as we went inside the plane. Bercolini seemed frazzled and no wonder.

Jericho County was number one on the storm's Top Ten Hit List. Under normal conditions, that part of the state would be just the place to be for a nice summer outing. Jericho, its biggest city, was surrounded by pretty countryside, dotted with resort lakes edged with summer homes, all perched on the edge of the Poconos, just about two hours' drive north of Philadel-phia.

The rain had added to an already turbulent atmo-sphere in Jericho, where the presence of the so-called

Keystone Militia had created a predicament if not major problems. *New York Lifestyle* magazine, in a March article, had profiled and interviewed several members of the Keystone Militia. There were shadowed photographs and anonymous quotes, since the alleged militia members insisted they could be the target of government reprisals.

I had read the story just last week. My spring had been taken up with my trip to Vietnam, my discovery of Jack's grave, and my part in the identification and capture of the criminal who murdered a Vietnam veteran and a young member of my staff. There were piles of catch-up reading to do, as I got back to the more standard business of serving in the United States Senate, and, I had to admit, I was working my way through the hefty backlog of Pennsylvania-related articles Milton had gathered.

The article on the Keystone Militia had held my attention—and, from the number of follow-up pieces in newspapers in the state, I wasn't alone in my fascination. It was like a cloak-and-dagger thriller, the more so because some of the quotes as well as the descriptions of gun caches and secret bomb schools seemed far-fetched, perfect examples of the Elvis-had-an-alien-baby school of journalism. Whether it was true or not, the phone calls I had personally answered the past two days, as part of my office's storm response, showed me that people in the Jericho area seemed more upset about the militia than about the deluge. Or at least about the magazine's description of the militia.

And this was even with the Jericho area's summer camps, bed-and-breakfasts, inns, restaurants, and summer rentals being hit hard by the bad storm.

"Nobody wants to spend their vacation getting shot at with an AK47. So tourism has fallen off, and business is hurting," complained Bercolini, who had decided that God's punishing weather was a weak second to the misery of magazine journalism.

I was annoyed. I had counted on having a chance to talk to him about his reports on the flooding in his district—as well as a couple of minutes to catch my breath before the real work of the day began.

But Bercolini's reputation in the House as relentless was not undeserved. He stayed hard on my trail as we passed the plane's Presidential Sitting Room. It was casual, comfy, like someone's southwestern-style family room—pale colors on the cushioned chairs, a TV, a pile of books and magazines.

"So I just took this issue on, face-to-face. Mano-a-mano, if you see what I mean, Norie."

I *knew* what he meant. It was hard to ignore any issue Bercolini took on, mano-a-mano. According to press accounts, he'd stirred up quite a storm with a double-barrel barrage: first, at a news conference where he condemned all paramilitary groups, then following up with an attack on the actual veracity of the magazine article. Bercolini practically laughed in the Keystone Militia's face, questioning the group's actual membership, insisting that a few "crazies" had pulled the journalistic wool over the eyes of *New York Lifestyle*:

"It's not like this so-called militia is a real organization. It's a couple of social misfits, roaming the woods."

"So now some conservative types are taking me on. Pundits, they call themselves. Bandits is more like it," he kept on, rapid-fire pace, as we headed toward the back of the plane, past the onboard Oval Office, with its horseshoe desk and its calming beige tones, past the conference room. We settled ourselves in the VIP workroom, at seats around one of the three tables. All this, and no sign that Bercolini was coming to the end of his monologue.

"I'm for the First Amendment—for free speech. I'm for the Second Amendment—the right to bear arms. But I'm not for a couple of thugs in khaki shirts running around the woods and pretending to be George Washington. So these right-wing groups are questioning my constitutional commitment. They're all creeps."

"People always want to read the Constitution the way it backs up their particular ideology," I responded. I was always happy to discuss matters of theoretical importance, since they usually had no importance at all. But my mind was on the flood areas and, anyway, Bercolini was singing to the choir. I hated hate groups, on both ends of the political spectrum.

"Some coffee, Senator? Or would you like to walk around a bit before takeoff?" One of the stewards was standing over us. The left side of the plane, to the rear of where we sat, was lined with support areas—a very large galley, a communications room, office support like faxes and printers. The plane was like a Pentagon with wings. I knew that upstairs, in the small second floor, there was a "rest area" for the President, where he could shower and catch a nap.

I wanted to take the tour, but I nodded "yes" to the coffee. Bercolini waved the steward away, making sure nothing would get in the way of his rap.

"But the Keystone is not all that I wanted to talk to you about, Senator. What I'm working on right now is somewhat related—but would really be important to you, considering your time in government."

"Okay," I managed. Did Bercolini remember that we were going to his district to inspect flood areas? If he thought an article would discourage tourists, didn't he realize that half the happy camping grounds were currently underwater? And I really didn't like the idea that he was pressuring me by pointing to my newly appointed spot, helping to run the government of the United States.

"In my district, we've got a lot of very specific problems," Bercolini said, almost echoing my thoughts. "Problems of crime. Of murder, I think. Not just people corrupting the Constitution, but people polluting the entire system. And it's very hard to get a grip on. That's what I've been working on."

"With the militia? Didn't you just say they were blown up out of proportion?"

"Well, yes and no. Not really. Stay in Jericho tonight. Let me show you around tomorrow. Let me lay out what I think's been happening. For years. It's murder, really Norie. And you—with your experience—you really need to plug into this."

He got no further in telling me why I needed to follow his lead. One of the White House aides signaled to me, then pointed toward the front of the plane.

"The President would like you and Senator Smith to join him for the flight up," the aide explained, motioning more vigorously as Bercolini grabbed my arm.

"The President . . ."

"Sure. Just let me find you when he peels off later this morning. We'll do the flood stuff and I'll be able to fill you in. And, hey, it won't be so bad for your campaign, either. This is really hot stuff."

Something Bercolini said struck him as funny, and I could hear him chuckling as I made my way to that southwestern sitting room in the sky.

The flight from Andrews to northeastern Pennsylvania was less than an hour. The conversation, until we got over the flooded area, was basically the President telling stories—about *Air Force One* and other presidents.

"Coming back from Texas late one night, Lyndon Johnson rang for the steward and told him he wanted a particular brand of soft drink. The steward checked the galley. No such drink was on board. So the steward woke the President's right-hand man. 'Just tell him

12

the truth, son. You messed up. There's none of what he wants. You're sorry, but the cupboard's bare.'

"Which the young steward did. LBJ told him to stand by, then proceeded, with the help of the White House switchboard, to call some high-up exec at the soft-drink company—and tell him that he was sorry that his company had gone out of business. 'What? You're still making that drink? Guess you just don't sell it to the government.' Nobody could sound as surprised as LBJ. The steward was probably trying to figure out how to throw himself out the plane's window. 'What? You do make that drink! Guess you don't sell it to the air force.' Pause. 'You do. And in Texas, too. Okay. Thank you and good night.'

"Now who was more crazed at that time—the steward or the soft-drink exec, we don't know. But the next time that LBJ's plane took off, it practically waddled down the runway, it was so filled with that soft drink."

We laughed, but the President held up his hand.

"That's not the end of it. Truth be told, Lyndon Johnson never asked for that particular soft drink again."

CHAPTER 2

The President, Senator Smith, and I—all stationed at separate windows in the flying Oval Office—looked down at the flood-damaged landscape, Smith and I taking turns at figuring out the geography, pointing out towns and landmarks. Aides stood by with maps and graphs, ready to answer any of our questions. But none of us talked much as, high and dry in the plane, we crossed several of the most water-soaked areas.

We landed at the Northeast Regional Airport, and, as we taxied to the hangar, Senator Smith mumbled something about "Now we're going to really see a national disaster. Hold on to your hat."

Naive me—I thought his remark had something to do with the flood. One minute off the plane, though, and I got it: He'd been telling me that no natural disaster was big enough to achieve every political agenda.

Our "small" D.C. official delegation grew like inflation. On board, our party included honchos from FEMA, White House staffers, and the Members from the flooded area. On the ground, our ranks swelled with the addition of any elected official who'd ever heard of rain. Now at invasion-force strength, we mounted our various four-wheel-drives and headed into Jericho City.

The rain clouds were gone, and the morning summer sun beat directly down. Unseasonable rain followed by unseasonable heat. The driver kept the air conditioner going full blast, but we rolled our windows down to get a better look. From what I could see, the town had been ready for a big, booming summer season. The drugstore, across the street from the school, had an enormous display of suntan lotions, along with a side window devoted to various mosquito repellents. One boarded-up window kept us from seeing what the sign above called "Susanna Ming's Swimming Sensations."

The motorcade pulled around the war memorial that sat in the center of the town's usual busiest intersection. We all got out, and stood there—the humidity, the crowd, the steam rising from the mammoth puddles all swirled together in front of me. Debris leaked out into the streets. Overturned trash cans and backed-up sewers left a sodden stench that I knew would only get worse in the heat of the hours ahead. The confusion that tragedy brings could have slowed our progress to a crawl—but not the President.

"Where are we going to hold the news conference?" he shouted over one shoulder as he plowed down what had been Jericho City's main shopping street. One aide pointed vaguely toward a large brick building looming ahead, which had to be a school.

"Get me someone to brief me and the senators. And I want somebody who's been out in the countryside. And where's Joe Henry?"

As if he had invoked a magic charm, Joe Henry—the President's right-, and some said left-hand man— appeared. With him was a large fellow in a bright yellow slicker.

"Okay," the President said, with no other introduction. "Tell me what I need to know."

I stood close by, Bercolini at my side. The Secret Service closed ranks to hold back the reporters, motioning for several of the crews to put down their boom mikes. Nobody was going to eavesdrop.

"The water supply looks okay, once the drains get cleaned out and the streets drain. But, outside of town, the roads are really bad. It will take at least two weeks to simply clean up the lumber. Cut up the trees. Get the debris carted away."

The President motioned the nameless Yellow Slicker to go on.

"Some local types want to say that two weeks will do it all. That it's important for summer business, for the season, to tell people that everything will be okay before the Fourth." The slickered man shook his head, shamed at the apparent lie.

"I don't want to know PR. I want to know real numbers," the President said.

"Two weeks *to start*. And, if the rain holds off, everything can be up and running—phone lines, electrical power, roads cleared, ponds and lakes skimmed—sometime by mid-July. If it gets hot and stays hot and stays sunny, heck, cut off a couple of days."

"Do you know what you are talking about?" the President asked as if the man was not accompanied by Joe Henry but was just some unknown citizen wandering around a disaster site.

"Sir, I am a vice president of NYNEX. I started with the army in Vietnam. I have laid cables and dug trenches and cleaned up after air attacks and after hurricanes. I know what it takes to get rid of a mess. That's why General Forester asked me to come up here and look over everything, not just the phone lines."

"And everyone appreciates it, Mister . . . ?"

"McDougal, sir. Mike McDougal. Maybe the Army Corps of Engineers or FEMA or some other government type or"—McDougal motioned to the school in front of us—"maybe some people who have to answer to a voting booth may tell you otherwise."

"I get the picture, Mike. Would you mind sticking with me as I prowl around?" The President had hold of McDougal's elbow, his new best friend. Bercolini and I followed them down the street. I was wearing

L. L. Bean hiking boots I had borrowed from Nancy Jackson, my personal assistant, and they were a wee bit big. But it was either keep up with the moving-at-a-trot President—or be trampled by the hordes of public officials and press types who were coming up fast behind us.

A makeshift podium had been set up on the broad steps of the school building. The President, with Senator Smith and myself acting like nodding bookends, served up what Milton had accurately described as "standard fare in emergency situations." FEMA people were introduced, and the President made a couple of remarks—mostly telling people in that part of the state that he knew just how hard it was on them. The press corps—the Washington contingent swelled by the dozens of locals—was in a feeding frenzy about how much help, how soon, but, most important, how. The President—straight from his sixty-second briefing by the previously unknown McDougal from NYNEX—sounded as if he'd spent the past several days just learning about the area, its particular economy, and the damage the flood would do.

"Experts tell me that a major part of this job can be completed in two or perhaps three weeks," the President outlined, in a slow, careful voice. "But—and here is my cautionary note—this part of the country is mountainous, with lakes and streams appearing around every bend in the road. We've got to get those roads cleared before we can be absolutely sure how long a finished job will take."

"And when might *that* be?" The question came from the rear of the auditorium. The voice sounded familiar, and I guessed it was one of the better-known TV reporters.

"That *might* be in three or four or five weeks. I don't want to give people false hope, especially since so many people hereabout depend on vacationers to make their living. But I am sure"—the President paused, giving extra weight to the words that followed—"very sure that everything will be in good operating order by the start of the second half of the season."

He didn't miss a trick. Back on *Air Force One*, Senator Smith had casually mentioned that people in Pennsylvania frequently rented vacation homes for "half a season," but that measurement varied from person to person. One place could be leased from Memorial Day to mid-July, with another the first half could run from mid-June until the end of July. The President had taken it all in and allowed himself a little leeway.

The questioner tried to get in a follow-up, but the President cut him off with a quick "thank you."

I remember thinking that if you had to be the President, it was much better if you were good at the job.

"There have been reports of looting here in the emergency area," the reporter with the familiar voice boomed into a handheld microphone. "Looting. And an increasing lack of personal safety."

The President had left us behind.

The Senators from New York and New Jersey had stayed on the plane and would accompany the President in his flyovers, ending up at a news conference in Newark. Senator Smith and I, each separate political suns surrounded by officials from our respective parties, had been doing informal Q&A sessions with the local press when the giant voice boomed out. Standing on the far edge of the steps, it was the reporter with the familiar voice and he was shouting into a hand-held microphone. Only it was no reporter. It was Hank Dugdale, my Senate opponent.

Dugdale certainly gave the impression he was in charge. His olive drab safari shirt came complete with general-sized epaulets. He was wearing a blue baseball cap with gold letters spelling out "FEMA." Dugdale looked more official than the president.

"Local police officials I have spoken to complain that once again they are hampered by a lack of sophisticated equipment. Priorities must be established that place personal safety first." He spoke slowly, carefully, like a high school valedictorian. "The federal government cannot merely stick a Band-aid over the open wounds of society. We must attack these problems where they start. And we must return to the values that made this country great."

I couldn't figure out the exact connection between the flood, police technology, and basic American values. As I was trying to make that logic hyperwarp, some fifty demonstrators appeared, all carrying signs announcing that the "Values Coalition Supports Hank Dugdale."

Bercolini was still at my side and still carping: "People around here can't find a pencil because of the flood and Dugdale's supporters show up with printed signs. Unbelievable. And how did he get a hat? FEMA didn't give us hats. My district has problems of supplies and sanitation, and Dugdale wants to talk about 'values.' I'll give him values. Let me take him on."

This time it was me grabbing at Bercolini's sleeve. The dozen or so local TV crews had quickly moved over to Dugdale's part of the front steps.

Dugdale was made for television. He looked like all those former romantic leads who wind up playing detectives on movies-of-the-week. Tall, he had blown-dry, steel gray hair. A deep streak of black shot back from his forehead. I swore he dyed it to look even more dramatic.

He didn't have to do much to doctor his already good looks. As infatuated profile writers keep insisting, Dugdale was a "youthful sixty." He was both dapper and macho, a persona he'd perfected over the past few years, ever since he left his job as director of state corrections. First, he wrote *Imprisoning America*, then quickly turned his book-tour TV appearances into an almost regular job. I thought he'd logged in more hours in the past year than David Letterman, since not a crime, not a trial went by without Dugdale having a chance to "expert" himself.

"Don't take him on. We'll just wind up in a shouting

match," I said, fearful that we'd come out the losers on the five o'clock news. But a face-off was apparently just what Dugdale wanted.

"Mrs. Gorzack, who has been appointed to represent you in the Senate, is right over there." He pointed his finger at me like it was a gun and I was target practice. "Ask her these questions. Put her on notice. See what she hasn't done for you."

The crowd surged toward me, chanting a slogan: "We want values for our votes."

"This is not pretty," I said to Bercolini as the steps below us quickly filled up with placards and people. The humidity had risen along with the sun, and the glare of the noon sunlight put a strange gloss on the faces in the crowd. In my years in state government, in my time heading up the state's public health department, I'd been picketed, protested, roasted, and blocked.

I knew the look of political anger. But I had never before seen the faces of dissent freshly minted by a demagogue, anger directed not at my policies or my politics but at my person.

"You know, this is my district and my hometown," Bercolini shouted into my ear. "I know my people. Even the ones who don't like me. And I don't know any of these jokers." He stepped down to meet the crowd. "Are you from here? From Jericho? What town are you from? What county?"

The crowd would have none of him. I watched Bercolini get surrounded by a half-dozen people, cut off

from the steps and from me. I saw Senator Smith starting back from across the street, toward me, motioning
to a couple of state troopers to follow him. I noticed
the steam rising up from the profusion of puddles
scattered down the street. I noticed every detail, some
strange instinct forcing me to observe the ordinary.

I tried to hold my ground. But the crowd pressed
against me. Bercolini was foiled in his attempt to break
loose, to get back up on the steps. The crowd was too
strong, shoving and shouting. It made me move, it decided my pace, step by step until I reached the broad
cement platform. If I could break a little to the left, I
could be back inside, I could get away.

But I couldn't. Instead I slid along in Nancy's too-
large boots, away from the door, now trying to put
space between myself and those angry people whose
faces were inches from my own, whose placards
waved above all our heads. Surrounded by shouts,
pummeled with questions, I couldn't hear my own
voice as I tried to slow them down.

"Norie! Senator! I'm coming. I'll getcha."

Bercolini's voice was the last clear sound that hit me
above the clamor of the crowd and the clatter of my
own body as I tumbled off the side of the Jericho
schoolhouse steps.

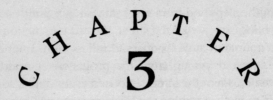

CHAPTER 3

A rose by any other name might smell the same, but hospitals smell like hospitals smell like hospitals.

Dress them up with bright prints or vivid chintz, you can't disguise the scent of rubbing alcohol and sheets washed in too much starch—the fragrance, the essence of my education as a nurse.

So before I opened my eyes, that smell reminded me where I was and that I was safe and that I ached all over.

"You're fine. You're just fine."

Nancy Jackson, my personal assistant, was acting a little too perky for the way I was feeling. Unexpectedly, she had materialized beside the bed, patting my hand. Reassurance is one of her strong suits, and she would probably say we were all fine in the face of an alien attack.

"You're not in the bed. You don't feel how not fine I feel. And, anyway, how did you get here so fast? I haven't been out cold for several days, have I?"

"I'm really tempted . . ." Nancy contorted her face into an evil little grin. "No. No. It's just the afternoon of the same day you came up here with the President. I was already in Philly when the accident happened. Remember, we were going to meet there tomorrow. Get on this campaign staff hiring thing. The President was so concerned he tracked me down and two adorable state troopers whisked me here. I've been in beautiful Jericho for about an hour."

"I'm kinda out of it. I saw several doctors in the emergency room." Pushing very carefully, I got myself to an upright position. My head hurt. Worse was the idea of how it would feel if I moved too quickly. "But I can't remember their verdicts."

"Terminally healthy, I'm happy to report. But you took a real bang on the head. Seems as you went over the side you managed a little back-flip action, so you hit your head twice on the same piece of masonry."

"Well, let's get out of here," I started.

"Nope. That's not the plan. The President had the White House physician call and you are under observation—probably for thirty-six hours."

"And what about my work? This is my stuff. I know about public health. I know about emergencies. I'm not going to let one little push keep me in bed."

"Milton is waiting in Washington. He wants to talk to you before you say anything about being 'pushed.' He thinks it's better if you leave it vague. So that you don't look too vulnerable and you don't get stuck in a shouting match with the picketers."

"Okay. I guess that makes sense. I'm still a little woozy. What happened to Bercolini?"

"He's fine. Shook up that he couldn't rescue you. I saw him when I arrived," Nancy said. "He wants to talk to you as soon as possible. Said he was going to make a couple stops and then head home."

"We'll call him after dinner. It'll hold until then."

"Yes, but this won't. You've got a visitor. Hank Dugdale."

Dugdale was carrying one of those floral bouquets that you can order by number on the phone, all stuffed into an oversized coffee mug decorated with one of those bright yellow Smileface Balloonhead people and "Have a Nice Day" written in childish block letters. It was ghastly enough to bring out the aesthetic police.

"Mrs. Gorzack. How are you?" He came dangerously close to the bed and I was afraid he was going to smother me—not with a pillow but with some macho cedar-infused men's cologne that he had obviously bathed in that morning. I had no doubt about three things: One, Dugdale was a good-looking man, with his steel gray hair all slicked back, all the better to see his jutting chin and his slightly crooked smile; two, nobody had a higher opinion of Dugdale than himself;

three, this guy was sporting a freshly pressed khaki outfit. Here we were, in the middle of a disaster area, and he'd gotten himself into yet another Ramar of the Jungle ensemble, with even more military doodads across the shoulder.

"I'm feeling pretty good, considering that I was toppled off a step and fell into a pile of bushes and slime. A little shaky, but the doctors say I'm just terrific."

"I know those people, whoever they were, certainly meant no harm." Dugdale couldn't seem to find a place to put his Smileface mug and kept carrying it back and forth in front of the windows.

"*Whoever they were?* Weren't they your supporters?"

"No, no. I wouldn't classify them as supporters. They were all members of the Values Coalition. It's a grass-roots organization. There's no coordination. There are really no leaders. Just people getting together to show support for the causes they care about."

"For an unplanned demonstration, they certainly had some wonderfully coordinated signs." I waited for Dugdale to respond.

But instead he plopped down his floral tribute and turned the offensive on me.

"So if you're okay, why are you still here?"

"For observation. Trust me, I'm not a fatality or even close to it."

"Good. Good. This is a fine hospital, I believe. Performed very well in the past few years, dealing with flood victims and the like." Dugdale had the wonderful ability to take credit for just about everything. Probably used the same possessive manner when talking about a sunset.

"This hospital, I know as the former director of public health for the commonwealth, is just another fine example of tax dollars at work," I countered.

He kept right on with his solicitous patter. Did I have someone to help me answer calls, here in the hospital? Did I need anything? Is there anything he or his wife could do—in addition to the prayers he and she and their prayer group were offering?

"No, I'm grateful for the offer. And very grateful for your prayers."

"I hope this won't delay the start of your campaign, Mrs. Gorzack," Dugdale crooned at me. Did it really bother him so much to call me "Senator"?

"No. I just think of it as a little R and R before I go back into battle."

My next visitor was little more upbeat.

"Hello? Hello? Hello!" A very tall, very thin woman with a lopsided nursing cap stuck her head around the door. It might have been at a funny angle, but I would know that cap anywhere.

"Come in. Unless I'm mistaken, that's a Mount Saint Agnes chapeau you're wearing. Very charming."

"I had to dig it out of the back of my locker. It's a relic, all right. Like me. I haven't worn it in years, but I thought it was good for a laugh. I was four years ahead of you, Senator. I'm Frannie Franklin. Really I'm Frannie Franklin Ford."

"And I'm Norie. You're on staff here?"

"I run chemo here. One wing over. Pretty big operation, since we serve a multicounty area. That's why I stopped by. To say hello. And also to see if I could take you for a little ride tomorrow. To meet some of the fellows. Vets. We seem to have an amazing number of Vietnam veterans showing up for our nuclear cocktails. It's like Saigon in the old days. Only we don't charge a cover."

"Yes. As long as it's approved by somebody in a white coat, I'd love to visit."

"I'll pick you up in my wheels about eleven a.m. Be there . . ."

"Or be square," I finished up. Gosh, we were getting old.

Nancy and I had soup for supper before she headed off to the Holiday Inn down the road. I watched TV, had my bedtime snack of two Lorna Doones and a ginger ale—one eats things in hospitals unthought of on everyday menus—and dozed off with some British mystery about a Cotswold vicar. When a light tap at the door woke me, I was confused for a moment and couldn't figure out what my friend, Lieutenant Tom Carver of the Capitol Police, was doing in the English countryside.

"Where are the floral tributes? Where's the candy? Aren't you an important elected official? This cupboard is bare!" Carver could fill up a room with a silent stare. When he was festive, the energy made the walls burst.

"We are in the middle of a federal emergency zone, Lieutenant," I said, pushing the lever that moved the bed that sat me up. "The goodies will be flooding in, so to speak, tomorrow."

"The goodies are here." Carver dumped the contents of two lumpy plastic bags on the bottom of my bed, creating a mound of candy bars. "What you need, I know, is M&Ms," he said, grabbing a bag for himself.

"I never told you this," I said, grabbing a bag for myself, "but when we played army when I was little, the only way the boys would let me play the nurse was if I brought the medicine. M&Ms. You're right. The perfect medicine."

"Don't limit yourself. Butterfingers. Snickers. How about that old classic Milky Way. Take just one bite of each. They're all for you."

I opened my own personal bag of M&Ms. I'd start small.

"What time is it anyway?"

"About two-fifteen."

"In the morning! Carver. Are you crazy? What are you doing here?"

As I spoke, I remembered that Carver's natural addiction to sweets hit record heights when he was under pressure.

"We got a problem?" I asked.

"Yes. A big one. I got a call at home. About eight

last night. Figured you'd need a friend up here. So I got my pals at the air force to let me hitch a ride. I wasn't going to have somebody tell you on the phone."

I didn't talk. All the bad things that could happen did happen in my head for the next thirty seconds. My mother. My brother. His wife. The kids. Nancy. My pals in Philadelphia. Everything and nothing just rushed my brain.

"It's Congressman Bercolini. He's dead. It happened about six o'clock last night. Killed on his way home, between here and Jericho City."

"A car accident! My God, Carver, are you sure? There are so many people using those four-wheel-drives. And you know he really knew this area. It's not like he would get lost or anything."

I waited for Carver to agree that my protestations were convincing. Which they weren't, not even to me. But Carver didn't talk. Just picked at his candy, sorting by colors the dozen M&Ms he held in his hand. He stayed silent—with Carver, not a good sign.

"What aren't you telling me?" I asked.

"I'm going to tell you everything." He paused and nodded, agreeing with himself. "It wasn't an accident. It was a carjacking. Bercolini was carjacked and then killed."

"No. You're wrong. I've had the TV on all night. I've been dozing, but I saw the news. Heck, I watched myself—and Bercolini. We were on the steps. Right before

I fell off." Something in me wanted to prove Carver wrong, prove that Bercolini was still alive.

Carver popped a few candies, then leaned forward.

"I notice you're not saying 'pushed off' or 'shoved off' or 'rammed off' in talking about your so-called fall."

"Well, Milton and everybody thought it would be better if we just downplayed the incident. We didn't want to make it seem like I was a target or anything. George Taylor—you know, the businessman from Philly who's my friend—he agreed. Getting pushed around makes me look too vulnerable. Not good for a woman candidate."

"That is what I really like, Senator," Carver said, signaling the sarcasm to come. "When you politico types decide that it's bad for your image to say that some people were trying to bushwack you."

"It doesn't matter," I countered, even though I agreed more with Carver than my advisers. "What matters is Bercolini."

"Okay, first some questions. Where was Bercolini standing when the crowd *accidentally* pushed you off the steps?"

"Nearby. Next to me, really. Until some of the pro-testers got between us."

"Did any of the crowd go after him—call him by name, or single him out?"

"No. He got involved because he was standing be-side me."

"Was it tough?"

"Yes. Awful. So hot. The people seemed to give off heat, especially the women, pushing against me." I shook my head.

"After you get hurt, the congressman comes here to the hospital. He hangs around to make sure you're okay. Do you talk to him?"

"No. He told Nancy that he'd call me later. He'd been at me all day about something important."

"We'll go back to that. So he's on his way home and he stops at an ATM. We know that because he had his ATM card in his pocket, not his wallet, along with a receipt timed five-fifty and a hundred dollars in cash. It's all there, so it's assumed the motive wasn't robbery."

"Who did it? Are there any leads? Why Bercolini?"

"Nobody knows. They'll check the film at the ATM. But I don't think they'll find anything. It's in a shopping center and there had to be people around. So we assume he leaves the ATM and somebody or somebodies get in the car with him, somewhere along his route. And they have him drive the car—a Ford Explorer— for like three miles past the ATM location. And then they kill him."

I couldn't ask any more questions. I couldn't absorb any more of the deadly details. I just kept remembering Bercolini trying to get back to me through the crowd, trying to rescue me. Carver must have realized my reticence.

"You want me to go on? The rest of the details are really gruesome and it's three o'clock in the morning."

"Now."

"The Explorer was found in the parking lot of the building where the congressman has his local office. There's some other federal stuff there, including a post office on the first floor. The congressman's body was jammed between two mailboxes."

I watched Carver's face and knew the story wasn't at its end.

"Not just jammed. Wrapped in brown paper, like a package. Tied with string. All very neat. And then, the pièce de résistance—printed in big block letters on the paper, 'Return to U.S. Capitol. Washington, D.C.' "

I think that's where Carver's story ended. I know that's when I began to cry.

Somehow, Carver located a big pot of coffee and we sat for a while, a strange pajama party, eating candy and drinking coffee and talking about Bercolini. Only Carver was full-blown into his interrogation and data collection mode.

"You said Bercolini wanted to tell you 'something important.' Do you think that some person or persons had threatened him? Was there any hint, a phrase, a signal?"

"One signal? Bercolini was like a walking flashing light, he was signaling so much," I said, the thought of his energy making me smile. "He kept on and on about this Keystone Militia. About the story in *New York Lifestyle* and how it was all blown up out of proportion and how it was hurting the tourist business."

"So he wasn't like on a crusade against them or anything?" Carver had an annoying habit of being able to ferret out information you didn't know you had. His method, however, employed for your head the same approach a dentist had in your mouth—drill, drill, drill.

"Well, he didn't like the militia," I said, pushing my memory for any more details. "But he put it down. Insisted it wasn't anywhere near as powerful as the way the media showed it. And he kept mentioning my 'experience in government,' how he wanted to show me around his district. I guess teach me a thing or two."

"Well, maybe it was good you fell off that stoop. Look, Senator," Carver said, dropping his usual kidding manner, "you got a lot of publicity with the murders this spring, a lot of press coverage when you helped figure it out. Maybe Bercolini had been threatened and wanted to talk through it with you. Although it would have done him a lot more good to have gone to the cops with any suspicions or threats."

"And the way he was killed? Why do that to his family?"

"Certainly the death of the congressman is supposed to look like a strike against the federal government. Thanks to the dumping of the body on federal property, whoever killed him managed to stress the point. They got what they wanted. The FBI moved right in on the case. They've got automatic jurisdiction, since that law was passed several years back making the threatening, assaulting, or murdering of a Member or a senator a federal crime, punishable by the death penalty."

"Is the FBI seeing a lot of violence from the militias, not just here but in other places?"

"No," Carver said, searching in his pocket for the notebook I knew he kept there. "Here it is. 'Paper Terrorism.' Since Ruby Ridge a lot of the more organized militias now hold these 'citizens' courts' and issue arrest warrants and find people guilty."

"And then?"

"Nothing, really. Although one FBI guy told me the way Bercolini was killed and his body dumped would be right in line with the militia's paramilitary pose and its hatred of the federal government."

"And you think that's right?" I asked.

"I think maybe I don't know enough. Like I don't keep track of all your colleagues. Could Bercolini have been a target for some piece of legislation or for some speech?"

"Every person on Capitol Hill wants to be some kind of lightning rod. How else do you get publicity? Anyway, Bercolini had a lot of causes. He was rabid on environmental stuff. And determined that everyone in America should belong to a union. But the unions should be squeaky clean. He wasn't pro–gun control, but he voted for the Brady Bill." I took a long sip of my coffee. "Now that I think about it, his agenda was like a litany of unpopular causes. Plus pushing at the Keystone Militia."

"Unpopular enough that instead of writing a letter or voting against him, he's carjacked and killed?"

"Carver, there's something about me, maybe it's naïveté, but I find it hard to believe that a United States Congressman is murdered only because of politics. I know you like to connect the dots, but I think there must be something else."

"Senator, as you and I both know, there's never a very good reason for murder. And I think politics ranks just about at the bottom of the list."

I nodded my agreement. Too quickly, it turned out.

"But," Carver added, "let's face it. The congressman *is* dead."

CHAPTER 4

Carver headed off at dawn and I drifted back to sleep.

A very smart night nurse ordered my breakfast tray held until nine-thirty. I was finishing my coffee when the calls started to come in. The President, my Senate pals Hilda Mendelssohn and Garrett Baxter, and, of course, my mom, Marie.

My mother was mildly hysterical about Bercolini's murder. The lid was off and CNN had switched from the mayhem of the flood to the murder of the congressman. As the reporter droned on about Bercolini's attack on the Keystone Militia and his other confrontational stands, the screen was filled with footage shot the day before—the two of us standing with the President and Bercolini trying to rescue me from the crowd—followed by gruesome pictures of the mailboxes where his body had been stuffed.

"Just come home right now. Sign yourself out. Who knows what kind of treatment they're giving you. I never trusted people from upstate," my mother warned. There is a tradition of regional prejudice among the various geographic quadrants of Pennsylvania, and my mother has never passed up a convenient bias. "Too much time in the woods. They're just too rural."

I used Frannie's arrival as a way of ending the conversation and hung up.

"Okay," I announced, climbing out of the bed and into the wheelchair, "let me grab a legal pad and we're off."

Frannie briefed me on the way to oncology, down two floors and one wing away.

"The six men we're going to see are all being treated on an out-patient basis. They're part of a protocol from the National Institutes of Health—and NIH is very interested, because we've got ten men with this rare form of leukemia."

"And they're all Vietnam vets?"

"All but one. And he was in the Peace Corps in Borneo."

I waved as I was pushed through the swinging doors and got a few feeble waves in return.

The men reclined in elaborate BarcaLounger-type chairs, like participants at a weird Roman feast. Each patient was hooked up to a clear plastic tube, each tube fed by several separate hanging bottles, bright colored, like the pastel and striped pillows. The room had the faux cheerfulness common to places of chemotherapy—a cartoon-crammed bulletin board, a bear dressed like a doctor, a hand-printed sign that ordered DO NOT TURN ON MOTOR WHILE NUCLEAR FUEL IS BEING PUMPED. I knew from my time in hospitals that such undergraduate humor hopefully dulled the edge of the existential dilemma, the dice throw on whether the dripping toxic drugs would correctly knock off the exact evil cell they aimed to eradicate.

We made the rounds slowly—Frannie, my chair, and myself—first greeting the two chemo-specialty nurses on duty, then going between the beds so I could meet each of the guys. Since the six were all Vietnam vets, they were naturally about my age, the age that Jack would have been, although the longish hair on several of them combined with the terrible thinness that treatment brings made them look much older.

We finished our rounds and Frannie positioned the chair at the end of the room, making sure that I was in view of everyone. I wasn't sure where to begin, but, as frequently happens when you get a bunch of vets in the room, they had a plan of action.

"So, Senator, Frannie called us at home last night and said you were stopping by. And we just wanted to thank you. And to tell you that we really need your help." The guy speaking I remembered was named

Raymond Aloyisus O'Dwyer because he had repeated it several times when he had introduced himself. Tied to his tubes, he couldn't move or even raise his head more than a few inches, but the strength of his voice belied both his horizontal position and his physical condition. He was tough.

"Exactly what would you like me to do?" I asked, ready for a laundry list of complaints, about the VA, about the NIH protocols, about the bureaucracy. Not what Raymond Aloyisus had in mind.

"We'd like—and I'm speaking for everyone here and the four other guys who get their blasts on other days—we'd like you to find out what the hell happened to us. Why we're all here. In this shape. With this weird cancer eating us out."

As he was talking, Frannie went and got a pile of paper and brought it to me. Talk about a Mount Saint Agnes girl always being prepared—she was as organized as a general.

"We asked Frannie to put together all our stuff. Our histories. Our physical conditions. Our meds. We've got a pip of a leukemia here. All ten of us do. And we're all from around here. But we don't know any women who have this disease. And we're all in our late forties or early fifties. Except for the one guy who wasn't in Nam. John, he's sixty-two."

O'Dwyer stopped talking and I stayed silent, looking through the papers on my lap. Frannie had done a series of charts on her home computer, showing the ages, the Vietnam experiences, the ethnic backgrounds—at least three scrutinized factors in rare cancers.

"What do you think *it* is? What do you think happened to you?" I asked.

They couldn't tell me fast enough. Where they had served. What they had done. What ammo they had used and what water they walked through and what they'd been bombed with.

"Now that there's all this stuff in the paper about Desert Storm and poison gases, some of us thought, hey, maybe that's what hit us in Nam," one man shouted out. "So we decided to contact government types. Like they tell you in civics class. Only then, you decided to contact us. In a way, I mean."

There were smiles around the room at his kidding manner, only the smiles didn't go very deep.

"Pete's right about Nam. You can't get an answer. Is the government just keeping us in the dark or what?"

"So some of us think it might be Agent Orange," one vet offered, the thinnest face shooting out from a Yankees baseball cap.

"And," another chimed in, "we don't know if there's other groups, just like us. You gotta understand, of the nine of us who served in Nam, one was navy and the rest army."

"Except for John, who was in the Peace Corps."

"Yeah, in Borneo."

Frannie called a halt to the explanations, clapping her hands and waving her arms like a referee.

"That's it," she announced. "Senator Gorzack is

supposed to be getting some rest. And it wouldn't be a bad idea for all of you."

I held up my hand to stave off her acting so much like a nurse.

"Okay, before Frannie drags me off, here's what I can do. I can get my office involved in this. I can get the Senate Committee on Veterans Affairs to get involved. A vet named Mike Kincaid runs it—you might have heard of him. He's been very busy trying to clean up some of the traditional paper jams in the VA. Kincaid's a good senator and a good guy." I paused. "He was with me in Vietnam when we got the remains of the MIAs."

"We're really sorry about your husband, Senator," one of the men said, and I just nodded my thanks.

"So we can get cracking. We'll look around the country, see if there are other places where vets are showing up with this leukemia." I looked around the room. "And we'll spend some real time and energy trying to find some experts to help figure out what happened to all of you."

"Thanks, Norie," the Yankees cap interjected. "It's a real bummer and you're just what we needed."

"I wish I had an easy answer," I managed.

"Not as much as we do, Senator," O'Dwyer said. "And that's the God's truth. Not as much as we do."

"So I'm really glad you took that spill off that schoolhouse step," Frannie announced, much to the shock of the two interns sharing our elevator. "The guys really need you to figure this out."

"They're so grateful for any help, it makes me mad that the government agencies aren't doing more already. Are we sure there are no more cases in this particular area? Are there any other major hospitals around here, where such cases would be treated?"

"No. This is it. We're kinda chemo-central. I've been in the ward now about six years. Since my last kid graduated from high school."

I swung around in my chair to look at her. "And how many kids preceded your last?"

"Four. All girls. My last, number five, was a boy. David. I stayed home until they were all in grammar school, then worked part-time and private duty until I came back to chemo."

"And your husband?" I asked her, ready for another flip remark.

"Tommy's dead six years. Right before I came back to work chemo." Frannie gave me a pat on the shoulder like she was comforting me. "I'd spent most of the two years before that in and out of that ward as a wife. I thought the least I could do was to put in my time there as the nurse."

Nancy was waiting for me. So was my hospital lunch. And, lined up beside the tray were several delicious-looking cardboard containers.

"Tell me it's Chinese," I said. Getting a happy nod from Nancy, I asked Frannie to join us. "Save me from myself. Between post-midnight M&Ms, a late breakfast, and an early lunch, I'm going to look like a 'before ad.' Speaking of that''—I grabbed the channel changer—"let's get the news."

I had a veggie dumpling within biting range when Nancy let out a shriek.

"I told you not to use that hot mustard sauce," I started, getting my dumpling back on my chopsticks.

"Not the mustard. Dugdale. Look, look," she shouted, sounding like some grammar school reader.

There was Hank Dugdale, a microphone in hand, looking like some over-the-top television correspondent with that FEMA baseball cap. He faced the camera doing what I'd learned was a "stand-up." That's another one of those high-tech, multimedia phrases that means just exactly what it says—a reporter *stands up* in front of the camera, at the scene of an event, and just talks.

And talks, and talks. Which is what was happening in Hank's case. For the first part of his report, he was in front of the schoolhouse, and the camera swung around to show the dozen or so "real" reporters doing their stand-up nearby. Each of them probably did a couple of minutes, but Hank had a regular telethon going on.

His angle was simple: The flood was bad, but the crime and destruction that would fall in its wake was a real terror. Apparently the U.S. Senate, both sides of the aisle, had promoted this tragedy by not funding local police departments to maintain what sounded like local civil defense armies.

Suddenly another clip of Dugdale filled the screen.

"He's in front of the hospital," Nancy shouted at the television, then ran to the window.

"No, I think this was taped yesterday, when he stopped by for a friendly visit." My words were echoed by Dugdale's.

"I've visited Mrs. Gorzack in her hospital room," he was intoning into the camera. "And I don't have happy news to report. Let me roll some tape."

There was a slightly fuzzy shot of the front of the hospital, and then, as the camera zoomed in to a second-floor room, Dugdale could be identified, pacing back and forth in front of a large picture window. Carrying that atrociously ugly bouquet.

"When I brought her flowers and had a chat, it was obvious to me that she was greatly shaken up by her fall, sustained when she tripped while chatting with some concerned citizens."

As Dugdale "reported," footage of the demonstration the day before filled the screen—not as the placard-carrying angry crowd rushed me but as they peacefully assembled in front of Dugdale.

"She's been greatly shaken up by her close encounter with the citizenry, and, although we offer her our prayers and good wishes for a speedy recovery, we are concerned that she will be unable to quickly return to the pressure of the campaign trail. Hank Dugdale, signing off, for Values Coalition News."

"How can he be the reporter?" Nancy blurted out. "He's the candidate."

It sure beat me.

As usual, Milton had an explanation.

"It's cable TV. They've got these five-hundred-plus stations to fill up. They can't be selling exercise machines and movie-star makeup and psychic connections all the time."

"But Dugdale can't just put on an ad and call it news."

"Maybe yes. Maybe no. We've got the party lawyers looking into it. Don't worry. Just get well."

"Milton, I'm happy for your concern. But there is nothing wrong with me. What's wrong is that this guy is on television, telling people there is something wrong with me. Explain again how he did it." I was furious and stoked my fiery anger with a handful of Carver's leftover M&Ms.

"The Values Coalition buys the hour. Or, sometimes, local cable operators are so desperate for free programming that they just put on whatever comes over the transom. Haven't you ever watched the nutcakes that come on late at night? Two weirdos sitting on office chairs, one interviewing the other about his successful approach to life planning. As if they have a life and still have time to do three a.m. cable shows."

Milton could sometimes make me crazy.

"But don't I get equal time the same as Dugdale?"

"No. Here's a catch—you don't even get to use C-SPAN footage in your commercials. And Dugdale can use it in his. You can't because you're an incumbent. No such rules apply to him. Anyway, if he buys time, you can buy it too. It doesn't cost much because it's public access cable. I've heard Dugdale was doing this. They have this show, with 'volunteer' reporters. They just hire local camera crews, like ones you would get to video a wedding. And then they put their 'volunteers' on the air."

"It just doesn't seem fair."

"Norie. We're in an election. Nothing is fair. Fair would be having a year to run this campaign. Anyway, I'm meeting you in Philly. With Kathy and George and the prospective campaign team."

"What campaign team?"

"Yours, I guess," Milton said, with a sigh. "All yours."

The rest of the day dragged by. I had the hospital version of cabin fever. I was impatient to be out and about, getting myself elected, finding Bercolini's murderers, or figuring out why leukemia had hit the vets.

I called Gracie Bercolini. I tried to remember what people had said to me when my Jack was first missing, or when I finally knew that he had been killed. Nothing seemed right, except to say how sorry I was and how much I had respected her husband and what a loss this would be for the Congress. Gracie wanted none of my sympathy, but demanded revenge.

"I want these people tracked down, Norie," Gracie rasped into the phone, her voice obviously shot from a day of crying. "I don't want these people to get away. They killed my Bobby. They're like animals."

"Gracie, that's what I'm feeling—"

"I told him not to go after these militia people. 'Don't make fun of them,' that's what I said. But he thought they were nothing. That they were bullies. And then there were these other deaths. Animals."

Animals, I thought. She must be hysterical. And why not?

"Gracie," I tried. "The FBI is here. The state police. They're going to find who did it."

"And give these creeps to me. I'd know what to do with them. Give them to me." Her sobs got heavier and, after a minute, someone else was on the phone.

"Senator. This is Joe Bercolini. My mom's upset. We're going to try to get her to take a pill and maybe sleep a little. Thank you for calling."

"Joe, I'm sorry. I didn't mean to upset your mother."

"She's Irish. My father used to kid her that she had a worse temper than the Italians. That she always wanted to get even with anybody who crossed him. I guess that's true with this too. She wants revenge."

"We all want the killers to be caught."

"I don't think you understand, Senator. My mom just wants revenge."

My experience was that nice people didn't run around looking for revenge. I remembered some piece of *Star Wars* trivia that must have come from my nephews—

49

that the third movie in the trilogy was supposed to be called *Revenge of the Jedi*, until somebody figured out that Jedi were too high-minded for revenge, and so it became *Return of the Jedi*. Not so, I guess, with mere mortals.

Revenge on my mind, my after-dinner snooze was fitful, my dreams strange and disconnected, ending up with one featuring a man-eating flower.

"They're chocolate. They're very good. They letting you eat sweets or what?"

"My God, Ralph, what are you doing here?" Inches from my head, munching on a chocolate rose, was political correspondent Ralph deSantis. "How did you get in after visiting hours?"

"I told the nurses I was your brother."

"I'm very touched, Ralph," I said, pushing myself up on the pillows. "But wasn't it dangerous getting here? It's a federal emergency out there."

"The roads are open. It's like a straight shot from Harrisburg. I got a big car. Didn't cost me anything. It's all on the expense account. Even the chocolate," he explained, carefully unwrapping another rose. "And, anyway, I told my sister from Pittsburgh I'd check out her cottage. It's about ten miles from here. See how it held up."

"Ralph, you give new meaning to 'two birds with one stone.' "

He took it as a compliment, smiled, and took another big bite of a rose.

"So this puts your campaign on hold, huh? That's

all right. So you got a slow start. This guy Dugdale is kind of a strange dude. A little too sincere for my money. You want me to push this lever and move your bed or anything?"

"No. No. I'm good. So he's too sincere?"

"Yeah, but sometimes that plays well with the voters. You've got a lot going for you, anyway."

He waited. Ralph was like a lot of political reporters—he wanted to play politics as well as write it. And now he wanted me to ask him how I should be running my campaign. If I did what he suggested, I'd get good coverage. I hated this. I tried to change the subject.

"What's the rumor mill churning out these days?"

"Same old, same old. Except for the stuff about 'the Gorzack Curse.'"

"Ralph, that's crazy." And it was, although for some reason it rattled me. Within days of my appointment to the Senate, a man was killed attempting to speak to me. Several weeks later, a staff person was murdered. Some of my political enemies started to talk about "the Gorzack Curse," that whoever got too close to me was in a life-or-death situation.

"Bercolini was with you. Now he's dead. You got bad luck, Norie. That's what people are saying."

"I don't need luck to win elections, Ralph." There I was, changing the subject back to just where I didn't want it to be.

"You might, with this Dugdale guy. Now what I'm telling you I can't write. Because I got no specific stuff.

But this guy is tied in with some questionable types," Ralph said, nodding his head.

"Are you saying he's tied in with the militia? Is the militia tied in with the Values Coalition?"

"If I knew something," Ralph said, peeling the last rose, "I'd write it. I just hear things. Anyway, one last piece of advice," he said, peeling the last rose. "Run like a girl!"

I laughed so hard I couldn't answer.

"No, really. A lot of guys try to run like he-men. Look at Dukakis with the helmet in the tank. Or Jimmy Carter. Remember all that sweat when he was running? Looked half dead. And how about his beating the rabbit that tried to jump into his boat? Hard to believe. And Dole—wearing his dress shirt and watch when he was exercising. You can't be somebody you're not. And you can't be macho. Heck, half these guys can't be macho."

"And what about issues, Ralph?"

"I hate issues. They just get politics all mucked up. Amateurs getting involved. Like give me a county chairman any day, somebody I can talk to about who's going to win the election, not who *should* win."

"Ralph, come on," I started to protest.

"No, politics used to be very clean. The other guy got his people out. You got your people out. And the one with the most people won the election."

It was hard to argue with logic like that. I nodded my agreement, and then felt my eyes sliding shut.

Ralph's monotone voice, as it droned on, lulled me, like waves hitting the beach.

In the morning, when I awoke, the only sign he had been there was the scattering of green paper stems and a pile of gold tinfoil.

CHAPTER 5

Carver drove down with me to Philadelphia. He spent most of the drive down asking what sounded like routine questions of the state trooper the governor had sent to ferry me through the flood area. He quizzed me on who lived in what town and what they did for a living and what salaries were like and if most kids finished high school, and I thought that when Carver had nothing to detect he obviously asked questions for the fun of it. I sat in the backseat and caught up on paperwork Nancy had dropped off at the hospital that morning and got ready for my first genuine campaign meeting.

The home of Taylor Technologies was a massive four-floor layout at Liberty Place, the glitzy downtown skyscraper complex, blocks from City Hall. George Taylor had built himself a high-tech playground, as high-tech as the company it housed. He'd paid four hundred thousand dollars extra to have the space left "unfinished," with all the ductwork, water pipes, and electrical systems exposed or behind plastic. Everything was finished in high-gloss paints—the colors I remembered from a big box of neon crayons my nephew wanted in the first grade. Hot pink ducts crossed lime green tubes and flowered down into buttercup yellow and grape and ripe peach offices and cubicles.

The wood floors had been stenciled—some with designs, others as copies of systems that Taylor Technologies had developed. George always said he liked to show how things worked and how his company worked, so all the offices, cubicles, and conference rooms had walls made of tempered glass. The whole atmosphere was ultra-upbeat.

I was feeling pretty good until I got to the door of George's conference room and was met by him and Marco, who tripped over each other in telling me that "our problem is solved." Nothing can make me more nervous than to have someone tell me a problem is solved before I knew I had a problem.

"I thought we were meeting about the campaign," I offered.

"Yes. But it's under control," George insisted, grabbing my arm and almost knocking me back into the elevator.

"I'm not an invalid," I said, trying to shake off their help. "And what problem? Twenty percent of my state is a federal emergency area. That's a problem."

"Don't you two start," Kathleen interrupted, coming out into the hall and using her best ex-nun voice to try to restore order. "These two will have you back in the hospital, they're so thrilled that you're okay."

Marco Solari, who runs the unions' political operations in Pennsylvania, businessman George Taylor, and Kathleen Burns, who runs United Way in Philadelphia, had been my friends and informal advisers for several years, so close that we always referred to ourselves as the Gang of Four. And now that the Senate race was finally here, it was hard to contain them.

"The campaign team is inside. You're going to like them. Christie's a little tough"—George still held my arm—"although not *too* tough. Just kind of the new-style woman in politics."

"What does 'new-style' mean? Does she wear Armani or that purple nail polish? Or"—this time I grabbed his arm—"does she just use foul language all the time? I can't take that, George. It's not necessary."

"Not the time, Norie, to have a discussion about manners," George countered. "You're up against the wall."

"I think your panic about my campaign is slightly overblown. I've done a good job in the Senate—and people know it."

"Nobody knows anything until you tell them. And unless you have a campaign no voter is ever going to find out what a great job you've been doing," George insisted, opening the door and ushering me inside to a conference room with a startling full-length view of City Hall, so realistic as to almost seem fake.

"Senator, hello." Christie Hamilton couldn't greet me fast enough. "Look at this view. Look at that statue of William Penn on top of City Hall. Isn't it something?"

"Yes. Something." I sounded cold, but I really dislike people who think they've invented a view just because they happen to find themselves in front of a picture window. "I love City Hall. I always think it looks like a big sand castle with all that plaster design dripping down the sides."

Christie took no notice of my clever architectural analysis.

"Senator, this is our media consultant, Charlie McPherson. And, for polling and focus groups—Josh Kaplan."

We all shook hands and nodded. Milton gave me a surprisingly serious handshake. I shrugged in return, and shot him a slight roll of my eyes. There was no response. Must have been a bad trip up from D.C.

Someone took orders for soft drinks or coffee and we sat down, chatting, saying the inconsequential things people say before the concrete business of a meeting begins. I tried to size up Christie. A size eight was my quick guess.

She was all black and grays—très tall, extra chic, with a whole-look kind of a thing, including her excessively large and expensive fountain pen. Now I think a fountain pen takes a lot of time and energy and maybe it's worth it if you're a nineteenth-century letter writer. But to go through ink and blotting and inconvenience just to point at somebody during a meeting or take a few notes seems an affectation that's a wee bit suspicious.

Charlie looked like he'd spent too much time in J. Crew. He was all aw-shucks preppy, as baggy and wrinkled as linen could be. The pollster Josh Kaplan was his exact opposite and seemed to have cornered the latent market in polyester. Which I didn't notice at first, since I was fascinated by his toupee. Josh couldn't have been more than twenty-five, except for his hair, which looked about fifty.

There were ten of us at the meeting: Marco, George, and Kathleen representing my longtime political allies; Nancy, who'd driven down earlier that morning; the consultants, Milton, and myself. That was nine around the table. Sitting off to the side was Stash Wolcyzk, an old friend of my dad's, a retired limo driver and, my mother had told me on the phone, my campaign's first volunteer. He'd apparently been directed into the inner-sanctum campaign meeting by mistake, but he seemed to be enjoying himself and, I figured, might actually know more about real voters than anyone else in the room.

We picked deli sandwiches from aluminum mesh baskets passed around by two of George's young assistants. I picked turkey and watched as Marco, who thinks cholesterol is a myth, chose corned beef. I couldn't help but notice that Christie, seated across from me, waved the basket away—the better to wear those Armani suits.

"So what I want to talk about first, Senator, is image. Let's see how image is created and watch our 'reel,' some spots that Charlie and I have created," she said. She raised her right hand, and, like an ancient goddess with a bad temper, brought on the night.

Not really. What she actually did was signal one of George's minions, who pressed a switch that flipped down blackout blinds. Two taps of Christie's fancy pen on the glasstop table cued another electronic response, and a massive TV monitor blazed on, with futuristic symphonic music and the flash of black-and-white photos with the words "Gardiner—Strong on America" flashing across the screen.

The "reel" was seventeen commercials long, ads from campaigns across the nation that were either shot by Charlie or managed by Christie. The candidates were all from my party, but I wasn't sure that they would have gotten my vote. They generally seemed contrived, with photos of candidates shaking hands with cops or in a multiethnic classroom or at a boot camp for teens or, of course, just being around the house with the wife and kiddies. Every single candidate was "strong," good-looking—and male. Every opponent was pictured as mildly dippy—photographs catching the opposition frowning, scowling, or, in one case, practically drooling.

The reel ended and Christie signaled the return of daylight. She bolted to the window and stood, arms outstretched, in front of the panoramic view.

"*This* is an image, Senator Gorzack. *This* is strong. *This* is Pennsylvania. And this is very much what we want," she announced. I couldn't agree more. At least if Christie agreed to her role as an imposter. Let her portray me in the commercials. Put my head on that skinny woman in the chic suit.

I'd worked hard on my image for the past thirty years. My thick hair was cut in a short, swept-back style, more blond than not as my hairdresser Lucien was heavy on the highlights. I liked simple, tailored clothes, St. John knits or Dana Buchman, and scarves—I was big on scarves, but I frequently felt that the scarf was wearing me instead of vice versa. At five feet four, I was tall enough not to be petite, but everything I wore still needed to be shortened.

My thoughts were drowned out by my advisers' cheers.

"Great. I love it," George shouted out. "Norie and William Penn. Looking down from that pinnacle that's ahead—and yet historic."

"George, what are you talking about?" I asked. "What would I be talking about—the restoration of historic buildings? City Hall has nothing to do with my being in the Senate."

"No, Senator, but Philadelphia does. *You* are Philadelphia. Hardworking, ethnic, a real reflection of William Penn."

"He was a Quaker and would probably now be living in a large mansion on the Main Line," I tried, then realized the meeting was running away from me. As the table bubbled about Christie's concept I leaned over to get a better glimpse of Penn, towering on his spire above the four floors of City Hall, his Quaker hat and stiff stance somehow signaling a reproof to the citizens scurrying below.

"I've always liked Billy Penn . . . ," I began.

"Well, there's language to change immediately," Charlie said. " 'Billy' is soft. A child's name. 'William' is strong. Adult."

"Hey, what's in a name?" Marco asked.

"I'd like to get to some of the issue material I've brought up from Washington before we get on this image thing," Milton said. He started to pass out the white folders he had stacked on the floor beside him.

"Let's hold that for a second," Christie said, sticking out her arm like a traffic cop. "Okay, now, we've got to make some decisions first. Before we get into issues. And those decisions are ones of time and scheduling."

"I'd like to do the process after we do the substance," I countered. Expecting a second from Milton, I was taken off guard when he rubbed his eyes with his hand and stayed quiet.

"Senator," Christie said, with the pen again, "a shooting schedule is substance. It is the difference between you being on the air—or left holding your issues in a wet brown bag."

Now there was an image. Christie was scary.

"Norie," George intervened. "Christie has a great winning record. She's got an ear—and an eye—for what turns a candidate into a success."

"That's terrific," I said, maybe halfway meaning it. "But in the seventeen commercials we just watched, I didn't see one woman."

"And I don't see what you're getting at, Senator," Christie said. "What difference does doing men or a woman make?"

"To me, a big difference. Some people will vote for me because I'm a woman—and some won't, for exactly the same reason. And why aren't we going to talk about issues first?"

"Because we haven't polled yet. None of us have any idea what issues are really key in Pennsylvania until Josh runs at least a preliminary poll. And a few focus groups."

"I think I have some key issues—before we poll. I have a certain set of visions for the state—jobs, education, health. And I think that my positions reflect the values that I share with a lot of other people in Pennsylvania. That's a good slogan: 'Visions and values.'" I sat back, feeling kind of smug.

"Maybe a good slogan for Dugdale," Christie answered. "He's got the values position staked out. He's already talking about morality, cleaning up government, getting the state ready for the next century."

"And because he's talking about some issues, does that mean I say nothing about what I believe in?"

"Of course not. But it's important to show you in

a certain style, to leave people with an impression of strength. Power. You have a marvelous sentimental image. People like you. They shared your pain when you found your late husband. We'll play to that. But you've got a lot to overcome, on this woman thing."

"And about my positions—on Social Security, education, health care? How do they measure up, strengthwise?"

"We're not asking you to change your positions, Senator," Christie said, sliding back into the conversation. "Let your image do your talking. Voters want to believe in people, not positions. They want to know you are protecting them."

"They don't want to know *how* I'm protecting them?"

"Not really. Josh!" she barked. "Josh!"

"Senator," Josh managed, looking up from under his hair, "I'm going to be looking for key phrases that will allow you to capture the middle ground. The people who are firmly for you—who like you for your issues—they're already ours. We're going to see what you can do and say to get the people in the middle to decide on you."

I took a long slow look around the table, at my consultants and advisers, waiting for one of them to speak out, to say that they were against my being packaged and promoted like some new kind of canned ham or deodorant. Bigger, better, stronger—get it all with one vote—Senator Norie Gorzack. My friends—and not a single supporting vote on issues.

"I'm confused." I really wasn't. I got it. I just didn't like it. "Don't I get points for being in the right?"

"Norie," George interrupted, "we're playing catch-up ball. We've got a few weeks to whip this campaign into shape. And a few months to make you a winner. I think we should put this all in the hands of the professionals."

I knew I wasn't thinking with a clear head. The consultants made me uncomfortable, and the real me obviously did something to their sense of political aesthetics. But George was right. I was playing catch-up and he, and the others, obviously thought I needed to be shaped up, before voters shipped me out. I trusted him. And Marco. They'd "been around politics" a long time, and I was still getting my card punched.

Christie ended the discussion by leaping out of her chair and speeding toward me, those purple-tipped fingers outstretched, like she was ready for a strangle.

"Great! Wonderful," she said, enveloping me in a tight hug. "This is going to be a campaign to remember. We'll treat you like the national treasure you are."

CHAPTER 6

George escorted me, the "national treasure," down to the car.

"That was as pleasant an afternoon as I've spent in a long time," I told him, mildly gritting my teeth. "There's nothing like strangers explaining how they're going to tell the world who you are. After they change you, that is."

"Norie, let it go," George snapped back, crankier than I thought my remark deserved. "You need consultants. You got consultants. Now you need money to pay consultants. A campaign and media cost money. Time to get to work."

"Raising money?" I rolled my eyes. "No, that's not what I do. First, I'm not a 'professional' politician. Second, you're the finance chair. You're in business. You ask them. I'm terrible at asking people for anything. Right, Kathleen?"

"Ask for checks? Norie can't ask you to split a lunch check," Kathleen agreed.

"Too bad. She's got to raise it. Get on the phone. Dial for dollars," George insisted.

"And who would I call?" I felt backed into the corner of what suddenly seemed a very small elevator. The door popped open before anyone could answer me, and I bolted out, through the lobby, the two of them following me. I still wasn't used to people recognizing me, so the big "hellos" from two pin-striped men put me even more off guard.

"Lists. Lists of regular party givers," George half shouted after me. "Lists of people you might know. Of people who are interested in issues you support. Local business types."

"Wait a minute, George," I said, turning on him, feeling more pressured than when the crowd pushed me off the steps. "I'm supposed to call up people I don't even know and ask them to give me a check."

"Yeah. And sometimes to host a fund-raiser. And to maybe ask their friends for checks. Or get their political action committee to give money. Yes. That's how it's done. It's legal. It's the way money is raised."

"Not by me," I tried to counter. Stash was waiting

by the curb with the car and I jumped in the front seat.

"Norie," George insisted through the open car window, "your consultants are ring-ready. They won't pull their punches. They'll keep you off the ropes. They are exactly what you need in your corner."

"If I was going to fight Rocky, sure. They're great handlers. But I'm a senator, George. And I'm not letting their high-powered pitch drown out what's important. I have my job as well as the campaign. I have a bunch of sick Vietnam vets sitting up in Jericho, counting on me. And I've got a dead congressman to worry about. I'm not losing sight of what's important. I have my beliefs."

I didn't particularly like discussing my ideology in an idling car on Market Street, but I was furious that I hadn't spelled out my personal politics during the meeting.

"Norie, the reason we love you is *because* of your beliefs," George said. "But you've never done a campaign. And they have. They know what they are doing."

"I'm not so sure," Kathleen volunteered from the backseat as the car made its way onto the Schuylkill Expressway and toward my mother's house. "They don't get that you're a woman. Or how people in Pennsylvania feel about you. I'm for women being tough, but I thought that Christie was about five degrees too hot. What's this all going to cost you, emotionally, that is."

I was looking through the packet George had distributed at the start of the meeting.

"I don't know about emotionally, but how does five million dollars hit you," I said, turning to look at Kathleen so she wouldn't think I'd been kidding. "The figures here say that Harris Wofford spent more than three million in 1991 on five months of television. That's about the time we have. Figure that a week in Pennsylvania costs five hundred thousand dollars—that we'll be running full tilt in the fall. And we'll probably run some ads before the August doldrums set in."

"So if it's no joke, let me make a suggestion," Kathy said.

"Okay."

"Get right on the phone."

"I'd have to call every person in the state just to raise one million," I insisted.

"No," Kathleen said, "you just have to phone the *right* people."

We pulled up in front of my mother's house.

"Is it a national holiday or something?" Kathleen asked. It was a valid question, since the front lawns on her block were dotted with American flags and bunting hung from several windows.

"No. It's just my mother. You've heard of Neighborhood Watch? This is Neighborhood Snoop." Stash chuckled from the front seat.

"Your father used to say it, Senator. 'That Marie. She could have been a spy, she knows everything.'"

Marie had obviously alerted the folks that the home-town heroine was returning home from her brush with death. "Norie. They can't push you around," one sign read.

"Give that slogan to our girl Christie," Kathleen quipped, following me in the back door. Since my father died three years ago, my mother had been sorting through his clothes and possessions, bagging them for the St. Vincent de Paul Society. My brother believes she's doing it one item a week. Her latest filled green trash bag was sitting in the tiny foyer, between the front door and the french door to the living room. It didn't matter since we all used the back door.

"You look pale," my mother sobbed, holding me close and pulling my face down to her. My mother, at barely five feet tall, was one of the few adults I ever leaned over to hug. Her tears startled me. She had been a little weepy since my brother, his wife, and three kids had moved to San Jose a few months before. And her show of emotion allowed me, for the first time since I had been pushed off the steps, to feel both fright and exhaustion. Mothers could do that.

"I am pale," I managed. "But I'm fine."

"The lieutenant's here. In the living room. And he won't eat a thing."

"That's because I stopped on the way here at Pat's Steaks," Carver announced. "Super sub with extra cheese and fried onions. I love Philly cuisine."

I had thought the lieutenant and I had come to a temporary parting of the ways when he delivered me to Liberty Place. But he was acting as if his drop-by at my mother's house in Northeast Philadelphia was an average occurrence, and I wasn't going to ask for details with my already worried mother standing there.

"Mrs. Kurek, I'm going to go over some details with the senator. Do you mind if we borrow your living room?" Carver asked.

"Sure. I'm running around to Mrs. McNally's on Pratt Street. She's had a terrible time getting over this summer flu and I said I'd drop around with some milk and bread." My mother, at the age of eighty, was still active in the parish's Sunshine Club. The elderly, she'd told me about three months ago, really needed visiting to cheer them up.

Kathleen mumbled something about using the upstairs phone to check with her office, and Carver—balancing two glasses and a pitcher of iced tea that he retrieved from the fridge—followed me into the living room.

I fiddled with the thermostat on the air conditioner. Old people are always too cold and their houses are always too hot. Carver settled the iced tea on the coffee table. I poured two glasses and waited for him to fill me in. But instead he wandered around the room, looking at the flocks of framed family photos.

"Whee-oo. Look at that hairdo. What was that?"

"A beehive. It required a half hour of teasing. But it did add three inches to my height."

"You white people do strange things," he said, laughing. "Some day I'll have to show you photographs of my gen-u-ine African Afro."

"I love this stroll down memory lane, but unless you're here in Philly to go to *American Bandstand,* I'd like a little more 'here and now.' "

"Good, since what I have to tell you is just about as up to date as it can be." Stretching, Carver leaned behind him and grabbed a brown canvas briefcase propped against the mantel. "This little model belongs to the local FBI office here. I hope I'll remember how to operate it, since my entire instruction was months ago from my son."

"The one at Cornell?"

"Yes. Mister Computer. He's the one who gets the full credit for what I'm going to show you. He'd called my office in Washington and left an urgent message."

Carver took a length of plastic cord and, unplugging the phone, hooked up the laptop to the outlet. I watched as he poked around, then heard the actual sound of a phone dialing, and, after a lot of static, a voice announcing that we were connected.

"Welcome to the Internet. Now"—Carver fished in the pocket of his blazer—"if I follow instructions . . ."

71

There was another two minutes of occasional typing, punctuated by Carver's attempt to sound like the background music on *Jeopardy!*

"Okay, let me sit beside you and show you where we are."

For me, going on the Internet was like going to outer space. I knew how to turn on my computer but I wrote on a quill-and-ink-style software system and was planning to ride my horse and buggy into the twenty-first century.

What Carter with his techie little laptop had punched up was the Keystone Militia Web page.

"Better living through technology," he mumbled, starting to scroll down the screen.

"Wait. I want to read this."

It was all in patriotic red and blue:

THE KEYSTONE MILITIA

This information is a service to the Patriots and Defenders of the United States and of the Commonwealth of Pennsylvania. Our founding fathers, the framers of our Constitution, knew what an Almighty-inspired document they drafted. And they knew protection was needed, especially to resist a National Guard, the unlawful and unconstitutionally organized militia. The right to bear arms, the right to organize a state militia, is one that must be upheld.

JOIN THE ARMY AND SERVE THE UNITED NATIONS
JOIN THE MILITIA AND SERVE AMERICA

What followed was page after page of quotations taken out of context, obscure court decisions, and an enormous diatribe about the configuration of the American flag.

"Bercolini was right. These people are just crazy," I told Carver. "Bercolini thought they were just a handful of nuts with a great sense of public relations."

"Bercolini might be very right, but he is also very dead. Let's remember that," Carver answered, as he kept scrolling down. He paused to let me see an obituary of Bercolini, which described him as "an enemy of the Constitution." It made me shudder.

Somewhere around page twenty-four he turned to me and said, "This is why I came up here today. This is why I'm nervous."

I watched as my face filled the computer screen. It was a straight-on shot, one that had obviously been taken at some event. And recently, too, since I was wearing my new yellow-and-white St. John knit jacket.

My face floated above a bright red headline.

WANTED. FOR QUESTIONING.
ELEANOR (NORIE) GORZACK.

This woman, appointed illegally to the United States Senate, is a strong supporter of gun control. She is now campaigning for election to the Senate. She is one of the Conspirators to form a Socialist One World government. Those who support her candidacy, those who support the United Nations, are working to treasonously subvert the Constitution.

BE MILITANT—IT'S YOUR CHOICE—FREEDOM OR SLAVERY

"I guess it's good for name recognition," I quipped, trying to make light of it.

"I think it's foolish too. The Internet is full of foolishness. I can conjure you up a Website that tells you about aliens landing in Times Square. But this is what got me worried," Carver explained, scrolling down more pages. "Here. This isn't so foolish."

What followed was an in-depth biography—my parents' backgrounds, my education, including grammar school; the details of my marriage to Jack and a complete list of jobs I had held. There were quotes from various magazine and newspaper pieces, with details like the fact I liked to cook, that I stayed with my mother in Philadelphia, that I liked to go to the movies by myself.

If that wasn't enough to set off a potent rush of paranoia, what followed put me over the top. There, on the Web page, was my schedule for the next three weeks: speeches, along with times and locations; town meetings, with the same kind of details; days I would be in Washington and others that I would be working from my state offices, in Pittsburgh and Philadelphia.

"How do they know this? I barely know my schedule. How did these crazies find all this out?" I shouted, grabbing Carver by the arm and almost turning over the coffee table.

"A lot of what senators do is public. Trust me, these

people know how to find things out," he said, rather casually I thought.

"Well, it's very interesting that some nuts who want to follow me have a terrific team of researchers, but they have to be stopped."

"No, Senator," Carver said, drawing out the syllables. "A lot of elected officials are just dying—no joke—to get their schedules out there. They want to be making happening appearances. Or at least have their speeches or news conferences covered by the media. So your office probably puts out a press schedule. Then, in D.C., there's a 'Daybook' put out by the wire services, listing all the stuff that's happening. Hearings. Meetings. Speeches. You gotta have that here, in Philly."

"So you're telling me," I said, trying to think it out as I was asking the question, "that my schedule gets issued by my press office, and the Daybook picks it up, and . . ."

"Senator, you want people to know your schedule. You're fighting for their attention. Especially the attention of the press. So anybody who has access to a wire service—like anybody with a computer or in a college radio station—can figure out where you are."

"Or"—Kathleen had apparently been standing at the doorway for a good part of our conversation—"someone who was pretending to be a member of the press could probably get your whole schedule right from your office."

"The Great Pretender. Hank Dugdale." I gulped my iced tea.

The two of them laughed.

"Sometimes I get a little scared by my own naïveté. Did I think I was campaigning in secret?" I asked nobody in particular. I then insisted that Carver show Kathleen the Website. Her little sharp intakes of breath accompanying the scrolling computer pages bolstered my belief that I was not overreacting.

"This is what I was telling you about, Norie. 'Paper terrorism.' These militias with their citizens' courts, their arrest warrants or writs or something. Kind of encouraging people to track other people down. Bad stuff. No doubt about it," Carver said, closing the lid on the laptop. "Bad enough that when I spoke to some of the fellows at the FBI they talked to some of the folks at the White House and, here I am. Hanging out with you, for a little while, until we find a more formal way of dealing with this."

"Dealing? Just shut it down. Make them take it off the Internet," I said. "Isn't that right? You know, maybe this is what Bercolini was worried about. If the militia was using the Web to track public officials. I understand that they can know about my campaign, that my schedule is public. But why should they be able to send out all this information about me?"

"Because, my dear Senator," Carver said, "*you* are a public official. Citizens get the chance to criticize you, to hound you, to make your life of public service real unpleasant."

"Citizens, huh!" I answered. "I thought that kind of harassment was reserved for my friends and staff. They all seem to be really on my case."

CHAPTER 7

Milton was. On my case, that is. No sooner was I back in the office the next morning, no sooner had Nancy stuck the flowers from the interns into a handy vase, no sooner was I behind my desk than Milton was in my office. Agitating.

Nancy had warned me about his mood, though my confusion about her current status with Milton put a cloud over her cautioning. I wasn't sure what the relationship of their "friendship" was. For a few weeks, the two of them had all the signs of a budding romance—but then, in the pressured days before my "accident" when a slew of late legislative nights was followed by the Pennsylvania floods, signs of wilting were noticeable.

That's when Nancy, bringing in food for one late-night session, refused to give Milton a tuna salad sandwich, saying that he hadn't ordered tuna and he wasn't getting tuna. I might be a little rusty on inter-personal relationships, but a refusal to compromise on the tuna was a clear signal there was a rift.

So when Nancy told me that Milton was "cranky"—making him sound like a tired two-year-old—I wasn't ready for the wrath of Khan.

"Senator, let's get through some of the issue material ignored in that meeting with your campaign staff," was the gentle beginning, as Milton plopped himself down, dropping the white folders I remembered from the campaign meeting in George's office.

"Milton, I was willing to make issues the center of the discussion," I started on my apologia. But there was no defensive stance with Milton, even when we were on the best of terms. It was all offense. Take your choice: Tac nukes or standard weapons.

"Why bother, Senator. Doesn't even *substance* have to be cleared with those hired guns?" Milton asked, managing to turn "substance" into a four-letter word. "You have to be careful now that significant legislation doesn't get in the way of a good commercial."

"But I thought you were involved in hiring those guns?"

"No, I thought we were all meeting in Philadelphia to interview the prospective hires and to tell them how to run the campaign. I got to the meeting a half hour before your arrival and George and Marco had the deal all sewn up. Everything but the contracts, and those have to be run by one of the election lawyers here in town."

"I'm sorry. I felt cut out too. I couldn't . . ."

"That's all right. Let's move on. What else is on our agenda?"

I told Milton about Carver's visit to Philadelphia and finding myself on the Keystone Militia's Web page. I admit it. I was looking for sympathy.

"So since these people know every place I'm going and everything I'm doing, Carver's going to give the heads-up to the local police. Just to make sure that everybody is on red alert."

"Knowing cops, I bet most of them either belong to the militia or have best friends in it," Milton grumbled. I always had to remember that Milton had a mild case of leftover sixties-itis. He thought most people in uniform were the enemy.

"At least *I* feel better knowing that somebody with a badge and some authority is out there, watching over me. In case these crazies show up again," I offered.

"Maybe it would make a good commercial. You know—senator under assault and standing up to face off the mob." Milton paused, and for a minute, I thought we were once again on good terms. "Course you didn't face off the mob. They pushed you off the step."

"Give it a rest, Milton." Now I was getting cranky.

"If you had a problem with the consultants, why didn't you speak up at the meeting?"

"You mean the coronation? Where the consultants were crowned king and queen of the campaign? Nobody consulted me about the consultants." He folded his arms and stared, a cold, hard look. I couldn't resist. I burst out laughing.

"Sorry. I am sorry. But to hear you. 'Nobody consulted me about the consultants.' It just sounds ridiculous."

Milton slammed his hand down on the conference table hard enough to make me think he might have broken it—his hand, not the table.

"How about 'laughable'? Does that describe how I feel? Imagine walking into a meeting I had found out about the night before. Meeting these three jokers who have barely visited a state I know backwards and forwards. And then to have my role consigned to 'issues.' I was doing 'issues' before you knew where the Capitol was, Senator. And before any of those *consultants* were allowed to vote."

This seemed a little extreme to me, especially since Milton was maybe three years older than Christie and Charlie. But I was not going to push the point, especially since I had a bad case of injured staff feelings on my hands—not to mention what harm he'd done to his hand with that one terrible smack.

"Are you mad at me—or at the consultants?" I finally asked.

"Senator, I'm mad that some pro-ams, like Marco

and George, get to walk in and big-foot everybody else out of the campaign. It's their choice. Since those two have to pay for the campaign, let them have any campaign they want."

"What about me? Aren't you supposed to be working for me?"

"Don't start questioning *my* loyalty, Senator. I was the one who wanted to take a four-month leave of absence, and go up to Pennsylvania and run this campaign. I was the one who sat down and wrote the campaign memo and pointed out the key issues and personalities. I was the one who figured out how to get the research done." He sat back, with a sadly smug look on his face.

"Milton, I have no idea what you are talking about. I've never seen a campaign proposal. I never understood that you wanted to go to Pennsylvania. Nothing. Where is it? Why didn't you just talk to me?"

"Where is it? I gave it to Nancy. Two, no three weeks ago. I left it at her apartment. I figured you had read it and, once we got through this flood stuff, we'd sit down and talk."

"I never saw it. I never heard about it."

There was no time to quiz Nancy about Milton's memos. I was late for my lunch with Hilda in the senators-only dining room.

When I first got to the Senate, I thought the Senate Dining Room was where senators would meet and discuss great issues of the day—but that's where senators hosted constituents, or lobbyists, or just the family at lunch.

The real business—although it wasn't all "great issues"—happened in a far more modest "Senators Only" room across the hall. Two oblong tables, one for each party and separate enough for some conversation, along with a buffet make up the entire decor.

I was amazed during my first days, and my wonder has still held at the civility of the Senate. We can be battling each other for hours, and then, as one senator enters the dining room, others will nod hello. Although I did get more than a nod on that, my first day back from my "accident."

Just as I came through the door, the entire lunch crowd jumped to their feet, waving and whistling. Hilda Mendelssohn, my mentor and the longtime senator from Ohio, was standing and clapping. With her was Majority Leader Phil Fox, making some kind of a noise I'd only heard in cowboy movies when they were moving the herd out of the canyon. Representing Wyoming, Fox was a professional westerner—a hunter, whose trophies covered the walls of his private office. Dead deer aside, Fox believed that no one could be as macho as himself, so both men and women flunked the test and were all lumped together as equals.

"Norie. Welcome back to the old corral. Thought the rustlers might have made off with you," Fox yelled at me.

"Does that make you feel like a heifer or what?"

Hilda added, taking me by the hand. "I was really worried."

"The flowers were beautiful. My mother is thrilled that you sent them to her house."

"You can't get flowers up in the flood area," Hilda explained.

"Dugdale did. He probably brought them on the same bus that the protesters traveled on."

"Wait," Hilda said, shushing Fox with her left hand and holding me with her right. "You're telling me those people who attacked you were not from Jericho?"

I was just ready to give her a detailed account when Fox banged the table and called for attention.

"Just want Senator Gorzack to know that we are pleased as punch that she's back with us. Gotta little gift for her," Fox announced to the twenty or so senators, swinging around one of the largest present bags I'd ever seen.

"Pray that it's not a dead animal," Hilda whispered in my ear. "Or a gift certificate to a taxidermist."

I bit my lip, but Hilda, caught by her own humor, let a giggle slip. Foxie continued, apparently ignoring us.

"When we go out from this Capitol, into our own states, into other foreign lands, we all take chances. Norie took a chance. But she's okay."

"What is he talking about," I whispered to Hilda. "I wasn't going into a war zone."

"So I want Norie to take something with her—

something that will always be with her, as a reminder of our caring and friendship." Foxie turned toward me. Oh, was it that feared dead animal? "Open it. Open it."

I pulled out the tissue and realized that whatever the present was, it was large and soft. And cotton. It slid out of the bag. It was a U.S. Senate sweatshirt, about four sizes too big.

"Something to keep you warm and safe," Foxie said with a smile. I smiled back. My Leader was an occasional non sequitur.

"Sometimes he's just out of it. He just starts off speaking and he doesn't think about what he's going to say," Hilda said. "Like all of us in politics. Anyway, by the fall, when you've spent ten nights in a row on the road and you're crawling into a bed in a Ramada Inn, you'll love snuggling up with your sweatshirt."

I pulled my chair over closer to hers. She'd filled two plates from the buffet with heart-smart items, so we could get right down to business.

"I hired my campaign staff. A woman—Christie Hamilton—who'll coordinate. And then for the media Charlie McPherson," I said, pausing to take a bite of salmon. "What do you think?"

"Interesting choices," Hilda said, her tone more reproving than her words. "I've never used them myself. But I've heard about them."

She started to sort through the salad items on her own plate and I couldn't help feel that my campaign suddenly had the texture of hearts of palm—a little soggy and a little too pale.

"Could I get some feedback?" I asked her.

"You've hired them. What's for feedback? Anyway, we should be talking about money. You've got a lot of catching up to do. Thank God there's some money in the DSCC pot."

The Democratic Senate Campaign Committee, like its counterpart on the Republican side, raises money for Senate candidates. This election cycle Hilda was the chair.

"Now you can't raise money out of your Senate office," she said. "You know that. But we do have a DSCC office just about two blocks away, so you come over there, and you do your phone calls."

"I hate it. The money calls. I'm just not going to be good at it," I told her, shaking my shoulders as if the idea of it gave me a chill.

"Do you mean you won't be good at it because you're too good a person to make those kinds of calls?" Hilda had turned in her chair and was looking straight at me. She seemed almost angry. "Because that's the kind of attitude that's going to push us into campaign finance reform that will only increase the power of people who are *not* the voters."

"I'm not being critical," I said. "I just don't like it."

"But it's part of the job. It would be great if the government financed all campaigns. But this way, you at least meet or talk to people who are interested in the issues."

"People who want to buy influence," I said, smugly.

"No." Hilda had shoved her plate away from her and was now fiddling with her fork. I wondered if she would soon use it as a weapon. "People who say, 'If you support our issues, we'll support you.' That's labor unions and the minimum wage. That's seniors and Medicare. That's environmentalists and cleaner water and air. And, yes, it's businesses and corporations. But if you are voting for the state and your principles, these people are not going to support you unless you support them."

CHAPTER 8

Money might be the mother's milk of politics—but meetings are the gruel of government. You might not like the taste and texture, but you must eat them all up.

Carver had spent the morning making calls to the FBI and the state police. He was waiting for me outside the dining room and we headed over to the office of the late Representative Bercolini. In my months in the Senate, it was the first time I had made my way to the House side of the Hill, since, common practice, the Lower House representatives came to visit the Upper House senators. But both Carver and I wanted a chance to go through Bercolini's files, hopefully uncovering some signpost to point to his killers.

There are 435 members in the House of Representatives, the number for most of the twentieth century. Each represents almost six hundred thousand people—that's persons, not just voters. Just like the Senate, the House has three office buildings, facing the House side of the Capitol from the other side of Constitution Avenue. But when the number of rooms in the three buildings is divided by 435 instead of the 100 in the Senate, the office space gets tight.

For most members, three rooms is the norm. One room is usually the personal office of the Member, the other two are for staff, crammed with desks and files for the allotted total of eighteen full-time and four temporary or part-time. For the House honchos—the Speaker, the leaders, the whips, and chairs of some committees—there are offices in the Capitol itself.

Bercolini's longtime secretary, Rose O'Connor, a woman in her late fifties who had passed the stylish stage of stout some pounds before, had set up coffee for us in the congressman's personal office. His desk had been pushed back against some bookcases, and a conference table pulled to the center of the room. Several open cardboard file boxes edged the table.

"We've been trying to get through our files. Jody Chang, the congressman's AA, is back in the district, dealing with the memorial arrangements."

"And I understand there is no funeral, except for the family?" I asked.

"No. Grace wanted it just very quiet. There will be a memorial service there. And one down here, in a few weeks. And, Senator, we'd like to have you speak at one of them. At least."

"Rose, I'll try to schedule myself for both of them. Now, I'm here to get up to speed on the congressman's agenda."

"Well, none of us were totally up to date on his various projects," Rose said, waving her arm in the direction of the boxes. "He liked to say he was his own best staff. He always had a lot of things going on."

"Like his concern about the militia . . ."

"Senator, let me interrupt. He wasn't 'concerned' about the militia. He was furious that they were getting this publicity. He kept putting them down, calling them little tin revolutionaries. Of course, every time he snickered, it just made them madder."

"Yes," I said. That jibed with Bercolini's conversation with me on the plane. I was thankful that with Rose I was dealing with a staffer who had some real knowledge of her boss, but I was quickly figuring out that there was no easy road map to Bercolini's political destinations. What could he have been hinting at— "something important" that would help overcome my inexperience?

"Well," Rose said, with a sad sigh, "so far I've sorted his various personal papers into boxes, but I still haven't read them through carefully." She pointed at one cardboard tower. "There's the 'environment.' Probably issue number one. Then there's the whole question of corruption-free unions. Third is the area of expanding where such unions could organize. He was just getting into this, but TAGNETs—those are the tracers put into possible explosives, like black powder and fertilizer—were like a new priority. And then he had his stuff—notes, governmental reports, newspaper articles—on various militias around the country."

"And what did he want, Rose? On TAGNETs, that is. I really don't know much about them," I said, realizing the question was out of order in what should be a targeted approach to figuring out Bercolini's files.

"Better use of TAGNETs in all possible explosives. Better follow-up on demands for any explosives. Better investigations, much more funding, when explosives were used," she said, her voice trailing off. "We had a whole plan for the fall. The congressman planned on using the two-week recess to focus on TAGNETs. And other stuff. But he was going to work from back in the district."

"Was that efficient?" I asked. "Wouldn't he have better information sources here, in D.C.?"

"He was a whiz on his laptop. We kidded him about it all the time. He had a Powerbook and there wasn't a program or an attachment that he wasn't the first in line for. So he'd E-mail back and forth all day, sending us stuff. And we'd do the same to him."

"And after the flood tour, what was scheduled?"

"He had this meeting with a union guy he knew. A Teamster back in the district. His second one in a week. I'm pretty sure it had a direct link to the TAGNET stuff. I should have the guy's name on the calendar."

Rose briskly raised her considerable bulk out of the chair. Her face had that wonderful smoothness, that pulled-tight skin that nature gives as compensation for a sluggish metabolism. Her crisp efficiency belied her phlegmatic portrait. Once again, I realized I'd erroneously bought into the image that TV and magazines were selling—in life, fat did not equate with fatuous.

She came back into the personal office carrying a stack of papers, all with the familiar three holes punched.

"I ran the congressman's schedule out of a loose-leaf book," she explained, smiling. "I started with him fifteen years ago, when he was a member of the General Assembly back in Harrisburg. Three years there. Six terms here. The one thing I learned was that he was always changing his schedule."

She sat down beside me and spread the papers in front of us.

"I kept the proposed schedule on green paper. Then, when a day or a couple of days were completed, I would fill in what he actually did on yellow paper. He was always telling people he'd get back in touch. So I taught him—" Rose caught herself. "I *asked* him to just stick their business cards in his jacket pocket. Or write their names and numbers on one of his cards. Then we'd xerox the cards and that would be the third color paper—white—in the loose leaf."

For the first time, Carver seemed genuinely interested. "Miss O'Connor, that is a system worthy of law enforcement."

"Well, it was overwhelming to keep it up. But it was the only way to keep track of his time—and his promises to spend time on an issue." She shook her head. "That's why I'm so disappointed, Senator, that I don't have more information for you on his 'Teamster friend.'"

"No phone number? Okay, how about the place they met last week?" Carver asked.

"Nothing," Rose said, sorting through the papers as if looking for the proverbial needle. "I can't remember anything specific, but I remember when the congressman mentioned the first meeting. He did say something about 'blowing up.' So that could easily be the TAGNETs. Or the President's anticrime bill."

"Or union corruption?" Carver added with a question.

"All those are possibilities, Rose," I said, hearing the impatience in my own voice. "But don't you, or Jody, have something on this meeting? There must be a name or a card somewhere. You did tell me there was another meeting scheduled, right?"

"Yes. The congressman told me. And I wrote it down. But there was no card. And it really was unlike him. He'd gotten so good at remembering to bring all the little pieces of paper. . . ."

She put her head down and started to cry. Her careful hairdo, all slickly puffed out and sprayed, bobbed up and down, a sad little dance accompanying the music of her soft sobs. I patted her back and stared at the boxes. I knew I'd find those "little pieces" carefully xeroxed and paper-clipped. I knew that this conscientious staffer, with her clerical mind-set, was the facilitator, the safety net that permitted Bercolini's high-wire, headline-grabbing antics.

"Rose, I'm not going to let the congressman—or his issues—fade away. I'm going to have someone from my staff over here tomorrow, going through these boxes, tracking down every possibility."

"Senator"—Rose lifted her head and showed me a tear-ravaged race—"I just feel so badly. I don't have a card on that Teamster. Not his name or his number. And the congressman had been doing so well with the names."

Bercolini had two big interest areas, unions and the environment. Rose said the FBI had been through most of the documents the day before, but Carver and I both thought it was worth a shot.

One thing was clear. On Bercolini's two big issues I had two big experts to help us out: Marco Solari, who'd been in organized labor for more than two decades, and George Taylor, whose business dealt with environmental technology and who chaired the statewide environmental protection group RiverWatch. I got them on a late-afternoon conference call.

Federal rules prohibit not just face-to-face fundraising solicitations but also fund-raising phone calls using any office on the Hill—but strategy conversations with consultants or campaign committees can take place, as well as conversations about fund-raising plans.

I thought we could cover both my campaign and Bercolini's issues. George had a different agenda and Marco was right with him.

"Norie," George told me, a little too crisply, "I, too, thought Bob Bercolini was a swell guy. His death is a tragedy. He was a terrific environmentalist. I bet he'd done more for rivers, for air, than anybody. But right now what we want from the environmental community is support for your campaign."

"Let me interrupt, George. Norie, this is Marco," he yelled into the phone. Marco had some misplaced belief that he must constantly identify himself on conference calls. He also seemed to think that the number of people on the call reduced the potential volume of his voice. "I have several fund-raisers set up with the unions. We need to get your scheduler on the ball. Get this moving along. We've got June and July. In August, nobody's around. Then it's September . . ."

"The Jewish holidays," George interjected. "By October, it's so close to the election that people think they've given even if they haven't . . ."

"And anyway," Marco picked up, "you've got to have cash to buy time on TV. So let's get this schedule happening."

I sat in my chair, looked out the window at my non-view, and said nothing. Finally George almost whispered into the phone, "Okay. We give up. Tell us what you want to do."

"I want to pick up the ball on Bercolini's issues. He was looking into something that he believed was really important. Something that he was convinced could help me."

"What would help is to get campaigning—" George began, but I cut him off.

"This *will* help campaigning. For example, I'm especially interested in finding out about TAGNETs. The tracers put in explosives."

"I know what they are, Norie," George said, interrupting me this time.

"So I want to try to help carry out Bercolini's agenda—an agenda he would have told me about if we had another five minutes. And, to be honest, I want to try and figure out what he believed and did that got him murdered."

"Great. So you can get in the same line of fire of some crazy people," George yelled, the whisper gone. "We're not going to let you do that. First, because we're your friends and we love you and we don't want you getting murdered. And, second, you've got a campaign to run. Not a vendetta or an investigation."

"This is Marco. No poking around. Too dangerous. And anyway, that's why we have an FBI and why Bercolini has House colleagues."

"Bercolini didn't let anything get in the way of his beliefs," I insisted. "His staff said he just started working on legislation regarding TAGNETs. Those are the tracers put in explosives and—"

"Norie, I told you, I *know* what TAGNETs are. And

I knew Bob Bercolini. Better than you did. But he's dead. And he's not running for the U.S. Senate."

"Norie, it's me, Marco. You should be working on your new committee assignments. Environment and public works is real perk, especially the public works part. You gotta start bringing some good stuff into the state. Bridges, highways, plants, postal distribution centers. What else, George?"

"Anything else she can lay her hands on," George said. "You're the incumbent, Norie. You've got to produce."

"I agree," I said, although I hated to put my representation in the what-can-you-do-for-me terms. "I want Pennsylvania to get its fair share."

"Fair share be damned," George shouted. "You want your state to get everything that's not nailed down by a senator from another state. First, because we need the industry and the jobs. Second, because you need to raise money from the people you help."

"George, this is Marco. Let me put my two cents in on jobs—"

"No, Marco, because we need a lot more than two cents. Norie, I get this feeling you don't want to do the money part of this campaign. And, if you don't"— George paused—"running around trying to figure out who killed Bercolini is not going to make any difference."

"And Bercolini was not always popular among union guys, Norie. My guys like to hunt. With some of them, a vote on the Brady Bill is enough to put a congressman in the gun-control column. Let's not confuse my people," Marco said, talking faster so that George couldn't cut back in. "Dugdale will make this a one-issue campaign. Give my guys the chance to work for you, to vote for you."

"You think these militia types are going to let you start in on them? That's who killed him. Why put yourself in their crosshairs?" George asked, and I could hear his self-satisfaction oozing out of the phone. "My county RiverWatch chairs are working overtime, with the floods and the faulty riverbeds and dams. They deserve your attention."

I hated to admit it, but George had made his point. I made one last attempt.

"But Bercolini tried to tell me something, when we were on *Air Force One*. And I don't think it was about the militia."

"Great. You turn yourself into a little investigator, like some half-baked committee staffer. And I'll bet you something, Norie." George was sounding quite irritated by now. "Next January, when the new senator from Pennsylvania is sworn in, you'll have plenty of time to investigate, because you'll be out of a job."

CHAPTER 9

The verbal attack by George and Marco had hit me like a truck, which was nothing compared to what hit the office that afternoon. The mail was twice as heavy as usual and, starting about noon, phone calls, faxes, and telegrams had started coming in, all questioning my patriotism, my voting records, my honesty, and, in every missive, my ability to beat Hank Dugdale.

"Dugdale doesn't miss a trick," Milton mumbled, pushing piles of papers to the back of my conference table, just to make room for yet another batch. "He had a news conference this morning, saying guns are a vital part of self-protection for people living in rural areas. He insisted that Bercolini could have saved himself if he had a handgun, and that the congressman contributed to his own murder by being for gun control."

"That's outrageous. Bercolini might have voted for the Brady Bill, but he was not a rabid gun control leader. And," I added, "I'm glad you're back, Milton."

"Senator, I'm not going to leave you, certainly not when you're on the Values Coalition's Most Wanted List. Dugdale and his group have a lot in common. None of them play fair."

Milton handed me a sheet of paper, with a large photograph of yours truly, and with a series of little boxes lined up under my name.

CHECK HER OUT, was the command of the bold black headline.

Where does Gorzack stand?
*** Does she announce herself as a Patriot?
*** Does she support ALL Amendments to the United States?
*** How does she stand on the Constitution?

What will Gorzack Do?
*** Affirm that States' Rights Must Return to the States???
*** Pledge That U.S. Troops Fight Only Under an American Flag???

"This looks an awful lot like my militia-sponsored Website," I told Milton. "It's called 'pin the rap on the Senator.'"

"No, what you see before you, Senator, is your charity dollars at work." Milton sorted through one of the folders he'd brought into the office. "It's a well-organized campaign against you—and it's being funded by tax-deductible contributions."

"Explain," I ordered him. "And then tell me how I can convince myself that everybody in the state of Pennsylvania isn't out to get me."

"Same question, really." Milton suddenly looked if not happy, at least not desperate. "Values Coalition is a tax-deductible organization. A 501-C3, as we call them in law school. Its intent is to educate people. It's forbidden from lobbying, at least not more than three percent of the time of its staff or with more than three percent of its funding."

"But lobbying is what the Values Coalition is all about. They want to change certain laws. So they picket, protest, write letters, fax."

"No," Milton said, shaking his head dramatically. "That's not 'lobbying.' They are not coming up here, on Capitol Hill, and meeting with lawmakers and asking that you take specific votes on specific legislation. They are 'educating,' they argue, on those issues—but that's not lobbying."

"This is the same kind of pressure Bercolini was under. His staff showed me the trash they were getting." I picked up the poster. "So you're telling me there's no way to stop this?"

"Sure you could stop this. You could sue. You could challenge their tax-exempt status. You could go to court and force them to release their list of contribu-

101

tors. But the U.S. Constitution wants to protect people's rights. And, by the time we went through the motions—and I mean *court* motions—the election would be over."

"But shouldn't we go after them anyway? Through the courts, I mean."

"Nope, I don't think so," Milton said. "Anyway, by the time the election is over, the Values Coalition is over. Because I think it's just a front group for Dugdale. It's a way Dugdale can pick up some big contributions from a few fat cats, and then use that money for the organization and the phone calls and all the stuff that for several months can make all of our lives a sweet little hell."

"And if we attack him about what the Values Coalition is doing?"

"Then we're the bad folks. We're doing the hated 'negative' campaigns. Dugdale, if he's smart, won't do a single commercial attacking you. He'll just let the Values Coalition keep on the offensive."

"Milton," I said, suddenly feeling quite *desperate* myself, "you've got to think of something. Quick."

"I'm working on it, Senator."

By early evening, Milton had even more bad news. A lot of the letters filling the in baskets were demanding specific information—how I would vote on a certain piece of legislation; if I was signing on as a cosponsor for a particular amendment; how much money my office spent on postage in the last year.

"This is impossible. We'd need a staff of a hundred to research all these positions. These people are demanding detailed responses on minutiae, and we can't keep up," Milton explained.

"I can't believe I'm saying this, knowing how I believe nothing is as important as constituent services—but can't we just, ah, I don't know . . ." I attempted a strategy.

But Milton was too quick.

"Can't we just send out the stock letters, the hated *ROBOS?* Nothing, Senator, would make me happier than to crank up the old robot letter writer, feed in twenty or so issue letters, and send them right along. But these requests are for itsy-bitsy details. And there's another problem."

"Of course there is, Milton. Nothing is simple."

"If we take a shortcut in our answering, we could be blowing off the League of Women Voter types who write in—not identifying themselves as a member of the League—ask a detailed question, get your answer, and then report back to their membership not just on where you stand, but how your office handled the information request. How do we guess which letters are real—and which, of the many, are from the Values Coalition creeps?"

"I don't know, Milton. This is really a problem."

"A dilemma. A real killer," he added, bundling his papers together and marching out of the room.

The crisis left Milton considerably cheered up. He'd

even engaged Nancy in several conversations, trotting in and out of my office like a somber golden retriever.

"Nothing picks that boy up like a real crisis," Nancy said with a sheepish grin.

"And does that mean that you are thinking about presenting him with such a situation?" I asked, being unable to resist girl talk about dating. "Like start seeing him again?"

"Norie, I can't stand the idea of, as you put it . . ."

" 'Quaintly put it,' is how I think you wanted to phrase it."

"Whatever. I can't stand the lack of transition between the office and the, for want of a better word, the *nonoffice.* When Milton and I were getting involved, it seemed like the work stuff seeped over into our personal time together. And then, in the office, the personal stuff made it kind of sticky."

"Do you think a lot of intramural dating goes on, up here on the Hill?" I asked, loving every detail of how the younger generation was handling all this stuff.

"Sure," Nancy said, with conviction. "But that doesn't mean that anybody knows how to handle it any better than we did."

The Senate had a pack of votes scheduled over the next few days. Watching the Senate on C-SPAN, a citizen might think that the Senators just stand around, waiting to be called on, but my schedule that week was packed.

I had two meetings with my legislative assistants on hot issues that were quickly coming up for a vote. I had a luncheon with the board of the American Association of University Women. There was a possible lake-dredging contract for a firm in Erie—a job that would mean hundreds of jobs over the next ten years, so I was getting together with the elected officials and dredging company execs from the area. All of this got topped off by several subcommittee meetings, an especially vital one concerned with a piece of public works legislation and a three-hour hearing by the whole committee on child health issues.

There were at least ten press calls a day—about my campaign and what kind of a schedule I would be maintaining in the state. Ralph deSantis alone took almost an hour during two separate calls. He had an early-warning system, he told me, and its lights were going off. Things were not going good in my campaign, according to the deSantis disaster detectors.

I told him everything was hunky-dory and that I would buy him a chocolate rose the next time I was in town.

Jammed, that's what my schedule was. But I didn't let anything keep me from my Wednesday lunch meeting with Mike Kincaid. I'd promised those vets up in Jericho that we'd track down this leukemia—and I was bound and determined to do just that. I knew Kincaid would be an enormous help.

We were set to meet over sandwiches in Kincaid's office, but, at the last minute, the location had been switched to Garrett Baxter's "hideaway," one of the unmarked offices given to senior senators and located right in the Capitol.

My set-for-fifteen-minutes meeting with the heads of a dozen Pittsburgh-area Rotary Clubs ran just a little late, so the two men were already seated at a small table when I arrived. This was my second visit to Baxter's hideaway, which rumor had it was top of the line, a corner room with views of the Mall and the Washington and Lincoln Monuments. I stared out for a minute, knowing that beyond a certain clump of trees the Vietnam Memorial glinted in the afternoon sun and that the recently chiseled name of my late husband's shone brightly.

"We didn't make a decision without you," Baxter said, jumping up to shake my hand. "You get *your* choice. Chicken salad or poached salmon." Someone on Baxter's staff had brought in beautifully done-up individual trays, each with a main course, small cups of soup, and two short towers of brownies.

"I've done some preliminary work," I told them. "I've talked to my successor at the Pennsylvania Department of Health who is running some questions through the computer system, just to see if anything turns up. Both of us, though, think there's little chance that we'll get any help there."

"That's a start," Kincaid said. "And I've got a plan. I'm ordering, on short notice, hearings under the Veterans Committee. We can look at the Jericho cases—

and try to track down similar outbreaks around the country."

"Great," I said. And it was everything I wanted. But I was a little disappointed that I hadn't been included.

"My staff in Pennsylvania could help out," I offered. "Maybe pre-interview some of the men."

"Help out?" Baxter laughed. "Mike and I think you should help run the hearings, Senator. Your background in public health makes you our most valuable resource. Besides, it's your state."

"I've asked Senator Baxter to sign on," Kincaid explained, "since he runs the Armed Services Committee. And some say the entire armed services."

I joined Kincaid in his laughter, while Baxter looked as though the joke had cut a little too close to the truth.

"Seriously, Senator Baxter gives us the punch if we do uncover a linkage between the vets' service in the army and their developing leukemia," Kincaid continued.

"Right. Also if we need information from the Pentagon, it's my job to make sure it's forthcoming," Baxter added.

"So I'm in? That's great." I grinned at both of them. "And, you know, I have just the right person to help us out."

I waited till the laughter died down. I am always a little too eager to throw myself into the fray, dragging various friends and staff along with me.

"Really. She's a skilled researcher and a whiz with computer data acquisition. She loves her data—"

"Like you?" Baxter asked, putting him and Kincaid into another round of laughter.

"Yes. I like details. Her name is Mary Devine. She's just come down from Harrisburg," I said. "It's part of my staff plan. The time has come to replace some of Senator Gannon's staffers, especially the ones who retired without informing anyone that they'd stopped working."

"So you've replaced some paper pusher with an Internet intellectual?" Mike asked.

"Not just the Internet. She'll be able to get access to the National Institutes of Health computerized info and really track down exactly how prevalent this rare strain of leukemia is turning out to be."

"If your Mary Devine is going to become that well informed," Kincaid suggested, "then let's send her back up to Jericho sometime next week. Let her research each of the men's cases. Where they served, what years they were in Vietnam."

Baxter was nodding agreement, but then he cleared his throat. It was not an agreeable sound.

"I just want to be sure that we've checked everything out. Norie, you better than any of us know that any research into a health issue requires ten times as much ruling out as it does finding out. So could Miss Devine also check out heredity and geographic factors. Okay?"

"Couldn't be better."

"Or better for you, Norie," Baxter said. "This hearing is good politics and good press."

"Speaking of politics, Senator, how's the campaign?" Kincaid asked, with what I was sure was the best of intentions. It was just that I couldn't stand any more criticism about what I was doing.

"Terrific," I said, hoping that it was just a little white lie. "Couldn't be better."

My general nervousness about the campaign racheted up several notches late that afternoon with a call from Christie Hamilton, campaign consultant extraordinaire. As Nancy announced her call, I felt a twinge of guilt. I was moving from the fast pace of the Senate to the faster pace of the campaign, and back again. I hadn't thought of Bercolini in days. I had to make the time to call his widow, Grace, and see how she was holding up. But, first, the campaign.

"I've got a great idea for our shoot Saturday," Christie bubbled into the phone. "We could really save some money if we did it in Maryland."

"The *state* of Maryland?" I asked, dumbfounded.

"Sure. What else?"

"But I'm the senator from Pennsylvania," I was naive enough to counter.

"Yes, of course you are," Christie agreed, sounding as if I had told her I was Napoleon. "But Charlie is already shooting another race in Maryland, and we can just piggyback you on. Same schools. Same senior citizens."

I explained that I thought it was a little problematic, even as a way to save money, since people might figure out that the shoot had not taken place in the state I was supposed to represent. She didn't argue, but I felt a little tenseness on her part. And a heightened eagerness on mine to get a look at the scripts for my commercials.

It turned out there were none. Not yet. They were coming.

"Christie, I have a bio. I have a life. I have some name recognition in Pennsylvania. And I would like to have scripts for the commercials."

"Senator, worry more about how you look than what you say. It's television. We're dealing with the image thing," she said. "Women are too soft. Your features aren't sharp, to be honest, and Charlie is worried about your chin."

"Is the chin a big problem in all your campaigns, Christie?"

"No, not really. Although we had a terrific problem with one rather young senator who wanted to do commercials on Rollerblades and when we shot it, had a chin down to his knees."

"I don't care about my chin. Or how far it falls," I said, all the while telling myself that I was too young to have a chin problem. "And I don't care much about the image thing. I'm worried about the vision thing. And the script thing. I want to see words. Words that some announcer will say. Words that I will say. I want to see what the commercials will say."

The long pause that followed seemed to indicate Christie's displeasure. I certainly had no way of making her happy, so I said good-bye and hung up the phone.

"I don't know exactly how you Catholics think, Norie, but fund-raising is not a mortal sin."

Hilda Mendelssohn was sitting across from me and we were sharing a Portobello mushroom. The two of us were tucked into one of the small banquettes in the front room at Galileo and were trying our best not to establish eye contact with any of the dozens of lobbyists and lawyers who seemed to be in full strength this night.

"I don't think there's anything *wrong* with asking people for money. I just don't like to do it. Hey, I don't like asking people for anything, let alone cash. And after the newspaper stories and the investigations . . ."

Hilda waved at a waiter to have him pour more of the Pinot Grigio. At Hilda's orders, we were cabbing it, so we could relax and make it a late night, which in Washington translated to about 10 P.M.

"But in order to *avoid* scandals, *you* have to raise money. You're asking people—not foreign governments. And if you are going to ask a citizen to support you with his or her vote, why not ask for their monetary support as well?"

"It just seems too, ah, I don't know. Too crass." I paused, embarrassed. "Anything I say is going to sound like some Goody Two-shoes who thinks fund-raising is beneath her."

"And . . ."

"Okay. You got me. I can't do it. At least not to people I don't know."

"They are not exactly strangers, Norie. They are longtime supporters of the Democratic Party in your state. They are used to writing checks. They're just people. Voters," Hilda finished up strong, poking her Portobello with a well-aimed fork.

"That's another question. People are one thing. But I'm not sure I should be taking money from political action committees. Maybe I should accept contributions only from individuals." I took a piece of bread, sopped up the olive oil that had leaked out of my mushroom, and stuck it into my mouth, feeling quite satisfied by both the taste and my pronouncement. From the look on Hilda's face, she found my views quite unappetizing.

"Fine. I'll tell all the women who make up Emily's List and all the men and women who belong to unions and all the families that belong to the Sierra Club that they don't count in your version of how government works," Hilda replied, sounding even more self-righteous than I had. "Unions and Emily's List and the Sierra Club are PACs."

"But what about businesses?"

"What about them? I bet your buddy George Taylor has a PAC. For Pete's sake, Norie, Marco's raising money for candidates all the time. But first he's making sure that the ones who get the contributions are favorable to labor."

"And do you think that's right?" I asked, only half

knowing what I myself believed. "Look at this place. It's crammed with guys in gray suits. It's a testimony to lawyers and lobbyists."

"Also to great food," Hilda said, starting to laugh.

"Okay. Make fun of me. I just think we could do all this money thing better. Cleaner."

"Sure. But," Hilda said, "until we revamp the whole megillah, until we are totally sure that one special-interest group is not going to sweep in on a tide of money and revamp our priorities—well, we better do our job to raise the money from people who support our party's agenda."

"Okay. As long as I never feel that I'm getting money to support someone else's agenda—okay?"

"Norie," Hilda said in her best maternal voice, "you're the senator. You know why you're asking them for money. And it's up to you to let them know that their money goes to support you. Not to change you. If you don't believe you're in charge of your own professional persona, what are you doing running for the Senate?"

She held the last syllable for a long time, like "Senate" was all in neon and flashing above the table.

"All right. Now what?" I finally asked.

"For me," Hilda said, "the rockfish with the olives, sautéed spinach and capers. And you?"

"For me," I managed, "a little humble pie."

CHAPTER 10

In the late 1960s, my friend Betsy Blair, a year ahead of me in college, got engaged her junior year. She was the first of my crowd to get a ring. Since I was starting to see Jack seriously and since back then everybody, even girls thinking about the convent, subscribed to *Bride* magazine, I monitored Betsy's engagement closely. We were both from Philadelphia, but Betsy came from a rambling stone house on the pricey Main Line, while my home was the modest twin off Oxford Circle where my mother still lives. I was sure Betsy would know how to do things right.

I was right. She did. There wasn't a potential social event that went unheld. There was an engagement party, a lingerie shower, a kitchen shower. She took all ten of us bridesmaids out for lunch after we were fitted for our dresses in the bridal salon in Bonwit Teller's. She went to St. Louis for another engagement party, this time given by her fiancé's parents, a dinner dance at their country club. It was all posh and all permeating.

Not that it was all fun. Betsy's fiancé was at Georgetown, next step Harvard Law School. He was really busy and Betsy spent most of her junior and senior years really hitting the books. Just for the heck of it, she took the LSATs, the entrance exam for law schools. She told me she planned on taking a few law classes, maybe at BU or BC so she'd have something to talk about when he went to work for a big firm.

Everything proceeded exactly along the storybook path we all knew it would—except Betsy never got married. Not that June. And not as recently as my college reunion two years ago.

Three days before Betsy's graduation, we all got neatly printed notes, informing us that the wedding—to which we'd been invited more than two months before but which had been on all our calendars for two years—was canceled.

"It's simple," Betsy explained, packing up her boxes as several of us lounged around her dorm room. "I don't know why, but since I was taking the LSATs anyway, I applied to Harvard myself. Just to see if I could get in. Well, I did. I got the letter in April, but I didn't tell anybody since Gerry didn't make it."

Collectively our undergraduate mouths dropped.

"And so," Betsy continued, "he told me our plans were changed, that we would stay in D.C. and he'd go to Georgetown Law, his second choice. It wasn't fair. It didn't seem right. And suddenly he didn't seem right. I got into Harvard—and I'm going to Harvard."

That Friday, Betsy was on my mind for several reasons, the most obvious her place as number one name on my fund-raising call list. Now a partner—judging by the firm's stationery, a getting-more-senior partner—at a big Cleveland law firm, she was probably the most financially successful person I knew from my growing-up years.

As I looked at her name, I couldn't help think about how the plans for her perfectly planned wedding, not to mention Gerry himself, got dumped when Betsy had the chance not just to go to Harvard but also to be something much more than she ever thought she would be.

That was exactly how I felt about being in the Senate. I never imagined that I would wind up representing my state, sitting around with senators whose very names were legislative legends. I was as surprised at being a senator as Betsy must have been that day she got the letter from Harvard, which, at that time, probably admitted like seven women out of every forty-two thousand acceptances. Betsy told me years later that her first semester, a professor announced to the three women taking his course that they were taking up spaces that belonged to men. But she stuck it out.

Just like me. Only I didn't want to keep taking the

Senate equivalent of the LSATs, which is how I thought about fund-raising. It seemed so darned small and demeaning, when measured against the stature of the Senate, to be on the phone asking people for money. Like I was selling vacuum cleaners or magazines.

But the campaign must go on. So here I was, during the "call time" that Milton had scheduled for me, sitting in a small office near Rittenhouse Square with a young woman named, unbelievable-but-true, Promise Blankly. Between us loomed a tall stack of papers and two double-line telephones.

Each page held a person's name, home and office phone numbers, and a short description of how I knew the person or why the person should know or like or want to give money to me. The system was easy. Promise placed the call, trying to get the person on the line by saying that I, Senator Eleanor Gorzack, was calling. I had asked Hilda about the nomenclature, since a lot of the targeted people were old and true friends and knew me as "Norie," but Hilda said that all the pomp and circumstance was necessary to cut through the deep resistance any caller would encounter from a secretary unfamiliar with the caller.

"Okay. So, Promise, let's get going. We'll start with Betsy Blair."

"Is that Elizabeth or Betsy, Senator?"

"Why not try *Ms.* Blair?" I suggested, wondering how long the afternoon would be and whether Promise had some kind of New England Puritan background or whether her name reflected her parents' participation in the sixties counterculture.

"Yes, the senator wants to talk to Ms. Blair directly. They are, um, they were, let me see . . ." Promise fumbled with the sheet of paper. "They went to school together. That's what they have in common. Undergraduate education. At Mint Saint Augnest."

That pronunciation took the cake and I took the phone. The afternoon would be endless.

I had listened to Hilda. I was following her campaign advice. I was calling. But the real issues—government, organization, scheduling—kept interfering with my planned fund-raising calls.

Three times I found myself on the phone with Milton back in D.C. At least twice Nancy called about some misunderstanding in the next two weeks' schedule. The schedule would be run out of the campaign office in Philadelphia, but, as of now, there was no campaign office, all proposed choices vetoed by Christie Hamilton as "unsuitable."

Despite my best intentions, I completed only four fund-raising calls. I foolishly felt rather successful. I probably spent too much time on the phone catching up with Betsy Blair, who said she'd put together a luncheon event at her law firm—and that I could earmark it for at least $10,000. I spoke to Johnny Jeffers, who headed up one of the AFSCME locals and he was certainly in my corner. The dean of the School of Public Health at the University of Pittsburgh couldn't have been better, promising to do a large reception in her home. She warned that it would have to be a $100-a-person ticket, since so many of the people on her list were in the lower-paying public-sector jobs. My fourth call, to a businessman active in party politics, was the easiest and probably the most lucrative. He said that George Taylor had spoken many times about me. That he "liked my style." And that he'd do a $25,000 event at his home any time I asked.

I carefully assembled my four sheets of paper and tried not to look at the still towering pile of names left untouched. Nancy had told me that the staffer working with me was supposed to get me on and off the phone, moving from contributor to contributor, with the least amount of conversation and time possible. But Promise was a gentle person who, after I shooed her away the first time, seemed hesitant to interrupt or signal me off again.

Sometimes being an effective, in-charge person doesn't do you any good. Good staff were people who could challenge you, get you to do things you might not want to do. At least that's what I thought in the abstract. There was no way to prove my management theory using any of my Pennsylvania staff as examples.

Like every United States senator, I was given a certain budget for state-based staff, an amount based on the population of my state. I had yet to make an "adjustment" in the personnel left by the late Senator Gannon, figuring that it would be less disruptive to leave them in their place until after the election.

In the case of state director Pete Mullins I knew that if I didn't move him he wouldn't expend the energy to move himself. Gannon had obviously owed someone a big political debt when he hired Mullins two years earlier. I felt I was still making payments on the loan. For Pete everything was a trial, a curse, a vengeance— and all the typical work of an office was a particular burden placed on his unwilling shoulders.

"This Mary Devine, now is she under Milton or under me, Senator?" he asked as I went through my appointment list early Friday afternoon.

"She works out of Washington, Pete, and so will report to Milton."

"Well, she's asking a lot of the state offices. Called up last week with a whole list of requests. Going to take hours for somebody to do this work," Pete said, rocking back and forth in his chair. I knew there were limits to plastic surgery, but surely Pete had to be more than the thirty-five years he looked. Maybe 103, considering his energy level.

"Let's make it a priority, Pete. She's working on the Kincaid hearings."

"Well, do I have to go up to Jericho for the hearings, Senator? I don't like to be traveling. Too hard for the staff to get me on the phone."

"Why not get a cell phone, Pete? Or a car phone? No, you don't have to go to Jericho." I could barely read the writing on the calendar in front of me. "Pete, do you think we could get somebody to actually type up my appointment schedule? We do have typists, right? You do have a secretary?"

"Yes. And no. I've got Mary Ellen Battle. And she's a good worker. But she's been really tied up with your new volunteer coordinator and I'm trying to do without."

"Without what?" I asked, more sharply than I had meant to. "What volunteer coordinator."

"Linda Vespucci. Now I know she's a close personal friend, but to have her here every day . . ."

"Who? Who hired her?"

"No, we didn't have to go through the hiring process because she is herself a volunteer, Senator. She's certainly brought a lot of people into the office the past two weeks. But it seems with every person comes a problem. Now she's doing a decent job, although her handwriting isn't the best. But some of *her* requests. I mean, I can't just order a shredder because she thinks it's vital."

I knew I was going to lose it, and I had no desire to get whatever it was back.

"Pete, I want to make sure I have the right Linda Vespucci, the one with the kimonos and the jewelry and the red hair. The one who thinks everything is a conspiracy—is that the one? And she's in my office and using my phones?"

"Not exactly, Senator. She's got her hair different now. Kind of streaky. Black and white. Like that woman in the movie about the dogs. Very dramatic, though. And she's also opposed to fur. On political grounds."

As I expected, Mrs. V. was delighted to see me.

"Great. Senator Norie. Looking good. A little drab I have to tell you. Like you're in the public eye. Right? And you're trying to catch people's attentions. Right? Still not enough eye definition." She was digging around in a massive tote bag before I could even defend my makeup choice.

"I got some of these samples. La-on-comb. French, you know. You buy one thing and they gotta like give you all the other stuff free. Only it's like small sizes. But, heck, take it, it's good."

She thrust several small shiny tubes into my hand and, before I could even say thank you, she was heading out the door.

"I'm off. I gotta lot of work to do. Home. On the computer. One of the kids got it for me. I'm doing like some sample letters for supporters to send to the newspapers about you. Pete told me I had to keep the campaign stuff out of the regular office. So I'm off to home."

"Linda, I need to have a little chat with you," I said, trying unsuccessfully to establish eye contact. "Lotta work to do"—that's what Mrs. V. had told me a couple months back, when she helped me figure out what was happening with supposed patriotic groups and their efforts to liberate MIAs. Linda had a lot of information. Some of it was actually accurate, although little of it had been sorted through by a logical mind.

"I'll catch up later this week, when you're back up here," she announced. "Anyway, I've got a lot of work today in the political chat rooms. Linda Vee Dot Com. With two *E*s. Love your office, Senator. Love helping out. I might have to move my operation down the street though, to the campaign office, if things really heat up."

Linda Vee with Two *E*s turned out to be the high point of my weekend.

I had a long and critical phone conversation with Marco and George, who basically told me that four fund-raising calls were about ninety-six short of my goal.

I arrived twenty minutes early for a community meeting in Chester and was met by a cheering crowd, courtesy of Hank Dugdale, who was finishing up a rousing attack on "professional politicians and longtime feeders at the public trough."

I then sat through a brilliantly orchestrated Q&A where people read questions from three by five cards about minutiae on procedural votes and line items in the budget.

On Sunday, I drove up to Harrisburg for a community forum on the environment that was attended by me, my staff person, Stash, and seven other concerned citizens. The round-trip took four hours.

At seven o'clock Sunday evening, I collapsed on the

sofa in my mother's living room and refused to answer the phone, even to Milton who called three times. I did nod my head when my mother told me Lieutenant Carver would meet me in my office Tuesday morning.

I headed back to D.C. on Monday morning on the eight o'clock Metroliner.

I put aside the required reading—a campaign memo and the morning paper—and instead dug into the massive envelope of information Carver had assembled for me, containing police and FBI reports on the status of the investigation of Bercolini's murder.

It wasn't moving very fast, that was for sure. Jericho was the center of Bercolini's district and he was well known. More than two dozen people had seen the congressman after he left me at the hospital and went by the ATM. Nobody remembered seeing him with anybody else. Nobody remembered anything, it seemed, except that they had seen him.

The FBI was beginning follow-up on crank letters, which Bercolini apparently received by the barrel. I thought that was absurd myself, since most cranks didn't have the wherewithal to track down the congressman during a FEMA situation, and then, finding him, capture him.

I was frustrated. I was sure that if I just had a little time, I could add to the investigation. But, truly, I could barely keep up with reading the newspapers.

Not that they were enjoyable this morning. The *Phil-*

adelphia Inquirer and the *New York Times* were full of news of my opponent, Mister Dugdale, who had put in a busy and productive weekend.

In addition to his smashing appearance in Chester, he'd spoken at a conference of retired police officers in Harrisburg on Saturday evening, then addressed a cable operators' gathering in Atlantic City. His only slip was missing the seven people at my environmental forum.

All of Dugdale's quotes seemed pithy and punchy. With the cops, he managed to attack Bercolini's murderers, while insisting "such random violence could not be used as ammunition against the Second Amendment. In fact, this attack could prove that everyone needed to exercise the constitutional right to bear arms." The police apparently loved it. As would the voters, no doubt.

All right, I told myself, so I haven't been getting this campaign under control. Wasn't that what my campaign staff was supposed to be about? I hunted in my briefcase for the folder marked "Campaign." According to the schedule, things cranked up Thursday, with a dinner meeting with Christie, Charlie, and Josh. We would review the scripts for the commercials and the polling data. Then, on Friday, a full day of shooting.

I made a note to check with Christie as to the appropriate clothes, makeup, whatever. I also noted that she was supposed to be in charge of my campaign schedule. I knew we were starting late, but all the more reason to get it together.

I looked at the next page in the folder, but that was yet another long list of possible donors and their phone numbers. Certainly not what I wanted to see on a Monday morning. So I tucked the folder back in my case and closed my eyes for the rest of the trip.

"This heat is getting to me," Carver announced, arriving in my office with two frosty iced coffee drinks. "I can hardly keep my M&Ms from melting."

"Yuck, what is this?" I yelled, having taken a giant sip from the cardboard cup. "It's like a liquid Hershey bar."

"Chocochino. Great, huh? Twice the calories and twice the caffeine. You'll need it for the campaign."

"I need something," I said, taking another sip and realizing that once I knew it was a liquid dessert, I liked it. "This thing is totally out of control."

"That's what I heard. Big scuttlebutt around the Hill is that you're running—but you don't know in what direction."

This was bad. I was getting political advice from Carver. But let him talk, I thought, going through a pile of invitations that Nancy had left on the coffee table. This conversation didn't deserve my full attention.

"You been watching your militia-sponsored Web page? No?" Carver asked, obviously pleased at my ignorance. "Well, you'd do a lot better if you'd monitor what the other side is saying. For example"—he pulled some folded papers out of his pocket—"I understand you're going to hold hearings on an epidemic of leukemia in Jericho County."

That got my attention.

"We haven't announced the hearings yet. Only senators and staff know about it."

"Somebody has a big mouth. Anyway, they seem to know everywhere you're going and everywhere you've been," he said, scrutinizing the paper. "You only got seven people at the forum in Harrisburg? Pretty thin, Senator."

"That's there, too? So embarrassing," I said, feeling more humiliated by Carver's knowledge than that of the Internet readers. "I know the campaign is iffy. But I'm not a politician. I'm a public employee, and, anyway, Carver, I hate it. I hate *asking* for anything. For money, for votes."

"You're not asking for advice either, but I'd start to take this into my own hands, Senator. *You* get on the Web. *You* ask people to turn out at your events. *You* challenge Dugdale to meet you face-to-face. Hey, if you don't want to be a senator, here's the trick. You won't be a senator."

"A home run," Milton announced, walking into my office and dropping a pile of newspapers on the sofa. "Take a look at the press coverage of your little ole news conference, Senator."

We were in all the Thursday morning papers—at least all the hometown papers, from Pittsburgh to Philadelphia and every town in between. The *Washington Post* mentioned it in a two-paragraph brief in the political wrap-up. And MSNBC had asked if I would do one of their call-in news shows the night before the hearing.

Kincaid had really been a friend, and had let me take the lead at the news conference, even though it was his subcommittee. "Senator Gorzack," he had said, "is taking the time and the expertise to solve the origin of this mysterious outbreak of leukemia." The reporters loved it. But we still had the hearing itself to get ready for.

"We need to get our witnesses in line," I said, looking up from the laudatory coverage. "We've promised a lot . . ."

"And we'll deliver. Mary Devine has talked to one-half the population of Jericho County and about a third of the people employed in a health-related way in the federal government. Not to mention the VA," Milton said.

"Okay, what next?" I asked.

"Now about the campaign," he began.

Unbelievable, but just when I was the least enthusiastic about my own campaign, every staffer in my Washington office seemed to want to pick up and move to Pennsylvania—and work for my election. It was complicated, since staffers had to leave the Senate payroll, usually by taking a leave of absence, before being hired by the campaign. Despite all the calls for reform on federal election rules, they prohibit any Senate staffers, except for three designated people, to even touch the financial reports when they come into the Senate office. Milton was one of my designated touchers, but he seemed to want a lot more hands on.

"I just don't think it's coming together, Norie," Milton said with a hint of whine in his voice. "You need me up there. These Kincaid hearings are going to take off like a shot. I know the issues. I know the state. You've got all these consultants—and nobody to actually run the campaign."

"Milton, I can't run Washington without you."

"Well, if you think you're running a campaign, you're not."

"I just think, Mary, that you have to have some control on your demands for information. Pete said you've been bombarding the Philadelphia office with requests," I announced into the receiver, taking out some of my Milton-induced tension on an innocent person.

"These leukemia stats are really something, Senator," she said, the excitement bubbling into the phone. "And you can't believe some of the links I've made. You as a public health expert—"

"Mary, I've got a desk full of papers and a day full of meetings. Cut to the chase."

"Okay, so all of these guys, except one, were in Vietnam during a three-year span, from 1969 to 1971. And they were all given certain shots. For example, all were given double doses of paratyphoid, because the army was really worried about some kind of chemical warfare. And the one—"

"Mary, I need some summary. What is the most important fact you've uncovered?"

"From the computer bases or from my interviews here? I've been linking up with the Centers for Disease Control. Also there are several Websites that the Vietnam vets run. Also a lot of stuff is coming out of medical centers."

"From any source," I said, my impatience with her punctuating my voice. We needed hard facts and good witnesses, not some vague theories about the men.

"Here it is," she said. "This will surprise you. All the men who are currently being treated at Northeast Memorial work in the construction industry. Except one. Nine do."

"And . . ."

"Well, Senator, don't those stats mean anything to you?"

"Yes, Mary. There are very few year-round jobs in an area where there are a lot of vacation homes. And construction is one of the biggest. Also these men were all enlisted men in Vietnam, which cuts the chances that they finished college."

"But I thought I'd isolated a statistic that wouldn't play out in the general population and—"

"And most of these guys probably drink beer. Or wear green socks. No. I don't think so. If *all* of them were in construction, that would be a sure sign of something. But, nope, I think you can't see the trees for the forest."

"You're a strong leader. Strength. Power. Muscle."

Christie Hamilton was giving us all a "little intro" to the next day's shoot. I'd come up from Washington late in the afternoon, and was sharing takeout Chinese with the consultants, Marco and Kathleen. George was off doing something technological, but we were using his office, since the campaign office still had only a light sprinkling of furniture.

We sat around in a circle reading our scripts, like people trying out for parts in a community theater group. The shoot was an all-day affair, involving six sites, all in the Philadelphia area—a school, a senior citizen center, a supermarket. In a second shoot, planned for late summer, we'd film in western Pennsylvania, in Pittsburgh, and near Lake Erie.

Christie explained that the footage from the two days would be all that was necessary for the entire campaign. It was standard operating procedure in campaigns, she said, to shoot sufficient film not just for the positive or bio ads, but also stock footage, so that whatever issues came up, whatever charges Dugdale made, our response ads would have an appropriate visual.

My orders had been to select five separate outfits—different jackets would do—so that it would appear that my visits to the various venues were both real and had occurred on different days. The heat wave was continuing—the ninth day of record late-June temperatures. The weathermen were already talking about the summer of extremes, with the flooding followed by a drought. So I had tried to find cool clothes that wouldn't look too summery when seen in commercials that would run in late October.

Men had it much easier during shoots, Christie had explained. "They just bring along a box of ties and pick a new one for each location."

I mostly would be filmed without sound, for future voice-overs, as well as doing a few short speeches, stand-ups, talking straight to the camera about key issues. That prospect added to my natural nervousness about the shoot, which was heightened by the scripts themselves.

"I don't understand the script," I said, rather innocently, half believing that I had lost the first page of my packet. "Listen to what I'm supposed to say: '*They* are coming into our neighborhoods. *They* disrupt our schools. *They* have taken our jobs.' Who the heck are *they* anyway?"

"It's a generic *they*, Senator. Middle-class people—

the people who actually vote—are feeling angry, displaced. It's an unfocused anger. The voters know that somebody is doing them in. And they want things to change. So we have to set it up that you, too, know that somebody is doing in the voters and that you will change it," Charlie finished with a flourish.

"But that's not what I believe," I countered.

"But that's what the polls say you must believe in order to win. It's not like you're talking about definite legislation. It's just a commercial."

"And why am I going to Valley Forge Military Academy? What does that have to do with my Senate race?" I managed.

"Well, the cadets are on vacation. But we've hired a dozen young men who'll be outfitted in fatigues and will be going through a heavy calisthenics. Really sweating it up. With a drill sergeant giving orders," Charlie explained.

"But I have nothing to do with fitness. I *like* fitness. But I don't *do* fitness," I tried.

"This has nothing to do with fitness, Senator. It's all about work camps for young offenders. It's an idea being debated right now in Harrisburg," Charlie said, at least not talking to me as if I thought I was Napoleon.

"I'm not in Harrisburg," I started. "I never plan to be in Harrisburg again—"

"Don't be too quick, Norie," Marco interrupted. "Look at Wilson in California. Went from the Senate back to the governorship."

"I don't care, Marco. What is this shoot about?"

"It's about your image, Senator. Your message. 'Tough Enough for the Job.' I think it says it all, don't you?" Christie said, getting up and starting for me. I saw some kind of touchy-feely connection coming up, so I waved her back into her seat.

"I don't think that's what I'm about," I started.

"What about the women's vote?" Kathleen asked, her question keeping Christie seated. "Isn't that a factor?"

"Haven't you heard of the angry men?" Christie asked me, waving those purple-tipped nails at me across the table. "You can get people to vote for you for sentimental reasons—but you can't be warm and fuzzy. You've got to be strong. Manly, if truth be told."

"When I went to the Hill, Senator Mendelssohn told me to 'be one of the gang, not one of the boys.' I'm not macho."

"If you're not strong, how will you defeat Dugdale?"

"I don't want to run a whole campaign *against* an idea. I want to be *for* an idea. I want to talk about what I've done," I said.

"Norie, you haven't had the time to do enough for the state, so let's stick with the slogan," George said. "Let's give the consultants a chance."

"I'm just not the macho type."

My wake-up call was a local morning TV show, where Hank Dugdale was featured, live, with his attack on the leukemia hearings.

"I fault Mrs. Gorzack for playing on patriotism," he told the blond bobbing head of the woman anchor. "Look at this headline, from the Harrisburg paper."

SYMPATHY IS THERE, NOT SUPPORT, was the headline Dugdale held up to the camera. Our meeting had run late and so everyone working on the campaign had obviously missed the evening news.

Now he and the woman anchor were sitting outside the studios of a network affiliate, somewhere out on the Main Line, sipping coffee and discussing the morning papers, spread out on a table in front of them. How did he get this kind of coverage?

"Senator Gorzack has all of our sympathy. She is the widow of a war hero," was his sappy attempt to disguise his vicious attack. The blond head continued to bob, even more when he added, "But heroism in her private life does not make her an able public servant."

Able? I'd received every brass plaque every citizens group gave, citing my work in public health.

"We care for Mrs. Gorzack. We honor her slain husband. But we do not believe that her emphasis on veterans is a solely selfless approach," the Dugdale attack continued. "I hope that Mrs. Gorzack's entry into politics will not tarnish the heroic glow of that marvelous thing that Jack Gorzack did."

Twisting and turning the truth—Dugdale was a champ. And then, in his lowest shot, he took Bercolini's death and turned it into an attack on the late congressman's top issue.

"Mrs. Gorzack's stand on gun control is exactly the

kind of uninformed attempt to keep citizens from being able to protect themselves. The death of Congressman Bercolini," Dugdale insisted, "is proof that people in rural areas need weapons of every size and shape for their protection."

I watched, first frozen then pleasantly mesmerized, as a familiar face rose up on the screen beside that of Hank Dugdale. A woman guest was pulling a chair up to the table, as if it were part of the planned sequence. The camera pulled around and caught the anchor, who looked terrified.

The visitor, middle-aged and with a pretty smile, turned directly to the camera as she, in one swipe, pulled Dugdale's minimike from his lapel and stuck it on her own dress.

"Hello," she said into the camera. "My name is Grace Bercolini and I'm here today to talk a little about my husband, since Hank Dugdale—who didn't know Bob and didn't like him—keeps talking about him all the time."

Dugdale tried at this moment to smile and reach for the mike, but Grace waved him off, like he was an annoying child, and continued to talk to the camera.

"I just want to tell all of you that this man is a hater and that what he is saying is nothing like what my husband believed," she declared. "My husband never thought that the people of America should turn the countryside into an armed camp. My husband was not killed by patriots. He was murdered by those who hate America and what it stands for."

She gave the camera a quick nod, turned the mike back to Dugdale, stood up, and walked off the set. I clapped my hands.

Stash knocked at the kitchen door. Darn! I wanted to watch every minute of reaction, but, in sixty minutes, I was going to be in front of the camera myself. I hope I did as well as Grace.

The first location was swell.

I was Little Miss Tough on Crime—SWAT hat on my head, my black suit jacket slung over my shoulder, staring at a crack house. Cameras rolling, I and an off-duty police sergeant who had volunteered his time strolled down along a massive cyclone fence, chatting about crime. This was a film-only segment. We turned a corner and came face-to-face with an armored vehicle. I was not getting in. I remembered Dukakis. No thanks, no tanks.

Before the next take, the sergeant told me he'd grown up in Philly, but moved to a development in Bucks County more than a decade earlier. He'd been a cop, he told me, almost twenty years.

"I can't wait until my time's in. You can't believe the filth we have to deal with every day," he told me. "These people—they're on welfare or they're taking jobs from Americans."

Wow, I thought, here's the perfect voter to see Christie's commercial. Too bad he's already in it.

"You're not giving them much of a chance, are you,

Sergeant? They either work. Or they have to get help. Right?"

"Wrong, Senator. The Constitution lays it all out for me. And for patriotic Americans. We are the People. Us, not them." He turned and flashed me a big American smile. Great! My own personal superpatriot.

I quizzed Christie on the way to the next stop about how that particular sergeant had been located. Referring to a massive leather binder embossed with double Gs, she came up with the information that the sergeant had written to me several times, about police and crime issues. And was thrilled to be part of the commercial.

"He was sweet. He told my office our shoot was much better than getting shot at the way he was used to. Darling, really," Christie said, managing the only time in our relationship to appear touched by something. I was going to reach out and touch her a little more.

"I think there's a good chance that if we check our mail, the sergeant's letters are all of the complaining kind. I think there's a good chance the ole sarge is a member of the Values Coalition and a Dugdale supporter. I think we better scrap that film until we find out just who he supports in this Senate race."

Christie started to argue and I was angry enough to not want to argue back. I told her to just hold it until the end of the day. I was angry. Angry at the advance work on the shoot, which was supposed to iron out the problems before the cameras started to roll. And, truth be told, angry at myself for letting people decide how and what I was going to stand for. I knew plenty of people on the Philadelphia police force and the state police who would have volunteered. But I didn't get myself involved because I was too busy running to take control of my own campaign.

I was beginning to understand what Hilda had told me a month ago, before it was clear that I was going to get the nomination and be the candidate:

"Senators are always up against two conflicting goods—one, following their conscience, and two, figuring out what the people want so that they can continue to represent them in the Senate."

Now I got it. You have to take charge of your own campaign. And you have to figure out what makes you comfortable while still allowing you to fight off the opposition.

It was a little late for that lightbulb to go on, since we were in the middle of an all-day shoot. But I was determined not to let the story of my campaign get written without my input.

"I wish we had all these people on our side," I complained to my driver, Stash. "It's a lot of votes."

There must have been forty of them, blocking the entrance to the Chester Lighting Company's factory and our last stop of the day. The carefully printed signs showed them to be Dugdale supporters, and they cheered every time a woman screamed into a bullhorn, "Hank Dugdale will protect America." Taking it all in were three camera crews.

"Norie, if I would've known that you needed people, I could've gotten you a thousand. A lot of people like you," Stash replied.

Wudda, cudda, shudda, as my mother would say. Not much we could do now, fleeing our own event. Or what was supposed to be our event—the happy rally of workers whose jobs were saved by their company getting financed by a Small Business Administration loan.

My film crew were seasoned enough to simply drive their minivan up to the entrance of the small factory and, seeing trouble, drive away. The car with Christie and Charlie was right behind and followed suit. Stash had kept a close eye on the cars in front of us and, without ever reaching the front entrance, did a U-turn in the driveway and had us back out on the street in a flash. As we turned, I tried unsuccessfully to spot Dugdale and wondered if he was once again reporting on himself.

My cell phone rang. Christie and I agreed to pack it in, she cheerfully pointing out that at least we saved money by keeping the film crew from going into "golden time," the astronomical hourly figure when overtime met the weekend rate.

"Where to, Norie?" Stash asked.

"Home, I guess," I answered. "At least I won't get picketed there."

CHAPTER 12

Saturday morning and I was wiped. I'd sat up too late talking with Kathleen Burns about the shoot and the protest.

"Haven't your consultants ever heard of gender gap polling? Don't they realize that this year it's good to be a woman?" she asked, only half jokingly.

Her conversation did little to calm me, and I found myself watching a black-and-white movie that ended somewhere around 2 A.M. The alarm sounded seemingly minutes later. By ten-fifteen, I was being yelled at by a dozen environmentally conscious citizens from northeastern Pennsylvania. Somehow weekends were not like this before I entered the Senate.

"We're finding traces of toxins in random testing of

the water supply. Not at a fatal or even a dangerous level. But to find them at all means we've got a problem. Somewhere."

The biologist from Jericho State College sat back and crossed his hands across his ample chest, bobbing his head up and down in complete agreement with himself.

"I hate, Dr. Roberts, to call your testing into question, but I would like to point out the presence of many of the materials you cite in many earlier tests," George interjected. It was at times like this I was pleased that the technological wizard was on my side.

"You're telling me you've found radium in our water supplies, George?" the professor asked, and it sounded like a rhetorical question to me.

"Sure. Especially if there's an old dump from the 1920s or 1930s nearby. Radium was just the thing. Watches. Clocks. It was as popular as neon is today," George said, pointing at the neon exit sign that flashed over the door. "And so, from time to time, we find these traces. But never at a level that's dangerous. Or even worrisome."

"How does this test compare with previous tests of the water, Dr. Roberts? Before the flooding, that is," I asked.

He hemmed and hawed and finally admitted that he had no comparison, having moved to the Jericho area less than three years before, and having thus missed previous flooding situations.

"But that's not to say that we aren't having problems, Senator," the woman whose name tag identified her as Sandra Stuart spoke up. "We've got weak riverbeds, ponds that are desperately in need of dredging and—I guess we should bring this up—some problems in getting contractors from outside the area to come in."

"Is there just too much demand?"

"No. It's the militia. At least the reports of the militia. And now, with Congressman Bercolini's murder, well . . ." Sandra looked around for someone to finish her sentence, and, when no one did, she continued. "People are just afraid. There's even rumors that one of the dams on the Reikers River—not a serious dam but one put in for summer swimming—well, that dam just collapsed and people are saying it was the militia. That the militia wants people kept out of that area."

"And what area is that?"

"Up in the northern part of Jericho, the tricounty area. It's close to a part of the county that really got developed when the interstate went in seven years ago. Lot of new people moved in, some commuting down to Allentown and over to Scranton," John Marquis, a longtime county commissioner, said. "But right along Reikers River—the one with the dam—that part stayed pretty undeveloped. Just a little too far out from both the ski areas and the cities to make it worthwhile to put in new houses."

I looked around the table. RiverWatch was an effective environmental organization that frequently managed to take its interest in the state's water as a rationale to push itself into any place or issue that water touched—forests, farming, housing, roads, even education. The RiverWatch county chairs gathered around the table were volunteer environmentalists who had spent years of evenings and weekends coordinating protests and testimony at hearings and leafleting and simply being the kind of good involved citizens it was hard to find.

"George, what you're saying about radium is all well and good," Sandra argued, "but we have a lot of people in our counties who think this is a big-time problem. I'm getting phone calls about Three Mile Island. If that nuclear blip there couldn't have poisoned the groundwater and it's just seeping up now."

"It's not technologically possible," George said, a little patronizing, I thought, about all of our general lack of such information. "The core of Three Mile Island is right now residing seventy miles from Sun Valley, Idaho."

"George," I said. "Don't kid."

"Seriously, that's where it was shipped. The people in Idaho aren't thrilled, but at least it's not in our backyard. Anyway," George said, "RiverWatch is happy that you're going to look into the riverbed and dredging problems, Senator. And I think we're all glad that Dr. Roberts is monitoring the water supply carefully enough that he's picking up seventy-five-year-old traces."

I looked around the table, realizing that my meeting with them had convinced the RiverWatch county chairs that something would be done, that I would be looking out for the environmental interests of their homes and neighborhoods. I guess their blanket appreciation prompted me to tell them about the Kincaid subcommittee hearings and ask that they, as individuals, be available to Mary Devine and her research.

The conversation moved on to my campaign, and, although Stash was signaling me from outside the glass-walled room, I allowed myself the luxury to be among people I thought of as supporters—and wound up throwing off my schedule for the entire day.

The schedule was already a problem, since, at my mother's urging, I was making a stop at Children's Hospital in North Philadelphia. It was, as she pointed out, located right on my route from the RiverWatch meeting downtown northwards to the Bucks County Crafts Fair.

My mother's best friend and archcompetitor in the fields of church service and neighborhood gossip, Jeanne Callaghan, had an eight-year-old grandson who had been hospitalized with a severe asthma onslaught. It was important for my mother, and for Jeanne, that I—the neighborhood celebrity—make a visit. I'd gone to grammar school with Patrick's aunt, Mary Ann, and had watched as she and Patrick's mother, Patricia, built their lives and families. I was happy for them, but a little envious that such expected satisfactions had not come my way.

I'd brought along two action figures, picked up by

my mother, and was received with the graciousness kids bestow when you've figured out what they really like, and I expected to stay a good ten minutes. But Patricia wanted me to talk to Dr. Margaret Hong, the hospital allergy specialist, about the problems with unlabeled and frequently allergic materials found in new homes. Apparently Patrick was highly allergic to the glue used in manufacturing the drywall in his parents' new rancher in Cherry Hill. No one had warned Patricia or her husband about the possibilities of allergic reaction to drywall, so the house was actually poisoning their child.

By the time Dr. Hong lectured me about the need for federal regulations and loaded me down with research papers and manuals on everything from household cleaners to paint to the contents of supposed organic garden pest sprays, I was a good hour and a half behind schedule.

Stash was cranky about the delay and gave me a little lecture about my needing someone to pull me away from meetings. I told him that Milton had wanted me to always travel with a staff person, but, since Stash was driving me, I hated to take somebody else away from their family on a Sunday morning.

"And what about security, Senator? Aren't you supposed to be having somebody along just to keep an eye out?" he asked as we went up the ramp to I-95 and he hit the gas.

"Yes. I guess. What did my mother tell you, Stash?" It had to be Marie.

"She said that policeman, from Washington, came last weekend and met with you and Miss Burns and that he told her you were supposed to have somebody with you and she was going to call him today, to tell him that you were traveling around by yourself. Just with me, and I'm not in my prime. So unless I could run them down with the car, I couldn't be much help," he finished up, cutting over a lane and pushing my new LeSabre to just five miles over the speed limit.

"I'm not going to travel around with a whole retinue of people," I insisted, more to myself than to him. "And I have to figure out what's strictly campaigning and what's senatoring. This event I'd probably do in my senator role, so that young guy, Dale Baum, is meeting us at the crafts fair, although he's probably worried because we're a little late."

"Well over an hour, to be exact," Stash said, and I took the criticism as a signal to look at my papers.

We arrived at the crafts fair as Dugdale, a crowd of admirers, and a great number of press people were leaving. It was just a little after three, but Dale, the press aide, told me that deadlines for Sunday papers were much earlier than during the week.

"That's why we tried to get you out here by one o'clock, Senator," he said. "I'm sorry that the schedule wasn't right."

I looked over Dale's shoulder at the departing press corps with their cameras full of Dugdale shots. I turned around and ran right into Stash's disapproving stare.

"I did this, Dale. Not the office. Not you. I just kind of drifted through my first two stops. And they were important. But there was no news coverage."

"What now, Senator?" he asked. "Want to walk around and shake a couple hands?"

Reluctantly, I agreed. We'd gone only a few feet when I was spotted by a coterie of tall, dark-haired women. Their hair, singular and collectively, was their most striking feature, their pale faces peeking out from Pre-Raphaelite dos. They all looked enough alike to be quadruplets, but they were merely sisters.

"The Johnson sisters," one explained. "I'm not going to introduce us all because you'll never remember all our names and that's not important anyhow."

"What's important is what's happening at our summer place. Up in the Poconos," Number Two said. "We've got this lovely cottage. Six bedrooms. One for each couple and then these big rooms with bunk beds, one for girls and one for boys. On Miller's Lake. Really more of a pond. North of Jericho. Lovely. Private."

"And, with the storm, we were worried, Senator," Number Three chimed in, "about the kids. Swimming and diving. All the broken branches and logs and pieces of docks and stuff. So we said, 'Hey, let's dredge the lake.' Do it ourselves. With our neighbors."

"The government can't do everything," Number One interrupted. "And it sure can't always do it on your schedule."

"The summer for us always begins right after school stops. We all stay at the lake—the four of us with the kids—for the summer. The men come up on weekends," Number Three said.

"So they dredged this week. And what do you think? They found all this hospital trash in the lake. Used needles. IV bags. A lot of stuff I'd rather not talk about. Poisonous trash," Number One said, starting to point her finger at me. "In our lake! And there's not a hospital for thirty miles. Until you hit Northeast Memorial. And they wouldn't dump their trash in our lake."

The Johnson sisters were a choreographed conversation. That—or being attacked by a series of machine guns armed with words. But they got their point across.

"I'm amazed I haven't heard about this. Nothing on the TV. Nothing in the newspapers," I said. There had been so much coverage of the flood and the attempts at recovery and this was certainly a wild tale.

"Why would we want publicity, Senator," Number Three said, shaking her head. "Haven't you ever heard of property values? That's why we're here in person. We called your office. Asked for your schedule. We wanted you, not a lot of federal agencies. First thing you know, hey, poof. Property values up in smoke."

"We could be the next 'Love Canal.' Imagine that!" Number Four finally spoke, then looked scared that she had said the wrong thing.

"So what do you want me to do?" I asked. I was

learning that when a constituent brought you a problem, they didn't necessarily want the help you thought they were asking for. The Johnsons were no exception.

"We want to have someone come out and look at the debris. The dredger cleaned away most of it. But he left a pile on the shore. But we don't want like an army or anything," Number One said.

"And we want the water tested," Number Two added. "And we want to know who to talk to in your office if we track down who dumped this trash in our lake."

"And," I asked, wondering how all this could be done and it not hit the press, "when do you think this 'trash' was dumped there?"

"It's mostly plastic. Plastic is like cockroaches. Doesn't go away. The dredge guy said he thought like several years. Because of the dirt crusted on some of the stuff," Number One answered. I wondered if she got to talk the most because she was the oldest or because she had the most hair.

"And he said it was like real pros. Because the stuff had been weighted down with rocks. Did we tell you that? Put in big clear plastic bags—like big balloons—and dropped in our lake. How about that?"

"How about that? Now I told those women I wasn't going to call in the National Guard, but it seems a natural for RiverWatch," I told George Taylor in a late-night phone call.

"Sure, Norie, I'll alert someone up there. But if it's

old stuff, the way the dredger said it was, there will be little we can do to put a source on it," he answered, then put me on hold while he got the other line.

I stared at the push-button phone. Among my primary hates have to be the invention of call waiting, answering machines, and double-line phones. If you want to talk to me, then talk to me. If you want to talk to somebody else, hang up on me and let the other person talk. And if you want to find out if I called you, stay home and take the call.

"I'm back. But I've got to hang up," George said, sounding a lot more rushed than he had a moment before. "Just understand that any red-flagged trash is disposed of pretty carefully these days. Once those used needles floated up on the north Jersey beaches— well, you know the rest."

George hung up and I curled up in my bed, piles of papers surrounding me. When I was appointed to the Senate in January, I gave up my Harrisburg apartment. Some things I moved to D.C. and others I crammed into my mother's house. I loved staying over with her, in the bedroom I grew up in, although my "three-quarters" bed held about half the papers I needed to sort. A friend of mine, a few years after she was divorced, told me she could never get romantically involved again because she used her king-size bed as a desk and, if somebody else was sleeping there, she'd have to clean up the magazines and the papers.

"Get hold of campaign," I wrote on the top of a

page, then stared at my handwriting. I flipped over to a blank page.

"Jericho County," I wrote at the top of the page.

"Keystone Militia," I wrote under it.

"Miller's Lake," I printed underneath.

"RiverWatch," was the next line, and "Bercolini's Teamster" followed, along with "TAGNETs."

Something was bothering me, something about Jericho. God, I almost forgot the most important item— the Kincaid hearings on leukemia. I printed that in.

It was a lot to be happening in one county and I kept thinking that there had to be some linkage. Since Mary Devine was interviewing the vets and their doctors, maybe I could use her to look into a couple of other problems. Although, looking at my list, I'd have to utilize my entire staff to get to the bottom of Jericho's murky questions.

And no matter what George said, I hoped Mary wasn't going to drink the water.

"**W**ith this arm, I could pitch a doubleheader," I jokingly told Kathleen during the seventh-inning stretch of the Phillies game. "You shudda seen me. I was shaking. I was helloing. I was meeting and greeting. I probably talked to more people there than the ticket takers."

"Norie, fuel up," Marco said, passing me my second hot dog. "Pressing the flesh is the hardest but the best kind of politics."

"Don't bet on it, Marco," George said, covering the mouthpiece of his cellular phone with his hand. "Now everything is television. I read where some guy out in California announced that the best political rally was three people gathered around a TV set."

I'd stood at the entrance to Veterans Stadium for an hour before the game, flanked by two young campaign workers who directed people toward me. The whole process made me feel a little foolish, like I was a sample of frozen pizza being handed out in a supermarket.

"Have you met Senator Gorzack?" the women would ask, pointing to where I was standing a few feet away. About half of those entering the stadium stopped for a quick handshake and a couple of words.

"What do you think of the Phillies, Senator?"

"What should I think?" I responded, rather diplomatically, I thought.

"They're in transition," came the quip. "Always in transition."

It wasn't all chatty, though. Maybe two dozen people shook their heads with a resounding "no" when asked to meet me. I hoped they all lived in Jersey.

It had been a jammed-packed campaign day—and I'd stuck to my schedule. First, early Mass with my mother, then services at an African-Methodist-Episcopal church in West Philadelphia. Congressman Chaka Fattah was sponsoring a "career day" with Temple University, and I stopped by for a half hour. I had a late stand-up lunch at the Italian market, then met the mayor and his chief of staff at the South Philadelphia String Band clubhouse, his honor's unofficial headquarters.

I did all this as I moved through the record-breaking heat that seemed to make me and everyone I met into a sticky sodden mass of wrinkles and dampness. There was nothing attractive about this summer in the city, and it was only George's promise that his stadium box was in the shade that had gotten me to the game. I looked a little worse for the wear and tear of campaigning in the heat.

"What ever happened to polyester?" I asked Kathleen, pointing to my black linen skirt. "I love natural fibers—when they're on the hangers. Give me chemically created clothes any day."

No sooner had I said that than a large shaggy green arm swung around my neck, the artificial hairs tickling my face. For one moment, I felt true panic—then I realized I was getting a hug from the Phillies Phanatic.

"George, get him to stop," I heard Kathleen shout. "He's too outrageous."

The Phillies monster-mascot had a well-known lack of inhibitions, and I had no intention of winding up on the front page of the *Daily News* being felt up by a man in a stuffed toy suit. With a shrug of exasperation, George got off his cellular phone and, between him and Marco, convinced the Phanatic to go annoy someone else.

"Dammit. I come to the game to see the game, not to get bothered by some hairy ape. People treat baseball like it was some kind of a carnival," George complained, then immediately got out his phone.

"Right, George. We should all take sporting events as serious business, the way you do. And if you like baseball so much, can you get off the phone for a few minutes and watch the game?" Kathleen asked him. "You're on that portable phone twenty-four hours a day."

"Some of us are engaged in money-raising and moneymaking activities," George snapped. "There's no complaining about my being on the phone when you come around looking for a big United Way check, Kathleen. Or when I have to raise the money to pay for Norie's consultants."

It was apparent that George was taking the heat in more ways than one. I thought I'd try to get his mind off the argument.

"About the consultants, George . . . ," I started.

"Don't! Don't analyze everything. Jeez, look at that." George jumped to his feet and started yelling at the Phillies outfielder who dropped the ball. We watched dumbfounded as the Giants brought two men home.

"Bad news," Marco said, sitting down.

"Bad news? I can't get a break," George said. "The Giants are in last place and we're losing to them."

"George," I tried, "you're taking this all much too seriously."

"Norie, I'm taking your campaign seriously. Which is more than could be said for you. I'm really tired of trying to pull all this stuff together. Look." He was half out of the box before he finished his sentence. "I'm going to head down the shore for a few days. I've got an event planned for you down there. And you try to get yourself into a money-raising frame of mind."

The next thing we saw was George's back as he ran up the steps.

"That's a little much," Kathleen said.

"No. He's just under pressure," Marco said, putting his hand on my shoulder. "George wants to do a good job on the campaign. And, to tell the truth, he talked to me and he and I are both upset that you're spending so much time dealing with the vets in Jericho and asking questions about Bercolini."

"Bercolini? I keep up. I meet with Carver and I talk to the state police or the FBI. But mostly I'm electing and not detecting."

"Is that a joke?" Kathleen asked.

"Yeah. But this campaign isn't," Marco snapped.

"Marco," I said, "I've been trying to track down this Teamster who talked to Bercolini. I can't come up with a name, and neither can any of the people on Bercolini's staff. I think he might be connected somehow to Bercolini's death."

"This is what I really hate about politicians, Norie. Every time there's a crime or a criminal you people want to finger some union guy. I'm sorry"—Marco got out of his seat—"but I'm just too hot and bothered to sit here and take more heat for something I know nothing about. And, Norie? You can't ask for union support with one hand and smack the unions with the other."

Kathleen and I watched as he followed George up the cement steps.

"Did I say the union guy did it? And do you have any complaints?" I asked.

"Well, my only complaint is that I don't particularly like baseball," she said, laughing. "And it is hot. Let's follow the boys' example and split."

What were split were the two tires on my new Buick LeSabre. The windshield was cracked on the driver's side—a straight line, top to bottom.

"Dammit," I said. "Somebody did this on purpose. How could this happen, right here, in a guarded parking lot?"

"Guard? I don't see any guard," Kathleen said, looking around. "Money collectors, yes. Guards, no. Anyway, how would somebody know it was your car?"

"Look at the license plate," I said, pointing to my new vanity plate that announced NORIE-1. I pointed through the rear driver's-side window. Piled on the backseat were hundreds of leaflets, along with two large signs proclaiming, MEET SENATOR GORZACK.

"Okay, so it didn't take a rocket scientist," Kathleen said, pulling her own cellular phone out of her handbag. "Let me see if anybody's in your campaign office. We'll take a cab there, unload this stuff, and then somebody can take us to your mother's."

The somebody turned out to be Josh, who was putting together focus groups but insisted on coming down to the parking lot and picking us up.

"While we're waiting," Kathleen said, "go shake some more hands. It looks like the game's over."

Which meant that dozens of friendly citizens offered to help, which we refused. Josh arrived, cheerfully got us settled in his four-wheel-drive with iced Diet Cokes, loaded up the back with the campaign material, and we were headed up Broad Street.

"Gosh, that whole thing lasted a lifetime," Kathleen offered.

"Just hours. And hours," I explained.

"Senator, I'm going to take you and Miss Burns home to your mother's, then I'll get the campaign stuff back to headquarters," Josh said. "The Auto Club will come tomorrow morning and tow the car."

"And shouldn't you report the damage?" Kathleen asked.

"I went ahead and called a police captain I know from the Rendell campaign. He'll send a couple guys down in about an hour, after the crowd clears out. You don't want to make the tire slashing an international incident. Especially after you getting hurt up in Jericho, Senator."

"Josh, you're smart," I said, and watched his ears turn red from the compliment.

"Not so smart that I've been able to figure out exactly what the polls are telling me, Senator," he answered. "I keep thinking we're missing something as we quiz people. And, hey, a lot of people we called last night already knew about you being on this subcommittee thing about the disease up in Jericho."

That's a little vague, I thought. "Disease up in Jericho" or "subcommittee thing" was not the punchy way I wanted my policies explained—and, what made it worse, the person doing the explaining was a campaign staffer concerned with my image and message.

"Josh, are you getting briefed sufficiently on my issues, from Milton or somebody in the Washington office?"

"Well, Senator, not really, although that's the way I've worked with Senate staffs in the past. This time, though, Christie," he said, working in a lengthy pause, "well, she's got a different approach. It's like with the woman thing."

Again, such clarity. If I hadn't been sure that Josh was both sincere and, on reputation, a good pollster, I would have believed I was chatting with the political version of Barney.

"The *woman thing*?" I managed.

"You know. The gender gap. Voting patterns among women in highly populated and or industrialized states show a marked preference for women candidates," Josh spewed out. The kid could talk!

"And in the polling for me, is the woman thing happening?"

"Yes. And no. It would be happening more if that's what we were pushing. You know, if our polls were about you and your stands on issues women are inclined to support, like education, health, jobs. But we're polling around the strategy for the commercials.

And they don't emphasize the woman thing that much."

"Great!" Kathy blurted out. "What a novel approach. Poll on what the consultants *think* the best strategy is."

"Yes," I cut in. "I'm getting the plan now. Don't let the facts get in the way of a good commercial."

Dugdale turned out to be one good commercial himself.

I almost had another unplanned face-to-face meeting with my opponent and his protesters, except Milton got me on the phone shortly after 7 A.M. and kept me there for more than an hour.

By the time I was ready to walk out the door, Dugdale was live on the morning news. It turned out he was protesting from a sidewalk outside my campaign headquarters.

"Mrs. Gorzack doesn't care about health," he bellowed. "She cares about headlines. She doesn't want to help workers become more prosperous. She wants to help herself become more famous."

All his scattershot criticisms seemed directed at my involvement in the subcommittee hearings. My campaign consultants had, in effect, patted me on the head and told me the hearings were a pleasant but ineffectual thing to do. But if Dugdale was this upset, I had to be doing something right.

I stood mesmerized, watching the set, as Dugdale slashed and burned my reputation. I got mad. And then I got madder. Especially when I realized that the large bunting-trimmed sign hanging outside my headquarters read "Senator Gorzick for Senator." At least my own people could get the name right.

"This is out of control, Milton," I complained as Milton jumped between piles of papers he'd arranged in a complex pattern on the floor in my office.

I'd canceled my Monday afternoon appearances before a small Rotary in Gettysburg, promising that I'd show up for their general membership meeting in the fall. And I got myself back to Washington as fast as I could. I needed some serious regrouping.

I found Milton had commandeered my personal office for his file-by-pile sorting technique and refused to have a sitdown conversation until he finished.

"Once I get these witnesses lined up," Milton muttered, dropping various pieces of paper like rose petals at a wedding, "I'll let you in on the really bad news."

"These are witnesses?" I asked, looking at the dozen-plus stacks. I was out of touch and it was no one's fault but mine. This was my bailiwick—vets and health—and yet I'd let other committee work and unimportant meetings keep me from doing everything I should on the Jericho syndrome.

"So how am I ever going to catch up?" I asked both myself and Milton.

"Get elected, stay around and get some seniority. Then you get staff up the kazoo. The perks of seniority. Committee staff. Leadership staff. For now," Milton grinned, "you've got Mary Devine. Our darlin' Mary, along with Kincaid's office, swear that these papers represent the best group of witnesses ever seen on Capitol Hill."

"Tell me," I commanded. At least I'd learned that when there wasn't time to read, there was time to listen.

"You've got doctors. Lawyers. Union reps. Real live people who actually represent someone. Not that anybody will have anything factual to say . . ."

"Milton, don't. So what's wrong."

He turned and smiled at me. I remember Barbara Dunfey in the third grade had the same look on her face when she told me, at recess one day, that she was sure she was coming down with chicken pox.

"The bad news is, Senator, that I'm called to jury duty."

"No way!" I begged. "You can't. It's impossible. You're a lawyer. We have to get you excused."

"The lawyer thing doesn't work anymore, even for real attorneys. And I've been to law school, passed the bar in D.C., but I've never practiced. And," Milton said, seeming to enjoy this all too much, "the District is so desperate for any breathing person to show up, that they'll take me—law degree be damned."

"Can't we get you excused? Say that you're vital to the national interest?" I asked.

"I tried, but those days are over. I couldn't even get another delay. It used to be easy to slip away. If you have a Juris Doctor, then there is no jury doctoring. But not now. It's 'one day or one trial.' I understand the White House deputy chief of staff served six days last month."

"And what about my hearings, to finding out what's happening?" I said, trying not to whine.

"The testimony will *sound* great. Like you're probing and pushing. But will we have an answer as to why these vets up in Northeast Memorial have leukemia? No. We won't," Milton said, flopping down on one sofa. I sat on the other sofa, across from him, and propped my feet up on the coffee table.

"Join me," I offered, and he followed suit.

"There is one witness problem," Milton said. "And that's Joe Hauser."

"A union guy, right?"

"Carpenters. On the Pennsylvania Building Trades Council. He's originally from Jericho. Mary went to talk to him about her theory, about the number of guys in the building trades who were sick," Milton said. "She said she mentioned it to you, but you said it was irrelevant."

I tried to recall the conversation, and did remember that the fact seemed unimportant then—and still did.

"So Hauser," Milton continued, "first tells her that he's got no info. That was last Wednesday. Then, suddenly, Hauser has like a vision and suddenly he announces that he's figured out the whole thing."

"What vision?" I asked, having trouble figuring

Milton's story. Maybe he was mentally already at jury duty.

"You understand Mary talked to Hauser. He said he knew nothing. But then, on Sunday afternoon, he has an interview with the *Jericho Ledger* and he tells them he's solved the mystery of the disease."

"And . . . ?"

"And that's all we know so far. He was supposed to talk about general health problems in the community at large with men the age of the guys with the leukemia," Milton said.

"That's good. I like the union angle," I admitted.

"But now we have no idea what's happening, except for his time slot. He's scheduled before the subcommittee—let me check—at about eleven a.m. And"—Milton scanned the paper in his hand—"he says he will reveal all in his testimony. What that is, we don't know. We can't take him off the list to testify. The unions would go ballistic. But it sounds like this guy has an elevator that doesn't go all the way to the top."

"I don't know. Head of the carpenters' union in Pennsylvania—Hauser is not a crazy. I think I met him a couple years back," I said, trying to pinpoint his face. "Do you know someone who would know him?"

"I used to have a great way to get the inside dope on any union guy from Pennsylvania," Milton said.

"Used to?"

"Yep. I had an impeccable source. Just call up Bob Bercolini. He always knew the hot scoop."

CHAPTER 14

"**H**ow hot is it?" one reporter yelled to another in the hallway outside the hearing room.

"Hot enough to put the First Lady in shorts?" the second one shot back.

"Better!" the first one answered. "Hot enough that the weather leads the news."

That had been the warning from one of the vastly overweight weathermen who populate early-morning television: Coming up was the hottest June 29 for seven hundred years. Or something like that. I imagined the singular good the weatherman did was to keep thousands of people from stopping for a donut on their way to work. "You wanna be *that* fat, huh? In this heat, huh?"

But Mr. Fatty was right on the money on the temperature. The heat wave had hit the eastern seaboard and was sitting here, day after day. Now the complaints and requests coming into the office centered more on the heat and its effect on the water level in rivers and lakes. Although the massive rains early in the summer had caused heavy flooding, the spring rains had been light and sporadic, and flash floods did not equal an equitable water supply nor seep down to the water table.

Down in D.C., days like this reminded Washington that it was indeed a city built on a reclaimed swamp. It was hot enough to force me to get on the Senate subway, first from Hart to the Capitol, then from the Capitol to the Russell Office Building.

Just the idea of the subway usually brought back the horror of my first days in the Senate. That's when a Vietnam vet had died trying to reach me as I got aboard a subway car. His body stretched across the tracks and me above him, trying to resuscitate—that was the news photograph introducing me to most of America.

Because I didn't like to think about that time, that day, my usual tack was to avoid the subway at all cost. But walking a few blocks in the steamy heat would have turned my hairdo from its crisp French cut to crispy French fried. And, as much as I liked to think that my substance, not my style, was what mattered, I wanted to look serene and senatorial in my black linen suit with the boxy jacket.

I was terrifically excited about this hearing of the Veterans Affairs subcommittee. Even when it was Public Works or Ag, I have to admit that I loved committee work. This was the stuff I saw as the real work of the Senate, what makes being a senator a senator. When I first got to Washington, like most Americans I thought of the Senate as rhetorical speeches on the floor—ideas and ideology clashing with high-tone rhetoric and, sometimes, in high fidelity.

But it was committees that made things happen. Committees, in fact, followed a process that was much like the one followed by most public health professionals. In public health, the focus was always on cleaning up a problem or making sure that a problem didn't reoccur. One used experts and studies and the personal stories of those involved to make decisions as to what should be done. That's exactly how a committee worked—assembling materials, weighing proposals one against another, and marshaling facts before making a decision or taking a vote.

I'd reviewed my briefing book the night before. My legislative director, on my own staff, had actually assembled the briefing book. For any committee or subcommittee hearing, the committee staff supplied a good deal of written backup—biographies of witnesses, issue papers on the topics, previous legislative initiatives, think-tank papers from the Congressional Research Service, and journal articles.

The committee staff is always bipartisan, although the majority members get the majority staff appointments and the chairman has enormous power in deciding where the resources of the committee will be spent.

Today's session was an oversight hearing, which sounds too much like "overlook," which is exactly the opposite of what it means. An oversight hearing "looks over" every aspect of an issue, checking out the topic to see if an investigation or legislation is necessary. Often such a hearing is used to check up on a specific agency—is the agency doing its job, or does it need specific prodding from Congress?

Since today's hearing was aimed at finding out everything that was known about the strange leukemia, I was delighted to see that Dr. Ramona Sanchez was one of the first witnesses. As the chief epidemiologist for the Commonwealth of Pennsylvania, she lived up to her national reputation as a crack scientific sleuth. A rising star at the National Centers for Disease Control in Atlanta, she'd been hard to budge—but I had successfully recruited her and brought her to Harrisburg.

The other leadoff witnesses did not make my heart leap, but rather my stomach drop. The Veterans Administration and the Department of Defense had racked up a poor record of bumbling and fumbling when asked to investigate Agent Orange and the Gulf War syndrome. Since there seemed to be no previous investigation of any kind of war-related leukemia, I had little confidence that the VA or the DOD would step forward to initiate any inquiry.

There were long lines of tourists waiting for a seat in Russell 305, so I went in through the senators' entrance, a back door, really, that opened into a spartan work space with phones and an area for the committee to caucus. That work space opened onto the dais.

I was the first senator to arrive, and I was *not* a member of the Veterans Committee, so I went down to take my seat among the witnesses. Ramona and I embraced and the TV lights snapped on. Big-footing was not in my portfolio, so I was antsy when the cameras followed me as I greeted the three vets who'd come down from Jericho County. According to my briefing book, there should have been two more, but one of the guys told me that the other two were having a hard time with some new medication.

Mike Kincaid came down to talk to the vets, as did Garrett Baxter.

"I'm holding up the hearing because the second panel of witnesses has this guy, Hauser, who's been making all the noise," Kincaid told me. "But he's still not here."

"I think we should go ahead," I offered. "Or the vets will get held over until afternoon and that's too tough on them."

The panel took their seats, and, since I was not on the subcommittee, I moved to the witness table. Then I began the required Capitol choreography, with music by Senatorial Courtesy.

"Good morning, Mr. Chairman," I began. "We the senators of Pennsylvania, the people we represent, and especially the Vietnam veterans of Jericho County who served with unwavering honor thank you for holding these hearings on yet one more possible tragic consequence of that war on those who served.

"This hearing on the possible link between exposure to chemical weapons and their current critical health situations is of an immediate nature. Your record, along with that of Senator Baxter and other members of the Veterans Affairs committees on concern for veterans' health care—a deep commitment to healing the wounds of war—are well known and well appreciated. All of America's veterans and these from Pennsylvania know we can count on you."

I paused for a minute, my kudos to the committee over, and got ready for the next set of steps in my little procedural dance.

"Mr. Chairman, I ask unanimous consent of the committee that Senator Alexander Garrison Smith's statement be placed into the record. He could not be here, since his presence was required at an investigatory hearing on corruption in federal procurement. But he wanted the committee to know of his support in your efforts to get to the bottom of this serious medical mystery."

Now, I got to the meaty part—my statement.

In a few paragraphs, I told the committee how the plight of the veterans was brought to me.

"When their country called, these men went to fight. Now we face a question of our courage to battle. Will we fight as hard for them to get to the heart of this dark matter? And if this government is found to be at fault in putting these men's lives in mortal danger not just once, but now once again, will we be as steadfast in our dedication to do the right thing?

"What happens to ailing veterans when they turn to their government for help? In most cases, worse than nothing! Administrators dismiss any possible link for a service-related injury. Veterans ask for honesty and they get an empty promise—a runaround tied up with red tape.

"Mr. Chairman, the Jericho syndrome cannot be another cover-up, like Agent Orange, or an evasive action, like the Gulf War syndrome. In each of these instances, it took congressional action to get answers.

"Today we are scheduled to hear from witnesses from the Veterans Administration and the Department of Defense. We will be told there is so little information that nothing can be surmised, that there are so many missing records that nothing can be investigated. Sound familiar?

"Sadly, in this case as in others, I believe only an independent study by Congress will allow the right questions to be asked, the crucial answers to be sought.

"Mr. Chairman, I do look forward to working with you on this problem."

Mike Kincaid smiled down at me.

"Thank you, Senator," he said, "for that compelling testimony. We will get to the bottom of this. And we need your help. Not just as a senator from Pennsylvania concerned with this issue, but as a public health professional, who can help us track down the killing links between these men and their enigmatic enemies.

"The committee extends to you an invitation to participate in all matters on the Jericho syndrome. Please join us, so that you may question the witnesses."

I gathered up my papers and went up and took my seat as an ad hoc member of the panel. It seemed like years, not months, since I had performed my first public committee duties, as part of the Select Committee on MIAs. A lot had changed since that moment, including my relationship with Garrett Baxter, who would, he had told me through Milton, "float in and out" during this day's hearings.

Ramona Sanchez was set for the first panel of witnesses, along with two doctors from Northeast Memorial and a researcher at NIH. They would all testify, my briefing book had told me, that they agreed that the men in Jericho County with that specialized leukemia really did have that particular specialized leukemia. It was a little frustrating, I knew, but the groundwork had to be laid.

Going through statistics, explaining both procedures and results, Ramona laid out the various tests and programs the men had been put through. The NIH researcher then agreed that what could be learned from established science had been attempted, and that what could be cured with established medicines had been tried. It was not a hopeful picture and I worried about the vets in the audience, what the negative statements would do to their outlooks and morale.

Next up on the schedule was a panel of three witnesses, including Joe Hauser. The other two witnesses walked up to the table, but no Hauser. I looked up and tried to locate him among the hundred-plus people in the audience, trying to match up a body with the photo shown to me early that day by Milton. Faithful Milton, I told myself, since he'd met me at the office at 8 A.M. for a "download" before he reported for jury duty.

"Don't worry," he had promised. "A judge will never let me serve. They'll never pick me. Yale Law School. More than ten years on the Hill. Come on."

Milton's photograph was an easy guide to finding Joe Hauser, especially after Milton explained that the union rep carried more than three hundred pounds on a rather short frame. He should stand out. Like the weatherman.

I felt myself getting nervous, anxious, probably because I kept remembering Milton's warning that the whole hearing procedure wasn't going to do very much to help those vets with the leukemia. Knowledge sometimes makes me antsy.

Hauser's absence was noted by Chairman Kincaid, who said we'd go ahead with the other two members of the second panel—a Veterans Administration deputy secretary and a member of the staff of the VA hospital in Philadelphia. The deputy secretary had come armed with literally pounds of material, all of which translated as "the army never made anyone sick, and, if it did, it was by accident."

"It's always like this, Norie," Kincaid said, leaning over and being very careful to cover his microphone with his hand. "It's having to sift through all the irrelevant stuff."

"I know," I said, wishing we could cut to the chase and afraid that the entire day would be nothing more than dead ends.

"So if you know, Norie, maybe you should look a little more interested in the witnesses. It's your people up there in Jericho County. Don't look quite so bored and impatient," Kincaid scolded, then released his microphone from his silencing grip.

I could feel myself redden under Kincaid's criticism. I buried my head in my notes, trying to regain my cool. I was trying so hard to concentrate that when the staffer from Kincaid's office leaned between us, I jumped.

He passed Kincaid a folded note. Kincaid glanced at it and I could feel him freeze up beside me. He let the army guy finish answering a question, then, with a quick look at the senators who bookended him, said an emergency had come up and we would be in recess until after lunch. We then all trooped into the anteroom.

Kincaid had a blunt, almost military manner, although I knew from my time with him on our mission to Vietnam that he could be a sympathetic soul. Today I was glad he opted for blunt.

"We won't be hearing from Mr. Hauser today, Senators. Mr. Hauser is the victim of a mugging. Just a few blocks from here, as he was walking from his hotel," Kincaid said.

"How's he doing?" Garrett Baxter asked, suddenly appearing behind Kincaid, who seemed startled by the question.

"Not well, Garrett. Not well. He was murdered."

I knew what Carver was going to say, as well as I knew he'd have an extra pack of M&Ms for me.

"Senator, you sure do bring out the murders. Of course, this weather is making everybody a little crazy, so maybe I can't blame it all on you," Carver said, walking me back to my office in Hart.

He'd been standing outside the anteroom when the subcommittee filed out, and I couldn't wait until we got out of earshot before I started peppering him with questions.

"This is no innocent murder, right?" I asked. "Hauser just wasn't attacked because he looked like a guy with a big wad."

"Hauser looked like a guy with a lot of big wads, from what my friends on Homicide over at the D.C. police are telling me," Carver said. "It took like three paramedics just to get him on the stretcher."

"We're terrible talking about a dead man this way," I said, reproaching myself more than Carver.

"The best jokes about death are made by undertakers. Of course, they always hate the jokes about undertakers. I remember, once, I said to a guy, 'We stab 'em. You slab 'em,' and he was really ticked off."

"So you think we're kidding about poor Mr. Hauser because we don't want to feel too frightened or too sad," I asked, deciding to once and for all take Carver on when he started to joke about death and murder. "Like maybe we should be afraid of some goblin showing up in the night and sucking our blood and leaving us like an empty shell. And that's why we kid about such gruesome stuff."

"Not really," Carver quipped. "We just like to make jokes. Nothing redeeming about it at all."

So I was back to the Carver-at-my-side routine.

The hearing dragged on through the afternoon, although all the press wanted to ask at the end of the day was whether Hauser was killed because he had "solved the mystery of the disease."

On the one hand I wanted to cancel the meeting and start calling people up—authorities, police and otherwise, demanding that they do something so that a citizen couldn't be wiped on the way to testify before a congressional committee. On the other hand, I knew the three veterans who had struggled to come to Washington for the hearing were hanging on thin strings—of hope, of health, and of resources. We didn't have the luxury to take time off and either mourn or seek revenge.

"Solve the disease? I don't think so," I found myself saying. "I believe Mr. Hauser was not a health-care professional, so I don't think he had done the scientific research to answer any health questions. What I think happened was that Mr. Hauser was a victim of a random violent crime."

Naturally, I didn't believe one word I was saying.

"This doesn't look good, does it, Senator? A witness cut down as he was coming to testify," was the question from my friend Diane Wong at CNN. It was a little dart, I knew, but I knew her queries always had a poisoned tip.

"Well, it's not good anywhere, anytime for anyone to be the victim of a violent crime. That's why many of us are deeply committed to gun control legislation," I said, figuring that if I was in for a nickel, I was in for a dime.

"Senator, on a more personal note," Diane hissed at me, "some people are saying that there's a 'Gorzack Curse.' That you can't do the job of a senator if you keep getting involved with violent crimes. What do you have to say about that?"

"As far as jobs are concerned, Diane, I'm more interested in science than in superstition. And I think that you, as a TV journalist, should be more interested in news than in rumors. If television doesn't concern itself with facts, can't people just get their news from those supermarket tabloids and not off their twenty-one-inch screens?" I asked. "And wouldn't that affect some other people's jobs?"

Having made that terrific analysis of America in the last decade of the twentieth century, I thanked the reporters and strode off. At least I was picking up some senatorial style.

"You're learning," Carver said, with only a hint of sarcasm.

"Yep, and if the election were four years from now, instead of four months, I might have a chance."

"Somebody thinks you have a chance," Carver said. "Or they wouldn't be doing so much to discourage you."

"You think the attack on Hauser was somehow connected to my Senate race?" I asked. "I figured it had something to do with all this stuff he's been putting out about solving the leukemia mystery."

"No doubt about it, that would affect your Senate race. You come up with somebody who can say that all those leukemia patients up in Jericho got sick because of A, B, or C—and you are automatically elected by proclamation. Automatic."

"And if I can't come up with any answers?"

"Well, you better be doing some more ordinary senator things, so that everybody back in your state is like liking you," Carver pronounced, with a heavy emphasis on the "liking."

Even Carver was beginning to sound a little like George and Marco: "Bring home the nuggets and don't get too involved in the murders." But, thankfully, Carver only sounded that way for a moment.

"So do you want to hear something interesting about Hauser?" he asked. I nodded eagerly. "He wasn't on his way to Capitol Hill when he was killed."

"No. Yes. Okay. So where was he heading?" I asked.

"To have coffee at the carpenters' building. It's about a two-block detour, between his hotel and the Hill."

"What do you think that means?"

"Maybe it means he was going to meet somebody else before he gave his testimony," Carver hypothesized. "We know he was heading there because he told the desk that if anybody came by looking for him, to send them over to the union offices."

We walked along not talking for several minutes, until we got to the fourth floor of Hart and the front door to my office, with its large colored replica of the shield of the Commonwealth of Pennsylvania.

Carver cleared his throat and I thought he was going to offer some insight into Hauser's murder.

"I really like Philadelphia and I'm looking forward to spending the Fourth up there," he said.

"It is an historic place," I agreed.

"Sure. But the food is the fame," Carver said with a laugh. "I'm thinking about funnel cakes. Philly cheese steaks. Those monster meatballs at the Italian market. Yes. That's historic."

"Carver, have I got a treat for you! Just wait until you meet scrapple."

CHAPTER 15

One day later, on Friday July 4th, Carver and I settled into a booth at the Mayfair Diner so I could introduce him to the miracle of Pennsylvania Dutch cuisine—scrapple. As my father once said, "If you expect to like scrapple, don't ask what's in it." Two ingredients I knew were cornmeal and pork parts.

"It is the only food I know that takes to either maple syrup *or* ketchup," I pointed out, spearing one of the thin, fried rectangles and holding it over my scrambled eggs for a closer inspection. "And, hey, look at the prices. Two eggs with Philadelphia panfried scrapple, just three dollars and twenty cents. That doesn't get you a coffee in D.C."

"I've never met a food I didn't like, until now,"

Carver said, holding on to his own plate, with pancakes and sausage, as if the scrapple might spirit the whole thing away. "Don't you think you should be eating more politically correct, since you're running for office and you're a health expert and all that?"

"Calories and cholesterol don't count when you eat in a diner, thank you," I said, slicing the scrapple up and dipping a piece in a puddle of syrup that was edging onto my eggs. "Of course, maybe I should take a poll on the subject. That's how politicians are supposed to decide everything these days."

"And what about the other side? Don't they figure out what people want the same way?" he asked. "Can't you both say the same thing?"

I slammed my fork down on my plate, angry not at Carver's question but something I just remembered.

"Sure. But then these creeps on the other side do this 'push polling.' A voter gets a phone call. The person on the other line is supposed to be a pollster. But instead of asking simple questions, they 'push' their own views. Like 'Did you know Senator Gorzack doesn't like the word *patriotism*?' "

"These people, I keep telling you, Senator, are not nice," Carver said. "But then, if they are all from Philly and they all had this kind of food for a long time . . ."

His cell phone startled him, and the entire end of our diner. People had waved to me on our way in and stopped by the booth before our breakfast came, but we had been left relatively alone.

"Yes, sir. I understand, sir," Carver announced into

the phone, looking more ramrod than I'd ever seen him. I'd just put another bite of scrapple in my mouth when he handed the phone across the table with the words, "It's the President."

"In the Mayfair Diner," I managed, then chewed madly for ten seconds. "Hello, Mr. President."

"Senator! Norie! I'm just checking in. I didn't like this thing about Joe Hauser at all this past week, and I've had every labor guy in the country on the phone. They're all pretty mad. Telling me it seems like a labor guy should be able to walk to his own D.C. office without getting whacked. Well, I know that."

"We're all pretty upset, sir, but I think that the FBI and Justice Department and—"

"I know, I know. But I'm just sitting here with a couple of the staff—Helen, Roger, Pinky—and we're talking about Hauser's saying he knew what this illness was, this mysterious cancer."

"Yes, but we don't *know* that he did," I said into the phone, all the while trying to shake hands with a prospective voter and not drag her arm into the maple syrup. "Hauser only said—"

"Lot of campaigning this weekend, Senator?" the President asked. He seemed to follow his conversational agenda no matter what you did on your side. "Lots of big-crowd public appearances, I would guess."

"Yes, sir. That's right. I'm doing the Freedom Medal here. At Independence Hall, with the vice president. Tonight we've got the fireworks. Then, tomorrow—"

"Terrific. Nothing like gearing up a campaign by patriotic appearances. Anyway, Senator, these crowds are tough. I want Lieutenant"—he paused, obviously asking someone in the background a question— "Lieutenant Carver to be with you *all* the time. And I'm having somebody from the Secret Service talk to the police up there. You know, Senator, I wouldn't mind losing a Senate election as much as I would mind losing a senator."

Carver was wired. In his ear, up through his sleeve, the thin wire ran, connected to something in some pocket, somewhere. I caught him showing off to Stash before we left my mother's house, like his recording device was some new car stereo or something. The American Male Love of Gadgets, I told him.

"I don't believe anybody can think and listen to one of those ear things at the same time," I insisted as Stash negotiated through the crowds around Independence Hall and finally pulled up at a side entrance. "How can you have somebody in your ear, telling you what's happening and then also pay attention to what you see is actually happening?"

"We learn it in cop school," Carver said, and, with a wink, flipped his coat lapel to show his teeny microphone. "First we learn how to talk into our coats, then we go to donut classes. I majored in lemon cream."

Stash laughed and I tried to, but the reality of the situation was as clear as the plug of plastic in Carver's ear: The White House, the Secret Service, and Carver himself thought I was in danger from the militia or whoever cut down Bercolini or whoever cut down Joe Hauser.

The car stopped and I reached out to open my door.

"Don't. Don't move. I'll come around to get you out," Carver said. So much for any attempt at keeping us all low-key.

"This is ridiculous," I mumbled. Carver ignored me, helping me out of the car. Both of us were quickly surrounded by flounce-shirted and -skirted Revolutionaries as we walked the few steps into the historic brick building.

"Who are all these wigged-out dudes?" Carver whispered.

"*Reenactors,*" I whispered back. "Volunteers. They show up with their costumes and, for battles, with their guns. Revolutionary War buffs or Civil War fanatics."

"You mean we don't know who any of these people with the muskets are?" Carver asked. "You mean they can just show up with a costume and get in the door?"

"Yes. But so what? You think I'm going to get musketed to death or something?" I asked back, sounding a lot braver than I felt. Maybe it was the attack up in Jericho County, but I was less sure of myself than I had been a month ago. Then, I found every crowd a group of friends or people I could try to win over to my side. Now I found myself looking into faces and wondering when a smile would mask a shove, when a polite question really was cover for just getting in close.

Despite my and Carver's misgivings, the hourlong ceremony proceeded exactly on schedule. The vice president presented medals to the honorees—a scientist, a businessman, and an athlete. Senator Smith, myself, and the recipients had each been allocated five minutes to speak, and I couldn't help but feel that the crowd was keeping a stopwatch on the results.

Although the presentation took place in front of Independence Hall on a bunting-trimmed reviewing stand, at its end, the ceremony participants were directed back into the Hall. We stood around the Liberty Bell, looking like people waiting for a bus.

"You should get out of here now, Senator," my colleague from the other side of the aisle, Senator Smith, said, leaning over me. "We're going to get led into some kind of a luncheon event and you'll never make the next stop on your schedule."

"How would you know about my schedule," I asked him.

"Norie, it's the Fourth of July. If you're not at seventeen parades, fourteen fairs and picnics, and at least a hundred and one fireworks displays, you simply are not the candidate," he finished up with a grin. What a class act, I thought, making my way out of the preluncheon crush. It amazed me that he and Dugdale could represent the same party. And, I told myself, if I wasn't a good enough candidate, could wind up representing the same state.

I whipped through the schedule and finished up late at night on Delaware Avenue, watching the fireworks. Since the actual holiday fell on a Friday, there was a lot more to come.

"If we get done in time," I told George and Carver, "I'm stopping at Vanity Fair in the outlet mall."

"Great," George said, "you're running for Senate and you're going to take time to buy lingerie."

"Speaking of underwear," Carver interrupted, "my daughter claims—"

I didn't let him get any further.

"I am not discussing any of my personal clothing habits with any of you boys," I announced. "Now, let's go over the next several hours' timetable."

Carver listed my events, starting with my ride with George in the Reading Holiday Parade. Although we were all heading to Reading in George's Town Car, waiting for us there was one of his babies—a 1927 Stutz Bearcat. We made our way through a couple dozen admiring onlookers. I dropped my large green tote on the floor of the passenger's side.

"There's just two seats," Carver said, pointing out the obvious as he walked around the nifty yellow sports car. Several teenage boys were also making their slow, circuitous stroll around the classic car. "So this is a problem. I can't protect you if I'm not with you."

"You can be right behind us," George offered. "These parades move at a snail's pace. A brisk walk.

Or you can follow in a car. Of course, if you don't think it's safe for the senator, Lieutenant, we'll put her in something else."

"What? A tank? That's the way I want my constituents to see me—protected from them by some military vehicle," I started. "No, I'm not going to parade in anything else. It's George's Stutz and that's that."

George was looking concerned, but it was a more simple problem—my ever-present tote bag.

"It's tight up front, Norie, so why not leave the bag in the Town Car?" he asked.

"No. I've got sunscreen. And my hairbrush. And the return post cards for possible volunteers. And my little camera," I said. "Anyway, George, my legs are so short that there's plenty of room for the bag. I just want to get my clipboard out . . ."

"Clipboard?"

"I have to say a few words at the end of the parade. And if I just keep the pages in my purse, they'll look like some school composition a sweaty-fisted kid brought home," I said, turning back toward Carver. "Now are there any other aspects of my life that you two would like to take over?"

Carver didn't blink. I caught George giving him a what-can-we-do-with-a-woman look. It made me dig in my heels.

"Nobody has made a direct attack on me," I announced.

"You got pushed off the steps in Jericho," Carver countered.

"Extremists. Anyway, maybe I slipped."

"Two people in close proximity to you have been murdered," he answered. "And, to be blunt, I think the President of the United States wants me up close."

"Close," I said over my shoulder as I walked over to shake some onlookers' hands. "Close is simply a matter of definition."

I've always liked parades. Also carnivals, circuses, and church bazaars. And, I was finding out, it was even better to be the star, riding down Reading's Main Street with George, waving to the crowds and, frequently, having people shouting back.

"Friendly shouts, George," I said over the parade noise. "I hope the lieutenant is picking up on the general friendliness of the crowd."

George nodded abstractly. Communication wasn't easy, since we were following close behind the Saint Helena's marching band. The tassels of their fez-style hats bounced in time to their music, which was a lot more pom-pom than pomp.

Up ahead I could see a quartet of American Revolutionaries, more of the "reenactors," I thought. There was little to think about as we crawled along, "Blue Skies" blaring out in front of us, the oppressive heat of noon almost on top of us. I kept my feet propped up on the tote bag and at least could separate my legs from the potential stickiness of the leather seats. I even managed to use my clipboard as an armrest.

My mind was wandering, and I couldn't help think

that it was an urge I didn't understand, getting outfitted in all that wool to stand around the "reenact."

A trio of the "colonists" stood happily waving historic flags with their circles of stars representing the original colonies. A fourth colonist had a flag, but his was modern, crisp, and complete with what looked like fifty stars. Right beyond the reenactors on the sidewalk a lone television crew had set up, and, as I vigorously waved at the camera, the fourth colonist bolted off the sidewalk and toward the car, his flagpole held out like a knight's jousting staff. A few people in the crowd screamed warnings and some jumped off the sidewalk after him.

But if I was going to be saved, I realized in a split second, I was going to have to save myself.

I'd obviously synapsed all the techniques from those 1950 movies with the pirates and the knights and the musketeers. I was no damsel in distress, but a buccaneer, ready for hand-to-hand combat. I whipped up my clipboard and flung it, Frisbee-like, at the renegade colonist. It whacked him right in the face.

I don't know who was more surprised—me or my supposed attacker. I couldn't ask him, since he was out cold.

"The guy's a kook."

That explanation came and came again from the Reading police captain as he marched in and out of the conference room where Carver, George, and I sat at a worn wooden table. I kept rubbing my fingers over the chipped and peeling surface, wondering about the pounds of troubles and sorrows that worked to give the desk the distressed look. I was feeling as distressed as the wood, with one problem or another removing layer after layer of my resilience.

"Somebody put the kook up to it," Carver was saying into the phone. He had several FBI agents on their way up from Philadelphia and was now talking to people in the Secret Service office in D.C. "It takes a lot of work. Renting the costume. Knowing where to stand. Having a television camera crew nearby."

The crew, it turned out, was an honest-to-goodness media representative from a local station. The station had been alerted to a "possible demonstration during the parade," and had been told that the specific corner where I had been rushed was the place to be standing. The report of my fending off—or as Carver put it, "Frisbeeing off"—the attacker was already on the air.

I had to admit that I looked pretty impressive, whipping that clipboard around. A lot more impressive than I felt.

The police had confiscated my clipboard, one sergeant saying that it was the first time he had a clipboard used in a felonious assault. And my attacker had turned out to be a former mental patient who was currently living in a halfway house. His therapist was out of town for the weekend, but a doctor on call had said he believed the man had taken himself off his medication.

"That's not so strange," I said to George, "especially

since the guy was a manic-depressive. Very hard to keep manic-depressives on their meds, since the manic phase of the syndrome is supposed to be extraordinarily exhilarating."

"Norie, sometimes I don't know where you're coming from," George said, shaking his head. "You get attacked by a crazy man. He could have run you through with that flagpole. And you're sitting here discussing symptoms."

"I guess I'm just a nurse at heart," I answered, only half kidding. "George, that's why I'm so concerned about these vets up in Jericho County. Do you think Hauser knew anything? What's the reaction of the RiverWatch members?"

George had an odd reaction. His face, already pinking up from the sun, turned a tomato red and he stood up and marched out of the office. Carter made a hissing sound and, when I turned, had put his hand over the phone mouthpiece.

"I don't think I would push old George, if I were you. I don't think life in the techno-fast lane prepares anybody for taking on a nut dressed up like George Washington charging your buffed-up antique automobile," he said.

"George is too tense these days," I announced, thinking that I didn't see myself as career oriented toward taking on a Revolutionary with a clipboard. Nevertheless, on that I was batting a thousand.

CHAPTER 16

Over Carver's objections, I went on with the Independence weekend schedule. I must admit that the general reaction from crowds around the state—thanks to the TV coverage—was more lively than I'd been garnering. It was hard not to like a five-foot-four woman who knocks out an attacker with a clipboard.

"But I'm not buying that this guy was just a random crazy," was the concept Carver floated about four thousand times as we covered the state from the Patriotic pageant at Kennywood Amusement Park outside of Pittsburgh to the lovely sunset gathering of the various environmental groups near Fallingwater, the Frank Lloyd Wright house in the mountains near Connellsville.

I marched in Hershey. I reviewed in State College. I made it to exactly the ninth inning in Pittsburgh. I had about seventeen versions of the average, all-American Fourth of July.

SHE'S A KNOCKOUT, the *Philadelphia Daily News* exclaimed in a banner headline. And although I was sure my more politically correct friends would be a little miffed at the slight sexism of the pun, I was delighted.

George was so overcome at the near miss that he begged off traveling with us, and instead met up with Carver and me Monday morning, very early, in Marco Solari's office near Society Hill. Sometime in the early 1950s, the unions had built what were then very modern three and four-story office buildings when the blocks near the waterfront were written off. Then came redevelopment, gentrification, and all the other similar movements that make people in old neighborhoods always hopeful. Society Hill was now quite fancy, with darling little town houses and the best restaurants. And, yes, several of the most modern 1950s office buildings a historic section could not want.

Marco was hosting this fund-raising for several dozen union reps, many of whom were already there when Carver and I arrived. George, I was told, was on his way up from the shore and might be a few minutes late. Kathleen Burns came in just as Marco was pouring coffee.

The amazing addition to the assembly was Christie Hamilton, who explained that she'd spent the weekend producing several of my thirty-second spots at

Modern Video, the elaborate production studios in downtown Philadelphia. We were, she reminded me, scheduled to review the proposed spots the next day in Washington.

Before I could ask any more questions about the spots, I became the one being grilled. The questions came fast and furious. The first were about the death of Joe Hauser, who was a longtime friend and ally of many of the men and women in the room. Then there were the queries—only some of them joking—about my propensity to attract violence and mayhem. "Your aim is getting pretty good," the woman from the Communications Workers told me.

Finally, after second and third cups of coffee all around, the conversation got around to the campaign. I was ready to launch into my "jobs for Pennsylvania and justice for workers" speech when Christie's voice piped up behind me.

"Wouldn't everyone like a sneak preview of Senator Gorzack's commercials?" she asked. My objections went unspoken when measured against the number of "yeses" from around the room.

A TV set and VCR were magically at the ready, and so, with an audience for both my commercials and my reactions, I got to see what I was selling the people of Pennsylvania.

"Boom. Boom." I knew it was the sound of a bass drum, but, for one moment, it sounded like a cannon. The face on the screen was my own, but the close-up was from a still photo that I couldn't quite place, certainly not from the shoot we had done ten days before.

As the voice-over began, chanting a paean to my bravery and patriotism, the camera pulled back and the full photograph came into view. I gasped. It was Jack's funeral, at Arlington, the President standing at one side of me, my mother on the other. I looked like I was ready to keel over and, as I always remembered too well from the terrible week, I was pretty much on the verge of doing just that.

There were a few more scenes—of my swearing in, of me in Vietnam, and of the Capitol itself.

"That's the bio," I heard Christie explain. A "bio" wasn't exactly what I'd call it. It was like a tabloid newspaper story, exploiting all the more emotional and personal particulars of my life. It was too close and it had little to do with whether or not I was a good senator.

Yes, I knew people were going to vote for me because I went to Vietnam and made connections that allowed certain MIAs to be identified. Yes, I knew that people felt close to me because they knew my and Jack's story. But I made the trip to Vietnam both as an MIA wife *and* as a U.S. senator. And I didn't want my emotions being played out, over and over again, in thirty-second spots all over the state.

This spot was important, Christie told us from the back of the darkened room, because it allowed people to view me in a sympathetic light. When that was put up against my "tough" image portrayed in the other spots, it made a complete picture. Right, I wanted to say, and I look like a complete dunce. The spot, except for the photographs, had nothing to do with what I or my time in public life had been about. Nothing about my working-class background, my education, my years and years of work in the public health field. Just the tragedy of Jack's death, and my role in solving years-long mysteries concerning the whereabouts of two dozen men who had been missing in action.

Before I could raise any objections, Christie was running yet another spot, this one showing me marching along with two policemen flanking me and a voice-over warning about the dangers of city life. This for a senator who believed that every corner should have a store on it.

"I think we're going to hold the rest of the commercials until *the entire campaign team has a chance to review them,*" I said, stressing every syllable as I stood up and blocked the TV screen. I motioned to Marco to open the blinds. There were staged moans of complaint, but I just smiled and insisted that until *we* knew what the entire commercial package would be, it wouldn't be honest to show part of what we were planning to air.

"What I'm here to do today is to talk about myself, not about the ads," I said, and as I made that intro I realized what was wrong with the ads. They weren't about me!

"Many of you know me because of my work in Harrisburg. Many others have been down to Washington, to see me in my office, to tell me of your legislative needs. And, in still other venues, we've talked about jobs coming to Pennsylvania, and of the real need for what I call 'nuggets,' which is the basic work of any senator—taking care of his or her state," I said, trying to gauge if I had covered all the bases.

"What about the time you're spending on this Jericho disease stuff, Senator?" the guy from the Service Workers asked. "Isn't that really the job of the public health people here in the state or of the federal agencies that are supposed to be dealing with disease?"

Before I could answer, another rep chimed in.

"And what about the idea that it might be Agent Orange?"

"Look," I said, "it might be anything. One of my staff people tells me that, with one exception, everyone with the disease is in the building trades."

"You think it's a job-related leukemia, Senator? Why hasn't it come up in other places?"

"I don't know. Yet. But I do know that as long as I'm your senator, my job is saving lives, saving jobs, and saving communities. And when a problem comes up—in any of those areas—I'm going to be there, doing whatever I can, whether or not it strictly fits the traditional job of what a senator does."

"Sounds good to me, Norie," one of the old men shouted. "Now how much is it going to cost us to get you elected?"

I thought I had done quite well. Marco thought I had flunked.

"You can't undercut your campaign advisers in the middle of a pitch," he shouted, pacing up and down the hallway.

The meeting had broken up, but he and I, joined by the late-arriving George, were holding a committee meeting in the hallway. George tried to move it into Marco's office, but the intensity of his anger made any such change of venue impossible.

"I want this settled now, Norie. You can't be both the candidate *and* run the campaign," he argued. "Christie Hamilton is the best money can buy. And you treat her like she was some volunteer worker who knows nothing."

"And you treat me like I haven't learned anything in this job. She might be the best you could find, but she's certainly not gotten a rave review from several of the senators I've been talking to," I countered, wishing I'd asked Hilda more about her obvious problems with my hiring Christie.

"Stop screwing around with Jericho. And this stuff about building trades. Gimme a break. You've got a union guy dead and the next thing we know it's going to be organized crime and criminals and everybody going after everybody with a union card," Marco said, the words almost spitting out of his mouth.

"What in God's name are you talking about?" I asked.

"Think of it. Bercolini, he knew a lot about unions. And Hauser, he worked for a union. What can I tell you, Norie? When it's not good for unions, it's not good for you," Marco shouted.

Just as Marco made the somewhat confusing argument, Christie came around the corner and down the hall toward us.

"Senator, I want to get a couple things clear, before we send these commercials out," she said, her brittle smile looking about one centimeter from cracking her face.

"I'd like to get a couple things clear, Christie. And the first thing is, no commercials are going out. None. Until we see and review them all. And especially the so-called bio piece," I declared, sounding even a little bit pompous to myself. "My husband didn't die in Vietnam to make himself into a commercial. And we're not using one inch of film that in any way takes the shine off his record or his life."

"But, Senator," she said, looking at both Marco and George for support, "Jack is the best thing you've got going for yourself. It's how we can define you to the people of Pennsylvania."

"What?" I shouted, sounding too much like Marco. "My late husband is my job definition? No way. I believe in certain things, beliefs that I think should be turned into laws. I believe that I can do a good job as a senator. I have a record of public service and public accomplishments—which you didn't bother to even learn. And I believe my opponent Hank Dugdale is a rabble-rousing despot who is a fearmonger and a professional hater."

I looked around at the three key people in my campaign. I had a finance chair who didn't think I was a good money raiser. I had a longtime friend and adviser who thought I was out to get him and everyone in his profession. And I had a media adviser who no matter how many times I told her what I believed and had done was determined to show me as a person and as a candidate that I was not.

George and Marco had been my friends for a lot of years. We had disagreements, but I knew them, knew that they were committed to me and the goals we all believed in. That was never going to happen with Christie. So I did what I thought was best for myself and for my campaign.

I fired her.

"I don't know if I would have done it quite that way," Hilda said, her voice bringing comfort even over the phone lines. "But she's no easy number. And her numbers aren't accurate anyway."

"What's that mean?"

"Her won-loss records. She doesn't count any primary losses. She counts primary victories, and if her primary-winning candidate goes on to win the general, she counts it as two wins. I had some problems about this when I did a forum last year for potential Senate candidates," Hilda explained. "I called her on it, too."

"What do I do now?" I asked, hating the plaintive, whining tone in my voice. "I've lost both my campaign manager *and* my media adviser. Charlie went along with her, like a package."

"And the pollster?"

"Unclear. Anyway, I couldn't see Christie doing much managing. She seemed to like going to meetings and explaining the ads."

"You need to hire somebody you like. Who likes you. I'll send a batch of commercials from various media types over to your office tomorrow morning."

"I just don't know where the campaign is going," I whined.

"If you don't get organized, it's going nowhere, Norie," Hilda scolded. "Every campaign needs a MOM—that's money, organization, and message. You hired consultants who wanted to package a candidate that didn't exist. You refuse to do your fund-raising calls. And, as far as a manager, don't you know anybody you can put in charge? It's not like a presidential race. You need somebody who knows the state and is well organized. Also who won't leave puddles of blood on the floor every time there's a problem."

"I got it. A Mother Teresa with organizing skills," I quipped.

"Norie, Mother Teresa *has* organizing skills. Or she wouldn't have gotten the Nobel Peace Prize," Hilda countered.

"All right. In my campaign, what comes first?"

"You're so late, everything's a scramble. I'll help you find a media consultant. As far as the money, I'm putting you together with Janet Fisher. Teeny little person with the biggest Rolodex in town. She's worked for a bunch of women's causes, and her people are your people. Build on your strength," Hilda insisted.

"I just hate the pressure of asking for money. Maybe it's fear of rejection."

"You think that's rejection? Go to the polls in November with a bad campaign behind you. That would be rejection. Now think about a campaign manager."

A campaign manager: someone who knew the state; someone who knew me; someone with organizational abilities. And, if I didn't get the right person, I'd lose. Which was what I said to Kathleen Burns that night in my next phone call, which was why she came down with me to Washington the next morning, which was how she wound up being the campaign manager.

Nancy Jackson really made it happen.

We all sat in my office—Hilda, Kathleen, Nancy, Milton, and myself—watching reel after reel of commercials. Time and time again, Kathleen would point out how a particular commercial would resonate in Pennsylvania—and whether or not she thought I could do a similar spot.

At the end of the marathon screening, we all got up and wandered around the room, except for Kathleen, who sat taking notes.

"Okay," she said. "My choice is Robert Welsh, the guy who did the two Illinois campaigns."

"He also does my stuff," Hilda said, "but I didn't

include my reel. I didn't want to give him a head start."

"It doesn't matter what I think," Milton started, and we all yelled him down. "But Welsh has done a Pennsylvania lieutenant governor's race. Six years ago. The candidate lost. But he was kind of a loser anyway."

"And once that's settled, all you need is a campaign manager," Hilda said. "I understand, Kathleen, that you've been fingered for the job."

"If elected I will not serve," Kathleen answered. "Really, Senator, I have an ongoing commitment to the United Way. And I've never run a campaign."

"But you've been part of statewide-issue campaigns. You are an organization genius. You're a great community organizer," I countered. "And you *like* me."

"And there's another reason you should take the job," Nancy said, walking across the room and looking down at Kathleen as she sat with her notes spread around her on the sofa. "It's the only reason, really."

"Okay," Kathleen asked, "what is it?"

"Just think about how you'd feel if Norie lost."

I didn't have to wonder how I'd feel. George Taylor was busy on the phone late Tuesday night telling me, in great detail.

"You will be at the end, I mean end of a really promising career, Norie. And you will have done this to yourself," he was telling me. "I think Kathleen is wonderful myself. But she's never run a campaign. She's never directed the spending of five million dollars."

"George, the entire committee is spending the money. The manager needs organizational skills. I have to have a schedule. It has to work. I need people to be there when I show up to speak."

"Norie, you need professional help. What you have now is a great volunteer effort. So what!"

My cellular phone started to bleep. I hated the fact I was suddenly a multi-gadget person.

The campaign meant I had to carry a portable phone. As well as my Senate beeper. And the little techno phone book that Nancy had filled with two thousand names of the people I might have to call up from the road.

So I asked George if he could hold on, and he told me that he had the RiverWatch chairman in Jericho County holding on his other line and that Mary Devine had stood him up that afternoon.

"I didn't know she was going to see him, George," I said. "What was it about?"

"Something about a 'poisoned pond.' She called me, asking for his number. But why should I know the total purpose of the meeting? She works for you. Don't you remember?"

I remembered. I'd asked Mary, since she was up in Jericho, to drive the twenty miles down to Miller's Lake and see what the latest dredging had pulled up.

"There's a lot of hospital waste that showed up

when a pond was dredged after the storm. I'm sure she was going to talk to the RiverWatch chair about that. Miller's Lake. But do you have any idea what could have happened?" I asked, without thinking that, of course, George knew nothing. As he told me.

"I have no damn idea, Norie. I know that your staff person made a key environmentalist sit around a hotel lobby for more than an hour waiting to have lunch with her. And that she still hasn't called her to apologize."

"George, I have to answer my cellular phone. Could you just hold on . . ."

He hung up.

When I answered the cellular line, so had the caller.

CHAPTER 17

We kept Josh.

He showed up in my office the next day with bales of papers and charts and graphs—and a written letter of resignation.

"Only that doesn't mean I want to go, Senator," he told me. "Only that I will go if you want me to."

"And what about your relationship with Christie and Charlie?" I asked him.

"Well, if I stay with this campaign—and if you win—you'll be winning against terrific odds. Not the least of which is that you fired Christie and Charlie," he said, looking as if he were analyzing the odds even as he spoke. "But *if you win*—"

"You mean *when I win*," I interrupted.

"Yes. Right. When you win, I'm going to be the genius pollster who turned the campaign around. I'm
going to be the guy on the phone to the *New York Times*
and the *Washington Post* explaining the numbers and
the issues. So I'll be the sought-after addition to the
next cycle's races."

"That's a pretty good reason for staying on, Josh.
Anything else?"

"I think you're terrific and I do think we can win.
Look at these numbers," he said, handing me a sheaf
of papers and starting to walk me through the pages.

I got Kathleen, who was back in Philly trying to
clean up some loose ends, and put her on the speakerphone. I brought Milton into the office and together
we went through a lot of numbers that added up to
one thing—I could win.

I would win if I played on the points I felt most comfortable with—my background in public health being
the best issue.

"People in Pennsylvania aren't sure exactly what
you're doing down here in D.C.," Josh told me, "but
they think you're hardworking and that you have their
best interests at heart."

"It doesn't make me feel exactly wonderful that nobody is quite sure what's happening," I started.

"But they think you *want* to do good for them, Senator," Milton interrupted. "And that's what I can make
happen here. I can be sure that you're right on the
money on upcoming legislation. That you are a lead

sponsor of several important bills. And that you get the credit for being the good senator you are."

"Or at least, will be," I corrected him. "Now I feel that I've got a campaign going."

Despite my best intentions, I spent the next several hours dealing with Jericho County, and so did Milton.

First item on tap was Joe Hauser, or at least the funeral of the murdered union representative. The services had been delayed until Hauser's son could return from Indochina, where he was working on the construction of a resort hotel. One thing I'd asked Mary Devine to do was to get my office the details of the funeral, so that I could at least make a try at getting to the services.

But Mary had fallen down on the job, and the funeral had actually been held Monday. The failure of communications made me mad, since I had been in the state, in Philadelphia, and it was a short hop to Allentown, Joe's hometown.

"But you can't blame her, Senator," Milton was explaining. "The Hauser family has really shut down. I guess the fact that Joe said he knew something, and then was mugged and murdered, really has them scared. Mary had told me Friday that she just couldn't get them to answer any questions as to time and place."

"Speaking of time and place, when did you talk to her?" I asked him.

"I haven't. Haven't got a clue as to where she is,

either. She's got a beeper. No cellular. But we're getting a low-battery response."

"Milton, you're telling me that we haven't talked to her in more than a day and we're just sitting here, saying how did she fall down on the job?"

"Senator, you said that. I didn't."

"I don't care who said it, Milton. Find her. Now."

Carver seemed a little low-battery himself when he crawled into my office early Thursday morning.

"Have a little sugar, Lieutenant, and make yourself at home," I offered, holding out the bowl of M&Ms I kept on my desk for Carver's frequent stop-bys.

"No. No sweets. I'm off them," he said, shaking his head in a slow, sad response. "That's it. No more. That's all she wrote."

I could feel a tremble all through my body. Carver, sick! With what? I thought. Diabetes? High blood pressure? It could be anything.

"And what brought on this dietary change?" I asked, trying to sound casual but dreading the answer.

"Senator, what do you think? I have gained weight. Seven pounds. Can you believe that?" Carver started the head shaking again. "Is that funny? Do you think my weight gain is amusing?"

I couldn't stop laughing. Seven pounds and this was the result.

"Haven't you ever gained weight before?" I finally managed.

"Never. Not an ounce. Until I got on the scale last

night, I believed I was the same trim and wonderfully in-shape person I'd been since I got through puberty."

Carver half sat, half slumped into a chair near my desk.

"I don't like this Hauser thing," he started.

"What's to like?" I countered. "The man's dead. Brutal mugging."

"I don't like some of the answers we're getting. Or at least the FBI is getting. They're in this too, since he was on the way to testify at a hearing."

"Anything new at all?" I asked, expecting there to be nothing.

"A little. That's what confuses me."

Before Carver could get his next sentence out, Nancy came running into the room.

"She's in the hospital. She was in a ditch for at least a day. Trapped by the air bag and the steering wheel. She's okay. She's conscious. Wants to talk to you."

I knew without asking that Mary Devine hadn't run off the road by accident.

It was late that evening when Carver and I finally got off the phones and were back in my office. Milton and Nancy were on their way up to Jericho, to get Mary and bring her back. The hospital kept insisting that she was fine to travel, but I wasn't having her come back alone. Carver arranged for a retired FBI guy to drive up and back with them.

"I don't think we want to start bringing in every law-enforcement group we'd need to get them from the District, through Maryland, and in and out of Pennsylvania," he explained. "Cops can't go from one jurisdiction to the other, so if they are escorting a car, they have to drop off at a state boundary and another police force picks up. This is where I always begin to question the intelligence of the Founding Fathers and all those little lines on the map that define states."

"Don't you let the militia hear you saying that," I kidded. There was something terribly sweet about Carver, Mister Follow-the-Rules, complaining about the complications such rules entailed.

"I don't think you should be kidding about the old militia, Senator," Carver warned. "This thing with Mary Devine certainly stinks of their pseudoparamilitary tactics."

"You think people ran her off the road exactly where they knew she'd really be in trouble?" I asked.

"These jokers are always running around the countryside, playing like they're fighting the Cong or something. Turns out, my friends at the FBI tell me, that very few of these guys they research ever served in actual military operations," Carver answered.

"And how's my militia-sponsored Website?"

"Interesting. They are always alerting the folks out there to what a truly poor representative you are—and exactly how they can track you down."

"I'm almost afraid to ask, but was there anything about Mary being up in Jericho and asking questions or being my staff member assigned to the subcommittee?"

"Senator, I've become an avid reader of the so-called 'Get Norie' page, and I don't remember anything about a staff person," Carver said, reaching in one large swoop for the M&M-filled bowl.

"Hey, what about your diet?" I asked.

"Senator," he said, "we've got to be using more calories figuring all this out. Have some yourself."

I took a handful, ate a couple, then started to sort them out by color on the top of my desk. I just couldn't get used to the blue ones.

"When I talked to Mary on the phone," I said, thinking out loud, "she insisted that she got a good look at the two guys in the pickup truck. She said they were wearing fatigues and that there was a big American flag painted on the truck door."

"Yes," Carver said, "that jibes with what she told the police in the emergency room. It's ironic. The poor kid was stuck out there, trapped under the steering wheel, and inches away was her cellular phone. Inches! She could have phoned for help and been picked up minutes after they ran her off the road."

That's what didn't make sense to me.

Here were the Keystone Militia, who knew every second of my public life. They'd obviously followed Mary from stop to stop. Yet, if they really wanted to do her harm, why not check to see if she had been hurt? Or, God forbid, hurt her if she hadn't been done in by having the car run off the road?

Instead, knowing that she probably had a cellular phone, they ran her off the road into a deep but grassy ditch, and let her get a good look at their fatigues and their truck.

"Maybe they wanted Mary to call for help. Maybe they wanted her to be found immediately and turn their description over to the police," I suggested. "Maybe somebody else wanted the militia blamed."

"Yeah, okay. Now tell me who," Carver rebutted.

"Let me figure out the 'why' first," I said. "Where was Mary going? To meet with the RiverWatch chair. Why was she run off the road? To keep her from that meeting."

"And the meeting was about a lake?"

"A polluted pond, really. When the floodwaters went down last month, turned out the pond had been a dumping ground for all kinds of old hospital waste. She was up there anyway, so I asked Mary to check on the most recent dredging and . . ."

"So you think the problem is a poisoned pond?" Carver asked.

"Maybe the poison did a lot more damage than the pond," I answered. "Maybe somebody has been dumping hospital waste all around the area and maybe my vets with leukemia were exposed to that particular water. And maybe somehow that has to do with the construction jobs."

"Senator, not *all* the vets are in construction," Carver reminded me.

"Yes," I responded. "But all the vets who have leukemia live in Jericho County and I'm beginning to think that murder might be like real estate—'location, location, location.' "

I thought I had struck a vein of truth when I connected the sick pond and the sick men. But it just didn't pan out.

"Senator, it's an interesting theory," Dr. Samuel L. Kantor from the National Institutes of Health told me on my fourth phone call of the next morning. "But it's a theory that has no basis. Cancer does not come from trash in the water supply. Now you can get a lot of other interesting diseases. And I'm sure the people around Miller's Lake should be checking in regularly with the local public health officials. But no—no way is there a connection."

I thanked him profusely, not bothering to tell him I'd received the same information from doctors and researchers at Sloan-Kettering in New York, at the University of Pennsylvania in Philadelphia, and at Johns Hopkins in Baltimore.

The doctors at Penn, who'd been sent samples of the water when I first heard about the hospital waste, were clear that some toxins were breeding in the lake.

"But they are the regular, old-fashioned get a little diarrhea or a little fever from a nonspecific infection style toxins," the chief biologist told me. "There aren't enough toxins. The toxins are not present throughout the water supply. And even if every lake in the area had been a dumping ground for such waste and the dumping produced such toxins, well, why don't you have any women or children with the same strange leukemia?"

"So it's either Vietnam—or, as my young staffer kept insisting to me, that they're mostly in the construction business," I offered.

"I'd jump on the construction business bandwagon. People on construction sites are notorious for not being careful. Suppose they were all involved with, say, asbestos removal. Different sites, mind you, but over a certain period of time," the biologist offered.

"And it's just in Jericho County," I said, sorting through the papers on my desk trying to see if I had any more questions for her.

"Not according to what I'm seeing, Senator. There are three clusters of such leukemias that we've been called in to help with or back up the lab work. Jericho County, sure. But then there's Salem County. Now that's men and women and they all seem to live very close. We wondered about a nuclear plant nearby. And there's that hospital near Havre de Grace. They're reporting leukemia that's very similar—but there, it's across the board. Men, women, children."

My mind was tripping over itself. Salem County. Where the heck was Salem County? And Havre de Grace? That was in Maryland.

Dammit. I'd been done in by those same state boundaries that Carver had been complaining about earlier in the day. The NIH had records of ongoing studies of longtime incidences of diseases. But the other two sites would be just like Jericho—just coming to notice as people got sick.

So there was only one cluster of leukemia cases in Pennsylvania. But there was another one in Salem County, *New Jersey*, and yet another one in northern Maryland.

All those dumb colonists, who wanted to have their own little state, their own little country, and so they had carved up the eastern seaboard like a jigsaw puzzle. It was probably a two-and-a-half-hour drive to get to all three of the sites, which were in three separate states.

Next time, I'd have a few things to say to the Founding Fathers.

CHAPTER 18

There are two places I could stand still, focus, and clear my head. One was in front of the Vietnam Memorial. The other was in front of my stove.

I bundled up all my legal-pad notes and told Nancy and Milton that I wanted them both in the office by eight the next morning. Then I walked out of Hart, past the Capitol, and down the Mall to the Vietnam Memorial.

It was the dinner hour, but the summertime throngs were still billowing under the trees. The Roosevelt Memorial had given all Americans another place to remember another time and a hero. I knew that for many of the older visitors, that was the structure that most embodied their hopes and history, as the Vietnam Memorial did for me.

In the years when my husband was still missing in action, I would visit the memorial and wonder when and if his name would appear on that roll call of fallen heroes. And I would try to smooth the fear that I would never know what happened to Jack.

Still, in the weeks since "Capt. John J. Gorzack" made its mark in the marble, I had not made a visit. Maybe I postponed the first sight of that freshly chiseled name because the sadness it underlined was such an old one.

So I sat across from Jack's place in history, I sat on the grass and wondered if the people passing his name had their own Jacks and Jimmys and Joes. And the sunlight slowly faded as the park rangers offered pieces of paper and instructions on making a copy of the name, whatever name was most important to you.

The sun was still working hard to keep the sky a paler blue as I walked the blocks back to my apartment. By the time, though, that I was standing in my kitchen, the skylight showed only an indigo sky.

I decided I'd make myself a little risotto and then realized that I hadn't really cooked for the several weeks since I'd first gone up to Jericho County. The floods, the emergency, the destruction—and Bercolini on the plane, telling me he had to talk to me about something.

Risotto was always a great way for me to logically think through a confusing problem. First, to make risotto, you need a little patience, because there are specified steps and rules to result in that extraordinary mixture of rice with its creamy broth.

Second, as I had learned from experience, don't always believe what the cookbooks tell you. Lots of recipes have details about splashes of white wine and being finished off with cream. Unnecessary, although you should permit a little butter and a little olive oil.

It takes eighteen minutes. Even when I am alone, I cook it for four because it tastes so good zapped the next day. Heat up some chicken broth and get the leftover cooked asparagus out of the fridge. Take a small onion. Mince it. Cook it a minute or two in a pan in some olive oil. Meanwhile, microwave the asparagus to get it warm. Take a handful of rice for each serving and cook it in the oil and onion for about a minute. Then, a ladle at a time, add the broth. Keep stirring the rice, although not as much as the cookbooks say you must. After about fifteen minutes, test the rice. Then add the warmed vegetables, then keep adding the steaming liquid until, magically, the rice releases its starch and a wonderful milky elixir softly envelops the cooked kernels. Add a pat of butter. Stir it in. Then salt and pepper and grated Parmesan.

Perfect. With a little salad on the side.

Only at my side I was having a large pile of papers, pushing, trying to make a link.

What did Bercolini say that day on the plane? That I'd be interested considering *my time in government* and *my experience*.

Maybe I'd taken this all exactly the wrong way. Here

I thought that Bercolini was on my case. After all, it was me who got the appointment to the Senate. Not him, or any other experienced campaigner.

But he wasn't talking about my campaign. He was talking about my experience in government, my government service.

"In public health," I shouted out loud to no one but the risotto. "Bercolini wasn't telling me what to do. He was asking for my expertise on public health."

I savored the connection I'd managed to make and my risotto never tasted sweeter.

I had a yellow pad filled with lists with little empty boxes drawn beside each item. I gave Nancy a copy of my list and told her that I planned to check them all off before the day was over.

A few of the calls she could make herself, I told her, and would she please bring the answers into my office immediately. Then I got down to some preliminary minor housekeeping.

Nancy got the Berks County district attorney on the phone, so I could check off George Washington IV. That was his name, the deranged man who tried to impale me during the parade. He had his name legally changed.

"And what was his name before?" I wondered.

"Walter Cronkite," the DA managed with hardly a snicker.

"His name was Walter Cronkite?" I asked, disbelieving.

"That was his name after he had it changed the last time, Senator. In the United States, you can call yourself anything you want to."

"Anything, regardless of a name already belonging to a famous personality? That's the federal law?" I questioned him, not really believing that august bodies like the U.S. Senate would do something stupid like that.

"Famous person. Living or dead. Doesn't matter. You can be Barbra Streisand or Barbara Bush or Barbie. Maybe not Barbie. Maybe that's copyrighted. But, yes, let me see." The DA paused. "Frank Watkins. That was his name seventeen years ago. He grew up here in town, seemed okay according to his high school records, but then had a breakdown a couple years past graduation."

"That's very sad," I offered. "Sounds like adolescent onset schizophrenia. Where is he now?"

"George the Fourth?" the district attorney asked in such a mean manner that I suddenly felt sorry for Mr. Watkins. "He's hospitalized for thirty days and after that, with medication, he'll be back on the street."

"Did the psychiatrists tell you anything about him, about why he chose to attack me?" I asked, hoping that the answer would be a "no." It wasn't.

"Only that Frank, or George, has been following politics quite closely and, in fact, has become devoted to your opponent, Hank Dugdale," the DA explained. "The police report says that in the group house where Frank lives, he demands that the TV set be tuned to the news all the time, or to some cable station that covers politics."

Hank Dugdale must have really been doing a job on me to drive that poor man to rush me with his flagpole, I thought. Of course, I didn't feel much sympathy when he was running toward me.

"Is there anything else I should know?" I asked the DA.

"Only that George was planning to change his name again. He'd filed papers with the county clerk. In his petition he said he needed a more patriotic epithet."

"And . . . ?"

"He wanted to be called 'Hank Dugdale.' "

With that out of the way, I got to several large, black boxes. Bercolini. Joe Hauser. Leukemia.

For this I needed Carver and Milton. I'd had Nancy track down the lieutenant, although these days he wasn't far from my front office.

"The Pennsy State Police and the FBI have identified maybe a hundred people Hauser saw or spoke to in the week before he was murdered," Carver began, reading out of his notebook. "Whatever he was going to tell the subcommittee had to come from one of those people. We're getting a copy of his home and office phone records and an entire team of interviewers will be following up."

I looked over the notes I'd made on my yellow pad. Under Hauser I'd underlined *union* and *Bercolini*.

"Marco Solari was really mad at me the other day,"

I told Carver. "Moaning about how Hauser and Bercolini were both deeply involved with unions. And it got me to thinking . . ."

"I'll buy that," Carver interrupted.

"Maybe we should eliminate some of the peripheral stuff and concentrate on the obvious stuff," I said, still reading off my sheets. "Bercolini wanted to tell me something. He was murdered. Joe Hauser wanted to tell the subcommittee something. He was murdered. What if Bercolini and Joe Hauser wanted to tell the same thing?"

Carver shook his head.

"That's a jump, Senator," he said. "You got a guy who's obviously the victim of a, let's call it, an ideologically based attack. The militia. And you got another guy who's trying to clear up a mystery about a strange leukemia that has affected a dozen or so Vietnam vets. These are not the same scenarios."

Carver made a lot of sense. Only I knew he wasn't right.

"You've taken your clues from me, Carver. All along, I've been thinking that Bercolini was somewhat sarcastic when he talked about my 'expertise.' Remember, he was one of what seemed like seven thousand politicians who thought they should have gotten the Senate appointment. Now I think he was being sincere," I said, and rustled through my notes, looking for a specific factoid.

"You think he knew something about the leukemia cases?" Carver asked.

"Think?" I joyously asked. "I know he knew. Bercolini's office has correspondence from at least seven of the men who are being treated at Northeast Memorial. And Bercolini met with at least one of them."

"And nobody brought this up to you?" Carver asked incredulously.

"Why should they, Lieutenant? I'm in the hospital. They tell me they are concerned. I think one of the guys told me he was contacting people in the government. To tell the truth, I thought he meant the VA."

I was a little embarrassed to tell Carver that piece of my detective work—that if I had asked another question that day, asked the guy who in the government he'd been writing to or talking to, I would have had Bercolini's name pop up on my radar screen.

"So you think this gets you off the hook with the militia, Senator?" Carver asked.

"Nope," I answered. "Whatever Bercolini was onto, whatever Joe Hauser figured out, somebody had to be doing something very illegal. As you told me, Carver, nobody goes around killing people for nothing."

I'd lied a little to Carver. I did think that what I'd figured out took me off the hook. Just a little, that is.

I could view the occurrences of the past few weeks through a truly clouded lens, coming up with a dark picture of my public life. Or I could see the random violence as related to one small, ugly piece of a somewhat badly functioning society—and the occurrence of such random crimes in my life as a happenstance.

I, of course, would like to always choose the latter alternative. And I could have kept that thought, except for a random meeting.

Carver and I were late for the 5 P.M. reserved-seat Metroliner to Philadelphia. We got to the gate just as the train was pulling out of the station.

"Okay," I told him, "you get new tickets for the six p.m. and I'll treat us both to one of those chocochino things you keep trying to foist on me."

I stopped and picked up some magazines and the two of us sipped our drinks and waited for the next train. There was a private lounge in Union Station that any senator or representative could use, but since at least some of the people heading up to Philadelphia might be actual voters, I wanted the chance to shake a few hands, say a few words.

Once on the train, we headed for the snack car, or, as Amtrak called it in a fit of nomenclature exuberance, the *café car*. Now it could have been called the diner—not dining, diner—car, since it had booths and served microwaved foods, including a dried soup that might be used for backpacking. But *café* gave a passenger a hoped for panache that fell as flat as a pancake.

Carver's chivalry shone through and he took the side of the booth that made him ride backwards. Which was pleasant and lucky, I thought, because I was facing the right way to catch sight of the two women making their way to where the attendant was serving up snacks.

"Norie! Senator!" the one woman blurted out with

a voice that verged on a giggle and I knew immediately—Eileen Fitzpatrick. I had gone through high school with Eileen, as well as, it turned out, her companion, Michelle O'Hara.

Eileen's giggle and her perfect smile made her easy to spot, but Michelle's dark brown hair had been so heavily highlighted and her once cheerleader figure had been so heavily filled out that she wasn't an instant recognition.

"Hi. Hi. This is great. Meeting you like this," Eileen said, enveloping my head in a cloud of some perfume I remembered from those gifts-with-lipstick purchase deals. "I'm sure not in Washington very much. Just down there today exercising my civic duty."

"And that was . . . ?" I asked.

Together, as synchronized as political Rockettes, the two whipped their purses up in front of them and displayed large Values Coalition bumper strips.

"Well, that's interesting. I know you weren't by my office," I said, trying to keep a steady tone, "so I guess you were visiting Senator Smith and some of the Members. The congressmen and congresswomen," I added, seeing that neither of them had any idea what the Member was a member of.

"Oh, no, Norie. That's lobbying. That's not what we're about. We were rallying. On the Mall. About immigration," Michelle said, flashing me a smile. "My husband, Pete Jankowsky, has a real problem about immigration. Our kids are having a hard time getting into the classes they want at Penn State because so many foreigners are signing up. For the classes the kids want. It's always those kind who are knocking our kind out of what's rightfully theirs."

I couldn't look at Carver. This woman had the political sense of a cocker spaniel, and, to be honest, old acquaintances could be forgot when all I remembered about the Values Coalition was getting pushed off that Jericho school step.

"I know just what you mean," Carver said in his chattiest manner. "My ancestors have probably been in this country for maybe two or three hundred years and I keep thinking about how people whose families came here, just eighty or ninety years ago, get so much more than their fair share."

Nodding at Carver and obviously not listening to his mockery, Eileen leaned toward me and asked, "Can I speak freely in front of this man?"

Before I could answer, Carver cleared his throat and explained that he was a police official, on a direct mission from the White House, and that anyone could speak freely in front of him. The only problem might be if he had to suddenly jump out of the booth to intervene in a life-threatening situation.

Eileen and Michelle again missed the obvious satire and started in on their rap about how the country needed to get back to basic values. I felt I was trapped in a Dugdale commercial.

"Moral values are what you have to uphold," Michelle insisted. "American values. Not these foreign ideas."

"I think I am for moral values," I said, hoping the anger wasn't seeping through my smile. "But I also believe—and I know Hank and I disagree on this—that all young children, regardless of where they were born, are entitled to some basic health benefits. Like inoculation."

"You mean even if they aren't legal, you'd give them medical care?" Eileen asked. "I think that's against the law, Norie. We can't be taking care of people who don't belong here."

"That's one way to look at it, Eileen, but I believe that American values—not Christian charity, but the tenets of American law—mandate us to at least prevent public health crises by restraining possible epidemics. Like whooping cough. It's sometimes fatal in children."

"Norie, I'm not worried about the health of foreign children. I am worried about the health of their minds. What about the books that are being read in public schools?" Michelle spit the question, and I realized she must have false teeth behind those ruby red lips and that a fine spray came out with each ugly pronouncement.

Before I could answer, the Tweedledee political polemics lashed out again, this time with the "us versus them" argument.

"We know, Norie, that you are one of us. And we just hate the idea that you're going up against Hank. Dugdale, you know," Eileen said.

"Yes. Hank Dugdale. My opponent," I managed.

Dugdale was not overwhelming his supporters with an overabundance of political sophistication. Maybe Christie Hamilton had been right and it was slogans that mattered.

"And what could be really bad are those negative ads. The ones that attack the other candidate," Eileen said. "Now we've all been to Catholic school and we all know that attacks are not what Christian charity is all about."

"Politics is not about Christian charity, but about who is supposed to be running the country," I tried to counter. But I wasn't sure that anything I said was registering. They both seemed to be reading from a script.

"I know you're going to agree with Hank Dugdale and pledge to avoid negative advertising," Michelle insisted. "Because we know you're the kind of woman who cares about what women like Eileen and me are concerned about."

The train was barely out of the station and I was wondering if I could make it to Baltimore. Surely, if these two women kept it up, Carver would have to intervene in a life-threatening situation—and I would be threatening their lives. Prejudice was always most hateful to me when it came dressed like an old friend. Eileen and Michelle had never been friends—but now they were presuming on friendship to try to pressure me, politically and personally.

Carver saved the day.

"I'm so sorry, ladies, but the reason I am on this

train to Philadelphia is to review with the senator the upcoming crime and capital punishment bill, which, you might know, extends the death penalty to about forty-seven misdemeanors." He smiled and nodded, like a cop letting you drive away after he didn't give you a ticket.

Eileen and Michelle were obviously all for us getting down to work on Carter's piece of supposed legislation, and, with a blessedly limited amount of hugging and kissing, they passed off into whatever car could receive these great American patriots with the welcoming gestures they deserved.

"It's a great country," Carver offered.

"Do I look that embarrassed?" I asked.

"Yes. But you don't have to be. If I spent all my time apologizing for the Black Panthers I'd never have time to remember what Dr. King was all about," he said. He pointed to our empty cups, and, when I nodded, got up to get us refills of regular old brew.

I stared out the window and waited for the Baltimore tunnel to envelope me. I wasn't like those women. I'd spent my whole life being different, practicing what I thought was the real Christian charity—acts they would probably see as heretical and unpatriotic. Like making sure little kids, no matter the country of their origin, had a chance for a better life because they were inoculated against childhood diseases.

"You need a vaccine to ride the train," Carver said, breaking in on my musing with more accuracy than he could have known. "I guess they fill the bill for 'it takes all kinds.' "

"I wish you were serving a cold white wine," I said, taking my coffee.

"They sell it, right here at the snack bar," Carver offered.

"No. It wouldn't be seemly for a woman senator to be belting down a wine. Michelle and Eileen might be put out," I said.

"Well, they obviously got what they wanted," Carver mumbled, slipping into his side of the booth.

"What? They wanted to have this confrontation?" I objected. "Come on. It wasn't pleasant, but it was all by chance. Random."

"Nope, not at all," the lieutenant said smugly. "Those ladies were bound and determined to meet up with you and talk to you and tell you all the evil stuff they were carrying around in their bright little pocketbooks and their perky little heads. They wanted you to hear all that hate."

"Come on. What if we'd made the five p.m. Metroliner? We would have never run into them."

"Well, that's not exactly true, Senator. When I went back to turn in my tickets, the ladies were right in front of me. They told the woman behind the counter that they had missed their 'friend' on the five p.m. and so they were forced to try and find her on the six o'clock train."

"I'll be darned," I managed.

"No, Senator. If you were to talk to those ladies, especially after your answers to their hate-crazed questions, they would tell you that you would, in fact, not be darned, but would instead be damned. That's true. That's what they think."

CHAPTER 19

Robert Matthew Welsh had a simple plan.

"We let the voters see who you are, and then they vote for you," he said, his broad Irish face lighting up. "It's easy, because we don't have to pretend you're someone else."

"But what about my being tough?" I asked. Kathleen Burns, Josh Kaplan, and R. M., as he was called, were all sitting in the suddenly authentic-looking campaign office. Kathleen must have visited every second-hand office equipment outlet in the tri-state area. The office looked real, like something happened there.

It was early Sunday morning, and the sunlight came through the now washed storefront window and glimmered on the steel chairs and desks. It was less than four months before the election, and I wondered if there was a glimmer of a chance that I could pull this off.

Here I was, taking advice on how I should present myself to a dozen million people from a man I had met once before, for an hour. It could make one nervous.

I did, however, like what he was saying.

"A media campaign can't remake a person. If you try, voters will always figure it out. There's some kind of mysterious chemistry," he said, using his unlit cigar as a pointer. "People know when they're being lied to."

"That can't always be true," Kathleen insisted. "Look at the people who get elected."

"Maybe people get elected who *you* don't like. But the voters like them. And almost always a winner's commercials show who the winner really was. Somehow, the camera acts like an X ray."

"Give me an example. Not just of a good commercial, but how it worked because of the candidate," I suggested.

"Ronald Reagan in 1980," was R. M.'s instant reply. "Reagan had run for the Republican nomination twice before. This time, in the primaries and the general election, he ran as the conservative he was. 'Government is too big and we ought to cut it,' was pretty much what his commercials said. He couldn't have run as a moderate. People would have known he was faking it."

"And if I'm not sure about what kind of a senator I

am"—my question slipped out on the table and sat there like a dead fish—"won't I be faking it and won't I get caught?"

"Nope, Senator. Not one bit," R. M. replied and in his answer captured the soul and exuberance of what would be the next four months of campaigning. "You will tell people about the senator you want to be. You'll know they'll want that senator, too, because you know what they need."

"That makes me feel much better, R. M."

"Just let me hasten to add, Senator, that you'll win because of your honesty. That—and the quality of your television spots."

Although scripts for the new spots still weren't written, R. M. was sure that little or none of the already-shot Christie-Charlie footage could be used.

"I've seen all the raw footage, Senator. The woman in the commercials isn't you. She doesn't talk like you. She doesn't relate to people the way you do. And"—he checked the faces of the other people around the table—"I don't think there's anyone here who wants you to go through the agony of reliving your husband's memorial service every time you turn on a TV."

"I couldn't think what they were up to. I understand that people would be sympathetic . . ."

"That's not all. Sometimes showing candidates, especially women, in situations where they triumph over tragedy is a very effective tool. Senator Dianne

Feinstein is a good example. When she ran for the senate in California, she didn't have much of a record of public service. But she had taken over as mayor of San Francisco when her predecessor, George Moscone, was assassinated. So her commercials showed her in the minutes after the Moscone assassination, taking charge."

I thought about that for a minute.

"I don't know if I could do that," I said.

"In some ways, you don't have to. We have a bigger, broader, more issue-oriented message. I've read the tons of information Milton Gant assembled—and I think that I've got a couple possible slogans. No scripts," he laughed and got slightly pink, "but the slogans will tell you where we're going."

"Shoot!"

"You're running against Dugdale. His issue is some nebulous thing called 'values.' Your issue is jobs. So how about, 'The minimum wage is a family value.'"

"I like that," Kathleen said.

"Or, what about 'Value hard work.' Or 'People First.' That's simple. It covers a lot of bases and it says who you are."

"I'd like to stress that I'm working for legislation that affects families, especially working-class families."

"That's another consistent theme, which resonates both with the voter—according to Josh's polling numbers—and with people's already established image of who you are. How about"—R. M. checked his notebook—" 'Fighting for Working Families.' I also thought 'From the People, For the People' would be good, considering your background."

"Anything else?" I asked.

"The President's numbers are really high and we should either shoot him for a commercial, or get some footage of you with him, Senator," Josh answered.

"And the commercials?"

"Okay, this is where it gets a little tight," R. M. said, squirming in his chair as if it already were. "There's just no time to do scripts, to focus scripts, to put them through the normal write and rewrite hoops."

"We didn't have any of that the last go-round either," Kathleen quipped.

"But if we don't have scripts . . ."

"We're just going to go out and shoot you, Senator. Thanks to Kathleen, we're going to follow you around to your campaign events this afternoon and tomorrow afternoon. It's good because you're in State College today and Pittsburgh tomorrow. Then we're going to shoot you at some ten places that Kathleen has scheduled, mostly around Philly, on Monday. We'll talk a little more tonight, about some things you might say conversationally, and then we'll just let you at 'em."

"Well, that's avant-garde, to say the least. What do they call this approach?" I asked.

"Cinema verité," Josh replied.

"No," R. M. said with a shrug. "It's really just shooting by the seat of your pants."

For all the admitted lack of planning, the weekend went well.

R. M. had asked me to pick out several outfits in which I felt comfortable. "Remember it's really hot and it's easy to get ragged looking," R. M. warned. "And, please, Senator, don't have your hair done."

"You don't want me to look my best, R. M.?"

"I don't want you to look different. We'll have a makeup person along. And she'll do what she calls 'fluff you up.'"

"I guess you don't have so many details with the guys," I said, feeling a little unsettled at the attention that had to be paid to how I looked.

"You can't believe the amount of 'fluffing up' some of your colleagues require," he explained. "Your *male* colleagues, that is."

So, slightly "fluffed" I went through my paces—R. M. managing to keep the camera crew out of the way most of the time during Saturday and Sunday events. Then, on Monday, I had the chance to talk to teachers, factory employees, seniors—my constituents—through seven hours of stops. I kept my proposed slogans in mind—and I felt comfortable talking about jobs and minimum wages and health-care benefits.

It wasn't until the next-to-last stop that my short-range plan and my long-range campaign began to cloud up. And this time both had to do with forces beyond the control of any politician.

"It's a mess up there, Norie," Milton boomed out of my cell phone. "It's like some biblical plague. First we get the floods. Then we get the heat. And now everything is drying up."

"How bad is it?" I asked.

"Very. I'm talking biblical. No exaggeration. First it was Miller's Lake but now it's everywhere. The heat is like some vacuum cleaner, only it's sucking up the water and leaving all this junk behind. The shores of some of these lakes and ponds are looking pretty ratty. No water. No vacationers. Good-bye economy of northeastern Pennsylvania. Unless you've got some idea of a lucrative use for filth and hospital refuse."

"I'll head right up there," I told Milton. "See if you can get me a state police escort."

"No, Senator. Get some rest tonight, and I'll get the schedule set for tomorrow," Milton ordered. "You're going to need every bit of energy to deal with this mess. And you're going to need to be briefed. I'll get Mary Devine on the phone to you tonight."

"Milton, Mary's supposed to be on leave, getting a little R and R," I argued. "She can't go up to Jericho or the Poconos."

"Mary doesn't need to, Senator. I called her about noon and by four she had a computerized command center set up here in the office. We've borrowed a techie from Phil Fox—and the two of them are plugged into every known informational source."

Despite the crisis, I had to smile. Nobody loved dealing with an emergency more than Milton. For a guy who was constantly harping about what was wrong with the police or the army, he could really throw himself into mobilization. Maybe all Milton really wanted was a uniform and a badge.

"Give me an idea of what kind of magnitude you're talking about, Milton. And don't use language from the seven plagues of Egypt," I ordered.

"We have—at last count—reports of at least seven large and more than a dozen smaller bodies of water where some kind of refuse is found. Hold on a second," he said, and I could hear him rustling through papers. "Your successor at the State Department of Health, Maurice Hite, was not helpful. Why have I never heard you mention him, Senator?"

"This is not the time or place, Milton, but I guess it's because Maurice is never very helpful. He doesn't particularly like me and I guess I feel the same about him."

"You want to talk about this?" Milton asked.

"Milton, you're beginning to sound like a therapist. Maurice and I were both state government professionals. Maurice spent a lot of time planning his professional future. I spent a lot of time doing my job," I announced, the hiss in my voice quite apparent.

"Okay. I'll never bring that up again."

"You can bring it up," I said, "but realize that when you do, I will put Maurice down."

In two hours on the phone that night I learned everything I needed to know about the impending crisis;

eastern Pennsylvania water tables; federal and state regulations regarding hazardous and hospital wastes; record heat waves; and values of vacation homes; insurance limits on damage caused by a third-party dumping; numbers of letters and phone calls received by my office requesting federal help in the clean-up; and the ability to date rubbish by the code bars on items such as glucose drips.

The next morning, with Carver driving—the over-the-road trips were too tough on Stash—I headed up to Jericho, accompanied by Kathleen Burns and, surprisingly, Milton Gant.

"I just thought we needed someone familiar with the Hill and our office to be part of the program," Milton explained.

I refused his questionably gracious offer to let me sit in the backseat, pointing out that we were in an Explorer four-wheel-drive and not a limo. Milton had left his pinstripe uniform behind, and instead was wearing a very faded plaid short-sleeve shirt and a pair of khakis. He looked a lot younger than his late thirties, and I could understand why Nancy once told me that out of the office, "Milton is a real cutie."

I didn't know what was happening with that relationship, if that's what it was, until Milton happened to mention Nancy's views on the campaign.

"She thinks you should be talking to more women's groups. She got stuff from Senator Mendelssohn on Emily's List," Milton said. "It means Early Money Is

Like Yeast—it makes more money grow. They raised well over one million dollars in the last cycle."

"I know what Emily's List is, Milton. But I'm not early. We're playing catch-up ball. Their commitments are probably all made," I countered. Why was I always so cranky about fund-raising?

"No matter," Kathleen's voice came from behind my left shoulder. "I've got a call into them anyway. I've given money through Emily's List for years and I don't see why they can't do a mailing for you, here in the state, if not nationally."

"Why not?" I asked, grouchy that every conversation seemed to turn into one about money. "It's not as if people don't have a lot of other things to do. With their cash, that is."

A sudden and deep silence descended on the four-wheel-drive like an avalanche. We drove on, mute, for several miles, with signs welcoming us to "Pennsylvania Dutch Country" and the "Honeymoon Capital of the World."

"You know, Senator," Carver said, keeping his eyes on the road but propelling his voice to my side of the car like a guided missile, "democracy costs a lot of money. Food costs money. Education costs money. Government sure costs money. But democracy isn't paid for entirely with your and my tax dollars."

I scrunched around in my seat so I could gauge his reaction when I flung back my answer.

"A democracy shouldn't be run by people who have to beg and borrow to get the money to campaign. It's just beneath the idea of a public official," I declared. "It's not what being elected to office used to be all about."

"Right. It used to be about the Teapot Dome scandal and about vicuña coats and about the Watergate break-in. Give me a break, Senator," Carver said, sounding angry himself. "You want a better government. You go tell people that they deserve a better government. Then all those people better get behind you because some other dude might not have their interests at heart."

"This is a lot like what R. M. told me the other night. I should just run as myself," I told the car, but myself in particular.

"Well, now, I wouldn't go that far," Carver quipped, and we laughed all the way to the next "the Poconos is Honeymoon Land" sign.

CHAPTER 20

It was no honeymoon at Miller's Lake. Or Christmas Lake. Or Goose Pond. It was real nasty, as one of the local constables kept repeating.

"I'm going to send my two grandkids off to camp, Senator. Can you believe that," he droned as he had walked beside me from my car to the pond's edge. "Live in one of God's wonder spots and there's just nothing to do but ship the kids off. To another state. Who ever thought I'd send my grandkids to New Jersey?"

This was our third stop, Goose Pond, a pretty place with some two dozen houses gathered in a semicircle around one side, and a large, white sand beach on the other. The constable had no information and was determined to direct all of my attention to his personal grievances.

I took the chance meeting of a summer resident to peel off from the constable and walk the perimeter of the pond with her. She told me that the beach had been a joint effort by the homeowners a decade before.

"A large piece of land on the other side of the lake came up for sale," Myra Snyder related. She came from Doylestown, and she and her husband and three grown children shared the largest house on the lake. "Some old woman had held on to the parcel for years. It had a lot of frontage but wasn't very deep. So to protect the beauty of the pond and also our investments, we bought the parcel as a group."

She and I walked through the afternoon heat. When we had circled the lake and come back to the beach, we stood on the white sand and stared at the fetid rubble that edged the shoreline.

"You can't believe how nice this used to be. We had the sand brought in, and, behind the fence, we put down gravel for a large parking lot. It lets everybody keep their extra cars on the other side of the pond and not have people driving in and out early in the morning or late at night and waking the kids."

I was always amazed at what lengths people would go to to sleep in on a vacation.

"And you've been here how long?"

"My husband and I bought this house almost twenty years ago. The kids weren't even teenagers. Now they're married. They've got kids. We thought it was a wonderful place for the family to spend time together—and a place for the kids to keep forever."

The constable and the state police had told Carver that most of the debris seemed to be refuse from eight to twelve years ago. Although it had first seemed that all the garbage was hospital waste, some large pieces of metal and what looked like industrial waste had appeared as the water dried up in Goose Pond.

What the four sisters had discovered by dredging Miller's Lake now seemed epidemic throughout the area. Ironically, the larger, more commercially developed bodies of water seemed relatively free from trash.

"I talked to a dozen people who have homes around the polluted ponds and lakes and they all had something in common," I told Carver, Milton, and Kathleen as we stood by the Explorer. "These people only use their homes in the summer. Maybe May until October. Many of the houses don't have central heating. And, according to Myra Snyder, it's well known which lakes have homes that have year-round residents. Or, like a few of them, retired Florida snowbirds, who head south at the first frost."

"If what you're pointing to is consistent," Carver said, "then the dumping is not like a random act. Some trucker or two who is getting rid of a load of garbage doesn't necessarily know the habits of the residents where he's dumping the trash."

"I figured out that at least some of this dumping must have taken place right after the big problem on the Jersey shore," I said, thinking out loud and trying to make some sense of the mess. "There was enormous press coverage, photos everywhere, with all those needles and yellow contaminated bags drifting in on the beaches. And nobody ever figured out, did they, who dumped all that scum in the ocean?"

Carver nudged my arm.

"Speaking of press coverage, I think you have an interested group right over there," he said, pointing past the Explorer to a minivan with a camera crew standing at its open side door. A woman was floating one of those banana-shaped boom mikes, and the cameraman had his lens trained straight on us.

"Come on," Carver said to me. He ordered Kathleen and Milton to stay where they were. We walked the few steps around the car and toward the minivan.

"Hi, Senator," the young woman with the mike yelled out. "How about a quick interview?"

"Go along," Carver mumbled under his breath.

I smiled as we got within a few feet. Carver stood off to the side, out of their line of vision. I could see him waving to someone behind the cars, who was also out of the camera crew's sight.

"Sure," I said. "I've got a few minutes."

The woman with the mike, who doubled as the reporter, got right up in my face with a quick first question about my impression of the pollution I'd seen that day. I answered her, and she came back with a slightly tougher question, about the total federal aid the area was receiving as part of FEMA.

When I started to list specific amounts of money, she cut me off and then came in for the attack.

"Don't you think, Senator, that a lot of this trouble can be traced to your general incompetence as a U.S. senator? Like why haven't you quarantined this area? Why are children still being allowed to swim in some of the large lakes and rivers?"

Her fastball caught me off balance, especially since it was aimed right at my head. In baseball, she would have been thrown out of the game. I started to answer her question, until I realized that Carver had signed on as umpire.

"Ma'am," he asked, his voice as gentle as a lullaby, "are you carrying your police press passes—either from a Pennsylvania municipality or from the state police? Could you identify yourself?"

The woman turned on him.

"I don't need a press pass to report the news, mister. And I don't need to tell you who I am. Who are you, anyway? Some private security?"

"No. I'm a duly authorized police representative. A cop. Like the two guys standing on the other side of your van. Officers," Carver yelled, motioning over two state troopers, "could you check on the credentials of this camera crew?"

"You can't do this," the woman screamed. "Put the camera on, Joe. Record what's happening. How these goons are trying to cover up this story."

"Ma'am," one of the state troopers said, "could you present your press credentials?"

"I don't need credentials. This is still a free country," the woman snarled.

"Yes, ma'am. This is a free country. But this part of Pennsylvania has been declared officially closed to all but residents of the area. So I'm sorry . . ."

"Don't touch me," the woman screamed. "I'll have you arrested."

Carver pulled me back from the fray as several more troopers arrived at the van.

"I'll have you arrested," the woman kept screaming. "I'm an American citizen and I'll have you arrested."

Carver pointed me back to the Explorer.

I climbed inside and Milton and Kathleen got in the backseat. I leaned over and turned on the ignition and the air-conditioning, but kept the windows down so we could follow the shouting.

After about five minutes of yelling and screaming, the woman finally produced her purse and waved around several chits of plastic-covered paper. The policemen examined the papers, then separated the crew from their equipment and, taking the video cartridge out of the camera, led them to several police cars parked nearby.

I watched as one of the troopers passed the cartridge to Carver. He threw it into the glove compartment as he got into the car.

"Confiscated," he told me. "I'm going to turn it over to the FBI and see what they can figure out from whatever stuff is on the tape. And the press credentials! Issued by the Dugdale campaign."

"Wow, they are daring," Milton said from the back-seat. "I can't believe how they faced you off and the state troopers too."

"Not daring," Carver replied. "Dumb. Arrogant. She's there, surrounded by cops, and she's telling them she's going to have them arrested. These people just don't get it."

I kept trying George Taylor from my cellular phone all the way back to Philadelphia. All I got was his machine. I left three messages, but it was early the next morning before he reached me at my mother's.

"George," I told him, "this is the time for your volunteer enviro-army. Get those RiverWatch members out there, talking to people who live on the polluted ponds. Somebody must know something. Somebody must have seen something."

I was in the kitchen and was trying to stretch my mother's 1960 turquoise phone cord about three inches longer than it should go. The coffeepot was just out of my reach and I asked George to hold on for a minute.

"Hi. I'm back," I announced cheerfully. "So now we've really got some issue stuff to go after."

"Where were you?"

"Getting coffee."

"Norie, you have the worst phone manners of anybody in public life," George scolded. I felt like seven generations of WASPs were telling me I'd used the wrong fork.

"Gee, I'm sorry, George." I was learning to take a bitter pill, which everyone who ever runs for office has to learn.

"It's just one annoyance after the other. You don't make your fund-raising calls . . ."

"I'm going to the DSCC—the Democratic Senate Campaign Committee—offices right off the Hill, every day this week. I've got call lists and a DSCC staff member to call with me," I said, suddenly feeling that no matter what I was doing, it wasn't enough for George.

"I'm going ahead and organize this fund-raiser at the Shore," he declared. "At least we'll pick up a hundred thousand dollars in one fell swoop."

"George, that's terrific," I told him. "Now about the RiverWatch members. Would you make some calls?"

"Norie, I'm making calls to get you elected. I'm also running a rather large business. Yes, I'll make the RiverWatch calls. But I'm getting damned tired of picking up the pieces of this campaign. Leave the investigations to the FBI and try to be a responsible grown-up for once."

I thought that was a little heavy of George, especially since whatever was happening in his personal life didn't keep him at home much. His best friend seemed to be an answering machine.

But I took it to heart and, for the next two weeks, spent the several hours that I could slice out of my day at this warren of offices the DSCC rents near the Capitol.

Since it is forbidden to solicit money from a contributor in a federal building, both political parties have arranged a rococo system, where the senator or Member walks the five or ten minutes to rented office space.

I felt like one of those magazine phone solicitors, sitting in my cubicle with the irrepressible Janet Fisher and dialing for dollars.

We worked off lists—lists given to us by organizations who liked my stands on issues; names left over from the late Senator Gannon; by the state party; by supportive senators who weren't running this time out. There were lists of men and women who graduated from college or grad school with me and gold-starred names of big party givers.

The system was simple, once I had Janet to set it up. Frequently, in the case of big givers, she'd call first and set up a telephone time with a secretary or assistant. Then I'd ring up. It was another Washington dance, like the flowery phrases in my speech that prefaced my real statement before Kincaid's committee.

Nobody wanted to put a big giver on the hook, so, by trying to set up a time to talk, it gave the donor a chance to say, "Thanks, no thanks."

All contributions were covered by the $1,000-a-race-per-person rule. If I had run in a primary, I could have received $1,000-per-person for that, too. But that wasn't all the money I could raise.

Contributors, as part of the $25,000 in hard money allowed in contributions each two-year cycle, could give up to $20,000 to the DSCC. Those amounts rarely happened, but some people would give $5,000. It could then be "earmarked" for my campaign, or become part of my "tally," which was the internal accounting system used by the DSCC and also by its Republican counterpart.

There was also soft money, money for GOTV—Get Out the Vote—and money given to the state party to help in organization, message, or noncoordinated media.

Janet always followed the book, which she knew as well as she knew how to dial with the eraser end of a pencil: "It's the only way to have any fingernails at the end of a campaign." She told me she liked to have the airport-at-Christmastime approach to calling—while I was on the phone with one potential giver, she had another one waiting on the other line. "I like to think of all those givers, just circling around in cyberspace, waiting to get their chance to talk to you," she said, I hoped jokingly.

As I was finding out, campaigns and the specialties they have generated are sometimes very weird.

CHAPTER 21

Nothing was as strange as seeing myself, over and over and over again, on television.

Dugdale had been on the air for several weeks, and, before R. M. went forward with our "buy," he wanted me to tell him how I saw the Dugdale message.

"Simple. Other people are taking away your stuff. Your government will betray you. No societal institutions can be trusted. If you learn too much, your prejudices will crumble," I finished up.

"I think that's right," he said, tapping his right foot against the floor in a silent little polka. I'd figured out that when R. M. was really targeting in, his brain got powered from his foot.

"So what are we going to say?" I asked.

"We're going to tell people what you believe. We're going to tell people why he's wrong. And we're going to tell people how bad things will be if you don't get elected."

"I'm right. He's wrong. Vote for me or the world ends."

"Senator, that's the spirit that will get you re-elected."

I was glad for his confidence, but I had a bigger quandary, one that would have the biggest impact on the campaign: answering Hank Dugdale's challenge to debate.

"You have to," was R. M.'s simple answer.

"But what about all the things that can go wrong?" I said.

"Like if you don't debate and he makes your not showing up the entire issue of the campaign? Can't do that," R. M. insisted. "You're just nervous because he's this big TV star and he's tall and has that deep voice like an announcer and he looks like everyone's uncle. Right?"

"Dammit, R. M., I don't need you on the other side. Yes, that's part of it."

"But, Norie, we've got so much going for us. We've got you." He grinned and I knew he was teasing. "We've got lowered expectations on your perform-ance."

"Great. It's a plus that people don't think I'll do well? Fab! That makes me so-oo happy."

"It should because every time you score a point,

you'll get double credit. And, of course, most important, you've got the world's best secret weapon for a win. You've got me to do both your debate prep and your debate negotiations."

"The prep I understand, but negotiations? For what, time and place?"

"Much more," R. M. said, and I could see this was a part of campaigns that he truly loved. "Number of debates. Choice of moderators. Can you ask each other questions or does all the interrogation come from a panel? Color of curtain. Number in audience. Who chooses them? And that's just the beginning."

"I can't see bickering about background colors," I said.

"You better bitch and bicker about the podium," he declared.

"Now I'm getting short jokes?"

"There are just certain things that make a candidate look better or worse. You laugh at 'background colors,' but your hair is going to look a lot more blond than gray when you're standing in front of certain curtains. And the podium? You have to insist on two—one for Mister Six-Foot-One Dugdale. And one for you. So you don't look like a cupcake or one of those student-senators-for-a-day," R. M. wound up, looking quite pleased with himself and obviously convinced he'd won the debate with me.

"So if it's so complicated, how do I win?"

"You win if you have the best line."

I shook my head.

"Impossible. One line?"

"You have to hold your own throughout the debate. You can't mix up New Jersey and Pennsylvania, for example. But if you have the best line, you'll be the one quoted and you'll leave Dugdale standing, holding his shrinking values in his hand."

"R. M.!"

"It's historically true. Look at Lloyd Bentsen and his debate with Dan Quayle. Both sides knew what Quayle was going to say. He'd been saying it the whole campaign, that he had 'as much experience as John F. Kennedy' when JFK ran for president. It wasn't what Quayle would say that was the problem. It was how Bentsen would answer him," R. M. explained.

"So it was lucky that Bentsen was so fast on his feet," I said, proud that I had gotten the point.

"No. It was lucky that Bensten had the right line written for him. Prescripted, we call it," R. M. clarified. "And we're going to do the same for you."

"R. M., why does it make me feel a little nervous to think that this election hangs on my ability to deliver a one-liner?"

"You need a one-two punch, Norie," Marco declared over coffee in my office later that week. "Now you've got commercials going. And they're good, I got to admit it. But you really need a strong GOTV."

"Whatever you say, Marco. I'm ready," I shot back. I was learning that no matter how little or how much you agreed with the political strategy advanced by one of your strongest supporters, at least you could tell them you agreed. I didn't think of it as lying, but simply as buying time until I could bring them around to my way of thinking.

This time, though, I had no problem giving the thumbs-up sign. Marco had a winning plan.

We were ready to meet with the national representatives of the building trades unions. The meeting had supposedly been called as part of a daylong series of conversations with senators and law officials about the death of Joe Hauser. A business agent in the carpenters union for a long time, Hauser was known to many of the key national union players on a first-name basis.

When I told Marco about the meeting, he offered to come down and "facilitate."

"Don't make the trip," I'd told him. "I can certainly sit down and talk with these guys about Hauser."

"Norie, the atmosphere in this country has made unions paranoid. Every time Congress convenes, there's a new law that somehow undercuts both the power of organized labor—and the job benefits a working person can be entitled to. An American can pursue happiness, but can't find a job. Heck, we're so busy shipping jobs overseas that we should rename the Department of Commerce. Let's call it *Departed* Commerce."

"I understand now. I'm going to make it very clear to all these union reps that I stand with them. On jobs. On minimum wage. On benefits for striking workers," I said.

"That's as it should be," Marco declared emphatically. "Your party is supposed to be for working people. How can a party be for working people if there's no work out there?"

The meeting itself, held a couple days later, started off like a real snorer. Milton had briefed me on every possible building trade issue and Carver had brought me up to speed on the Hauser investigation, which was moving slower than a snail.

A few men—they *were* still all men in the upper ranks of the building trades unions—threw out some questions and I answered them. How long had I known John Hauser? Were there any special task forces looking into his death?

"I don't like it much, Senator. Every time something happens to a union guy, then there's all these questions raised about organized crime or the boys or whatever. Joe Hauser said he knew what those men were dying from," the fellow from the plumbers named Ralph said. "All I can tell you is that if Joe knew what happened to those guys, then that's why he got killed."

"And there's all that stuff they're putting in the lakes up there. That's gotta be some trouble," Marco put in.

"I know a guy in the Teamsters, kind of a renegade, who's been complaining about nonunion truckers for years. Saying they use a couple lakes up there like a sewer," one of the men said.

"See, I know I'm right. There's got to be a link."

"Yes," I agreed, "I thought so too. But then I talked to these researchers who told me that three such outbreaks of this rare leukemia have occurred. So, first, it couldn't come from poisoned lakes and be hundreds of miles away. And, second, experts keep telling me that if the problem were in the water supply, then it wouldn't just be men of a certain age who are coming down with the leukemia."

"Senator, I used to have Joe Hauser's job before I moved up to the national. All these guys in Jericho, they're all in the construction business. I saw that in the paper, in that story in the *Washington Post* on the guys, after some of them were at the hearing," another rep said. He was a young guy, a least a decade younger than the men with the Jericho syndrome and maybe twenty years younger than most of the other men in the room. He seemed unsure if he should speak up and kept staring at some spot on the wall behind Marco's head. "Is everybody, everywhere who has this disease employed in the building trades? If so, we've got a hell of a problem on our hands."

A "problem" put it mildly. The nervous young man was absolutely right on target. It took Mary Devine about thirty minutes to track down the information. It would probably take me another three months to apologize.

"Almost every single one of the men—and it's all men—who have been hit with this leukemia are in the construction business," I read off the pages Mary was still pulling off the fax. "In fact, almost every one of those affected is a carpenter."

There was a general outcry that the unions would help, and I decreed that indeed we had research jobs for everyone.

"We're going to answer a thousand questions about each one of these men. And each one of the job sites that they worked on, either singly or together," I announced. "It will take us several hours to get the questionnaires together, but by eight a.m. tomorrow morning, we'll be ready to go."

"And we will too," the plumbers union vice president shouted. "I tell you, Senator, you're the kind of guy"—he paused and a loud laugh went around the room—"the kind of senator we like to have in office."

"So keep her there," Marco added.

I had learned the lesson of a good public health official all over again. Don't leave any question unasked. Don't take anything for granted. Make sure you apologize to your staff when you lead them astray.

"Gosh, Senator, I'm feeling guilty because I didn't push my hunch more," Mary told me as we pored over the pages spread out on my desk. "To tell you the truth, I was going to try and track it down on my own. But then I got run off the road . . ."

"And I'd already run you over," I said, "with my know-it-all attitude."

"That's what I want to hear," Milton announced, coming into the office, carrying large plastic bags that

I prayed contained Chinese takeout. "A senator who doesn't blame the staff."

"Milton, don't be silly," I said, grabbing one of the bags and starting to spread out those delightful little white cardboard containers. "I'm going to blame the rest of the staff. I'm just not going to blame Mary."

"Not all the praise should go to Mary," Milton said with a self-satisfied smirk. "How about your loyal AA who, with your colleague Senator Mendelssohn, has set up what I believe will be a hundred-thousand-dollar trip to southern California."

"Milton, how could a trip cost a hundred thousand dollars?" Mary asked.

I knew the correct response, and I gave it.

"It's a fund-raiser, Mary. It's a fund-raiser and I don't want to do it," I declared.

"Senator, come on. This is a classy event. No problema. We'll do a twenty-five-thousand-dollar lunch downtown, and then, in the early evening, it's a seventy-five-thousand-dollar buffet dinner in beautiful Beverly Hills. What could be bad," Milton asked, obviously rhetorically, "and I can even make the trip with you. It's set for the weekend after Labor Day."

"That makes it a 'no' on two grounds," I said, stabbing a dumpling with the end of my chopstick. "I do not want to go to Los Angeles and raise money. And I certainly am not able to do it on that weekend, with all the various events I've already got scheduled."

"You go out from D.C. on the first flight on Friday morning. You come back on the last flight on Friday night," Milton countered. I realized he had stopped eating to concentrate all his energy on this conversation, but I was tired and hungry and I wasn't going to get into a spitting match with a staffer. That's how tired I was.

"It's not the image I want," I finally said, before I took a large bite of a pancake-wrapped moo shu pork. "I think it would turn off my supporters, seeing me at some glitzy event, yukking it up with movie stars and moguls. Doesn't fit my image."

Milton stood up slowly and wrapped up his paper plate and napkin. He never took his eyes off me as he twisted them into a long roll. When he finally had squeezed the paper into a tight cigar, he turned slowly and walked out the door.

Milton could be a killer when he wanted to.

I couldn't have been more fawning on the phone machine to George late that night, and this time I got him to pick up the phone on my third try.

"With all this crisis stuff happening," I told him, almost swooning with appreciation, "I feel like I sometimes take you for granted. All the time, all the effort, all the trouble to raise the money so I can run."

"Norie, you are no more trouble than my second wife"—George chortled at his own joke—"and we all know what a tornado she was. Seriously, I just want to keep you on track and off the let's-investigate route."

I know that if I went into the union meeting with him, he'd be all over me for not using the opportunity to ask for a few checks. And I knew Marco would fill him in the next couple days. So I decided to avoid that discussion, as well as forget to fill him in on why I was not going to Los Angeles the second weekend in September. Why spoil a good thing?

"We've got a wonderful crowd coming down to the shore for the August twenty-third event," George said. "Lots of business types. Lots of environmentally interested people. And a beautiful house for the event. Right on the beach in Longport."

"I thought we were using your place, back on the bay. Casual. Like clams and beers," I said, wishing I had a helping of both right now. Chinese food does leave you really hungry.

"Norie, this response has been so extraordinary that I called up a friend of mine, Larry Shields, and he's going to host the event at his place. The house itself is a draw, Norie. Beautiful. Very modern. Lots of chrome and glass. Nothing funky about Larry."

"George," I pleaded. "Could we still have the clams?"

CHAPTER 22

I walked into Marco Solari's office and, whoops, Hank Dugdale was looking me straight in the face.

"Surprised to see me, Norie, baby," the gray-haired hunk mumbled with his signature grin. I'd seen Dugdale make it a hundred times on television. "Let's duke it out."

I plopped into the nearest chair and hoped I could stop laughing before the date of the debate. R. M. and Marco were jumping up and down, howling like the two juvenile delinquents I knew them to be.

"He's great, isn't he?" Marco shouted at me. "Looks just like the creep. Let me introduce you."

"No way," R. M. interrupted. "This is too perfect a

look-alike. Nothing could be better for our practice. Let's just call him 'Hank' for now."

I thought of the reenactors from the Fourth of July. Here was the first modern-day reenactor.

"Hank" stood quietly at his podium, leafing through his notes. I walked to my own podium and laid my hefty debate book down in front of me. This three-ring binder contained the minutiae to answer any question any person, living or dead, could possibly want to know about Pennsylvania and its people.

"As usual the staff has overprepared the debate book," R. M. announced, shaking his head in solemn disgust. "Notice I'm saying this *before* the arrival of detail man Milton Gant, who, I know, wrote every word of that tome with his own life's blood."

Things were obviously glowing on the staff home front. For one strange minute, to paraphrase the tombstone of W. C. Fields, "On the whole, I would have rather been in Philadelphia."

R. M. had his own copy of the debate book, conspicuously much thinner than my bulky volume. Several yellow Post-its were peaking out on the side. I bet he was a kid who had underlined every book he read. He and Marco were huddled in the back of the room, whispering. It was obvious that R. M. believed in people keeping to their assigned roles, and, when Kathleen arrived, although she nodded hello to everyone, she was directed to one of the three panelists' seats without any casual conversation.

The debate strategy R. M. had worked out was designed to keep me out of Dugdale's clutches while allowing me plenty of room to throw some power-house punches of my own. The procedure agreed upon by the two campaigns called for two sets of questions—first, from the three panel members, who were a newspaper editor, a television political reporter, and a member of the League of Women Voters. Then, in the time remaining, Dugdale and I would be allowed to question each other. We wrapped up with four-minute speeches.

"Dugdale is a mile wide and an inch narrow, so he could go on forever skimming across the issues," R. M. said. "We want to get you in and out before he realizes you've been there. So keep your answers on the message and try to keep your questions as clear and concise as possible."

At R. M.'s request, we'd all been working on what he said was the most potent weapon for a debate—the ultimate squelcher line. So far nothing had surfaced.

"Just think," he had told us during our last conference call, "of something that would get you the ultimate smartass award."

"In other words," Kathleen had footnoted, knowledgeable from her years in the convent, "a line that if said to an eighth-grade nun would have earned you a month's detention—but would have made you a legend in parochial school lore."

We all heard the admiration in R. M.'s voice when he told her that she should use her verbal talent and come up with the line.

Now he was pacing the back of the room, glancing at our pseudo Hank and at me, paging through whatever remained of the debate book. A young woman attorney friend of his came in and he did a quick introduction of "the television reporter." Kathleen was, of course, "the League of Women Voters woman," and Milton, who rushed in a moment later, was the newspaper reporter.

"A few caveats, Senator," R. M. began. "Try to forget most of what is in this debate book. It's too much detail. Too many hard issues. Facts, facts, facts. We'll get it boiled down tonight, to twenty-five possible questions and the four or five things you would say over and over."

Milton, the progenitor of the now practically defunct debate book, tried to interrupt. R. M. shushed him, saying that panelists weren't allowed to interrupt the moderator. "I'm always the moderator in practice debates," he proclaimed with a grin, "because that's the way I get to run everything."

We began.

The "Hank" was good. I knew from Kathleen that he was a practicing attorney from Gettysburg and a political junkie. He had Dugdale's style and a lot of his verbiage down pat. It was curious: When I heard these same lines from Dugdale, they brought on a visceral response. But now, with the "Hank" reciting them—even with his peppy delivery—the lines seemed to fall flat. Still I knew that when Dugdale stepped up to bat, he could hit those same old chestnuts out of the park.

By the draw, I went second with my opening remarks. Whether that would happen in the opening debate would be decided in the minutes before the real event took place, but R. M. said that second place was more difficult—and if I drew to go first, it would just be a little icing on my already practiced cake. A "cake walk," he said with his usual loopy grin.

My three-minute opening was a quick-paced reiteration of the messages of my campaign spots. Back and forth we went for an entire hour, a total practice debate, before R. M. called for a break.

"Here's what you must learn, Norie," R. M. began. He'd dropped the "Senator" several days before. It didn't bother me since I knew he called at least a dozen other senators by their first name. But it had engendered a strange switch in Milton's behavior. Although he'd occasionally called me "Norie," "Senator" was his almost constant appellation for me. That now was dropped and it was "Norie" all around. Strange, like he was jockeying to show he was as close, as familiar, as R. M.

"Rule one," R. M. broke into my thoughts, "no matter what Dugdale says, charges, demands, asks, or whines about—don't get off message. You know the five things you have to say. You know you must say them over and over. Don't let him draw you onto his playing field."

"But it's supposed to be a debate," Milton interjected.

"And that's what it will be," R. M. countered. "For

example, every time Dugdale brings up a 'family value,' Norie can answer by bringing the issue around to her position—'The minimum wage is a real family value.' But that's not what it has to be."

He waved his briefing book in my direction. He had this debate totally thought out in his head and in his stance. R. M. would have made a formidable candidate, and I speculated why he was a consultant and not the candidate.

"Norie, you only win if you are the one whose message is standing there at the end of the hour," R. M.'s voice rode on. "Dugdale's message can't stand up against your message. He's talking about vague values. You're talking about concrete jobs. You don't have to point out that his remedies don't do anything to help people. The listeners will figure that out themselves."

"Does she need to get great ratings to make this debate work?" Kathleen asked.

"Nope. She just needs the ten most important political writers in the state. She needs to show that she's in the race and she's capable of winning the race. And . . ." R. M. paused, waiting.

We yelled out in one voice, "And she needs to have the best one-liner."

Two days of rehearsal and I could probably play Dugdale myself.

R. M. was tough but he kept insisting that Dugdale would be tougher.

The second day he allowed me an hour to make phone calls from Marco's office. Milton was still in the debate mix, but Kathleen had gone back to the campaign office at the end of the first day, while "Hank" was heading back to Gettysburg as I dialed.

Marco had been tracking down the "Teamster friend" of the building trades rep who had complained about midnight dumping. I thought it was a long shot, but any solid information we could get would be more than we had.

Little new information was coming in from Jericho County, except for a flood of constituent complaints that the lakes were drying up too fast and the federal government was moving too slowly. I thought that if someone like the "Teamster friend" had at least the name of a trucking company, we would have our first solid lead.

Mary Devine did report that more and more information was being accumulated, now including massive amounts of data on building materials used and the time of year that various projects were constructed. I guess computers and their ability to collate such extensive research made the process more complicated and the goal, although reachable, a long time in achieving.

I wanted results and I wanted them now. Or at least I wanted to get this Teamster on the line. Marco had finally come up with a number for him. For three days, ever since Marco gave me the number in State College, both Nancy and I had been trying to get something more than a message machine. In what sounded like a child's voice, it told me the same nonsensical message: "Nobody's home. We're on the roam. So leave your word and it will be heard."

Then, to make my teeth grit more, the voice said, "Beep. Beep." It wasn't the machine making some rattling metallic noise. It was that cartoon cutie saying, "Beep. Beep."

Only this time, a woman answered the phone. She took me off guard and it was only after she said hello several times that I said hello back and introduced myself.

"Really. A senator. Great. Are you calling for my vote? I'm not sure I'm registered."

"No. I'm looking for Jake Singer. Is this his number?"

"Not really," the woman, Opal Gates, said, and my heart sunk. After all those "Beep beeps," and it was a wrong number. "He's my uncle. I let him use this number if he needs to leave it for somebody. Do you need to reach him?"

"I do," I said. "Yes. Can I leave a message with you?"

"Sure," the woman replied. "But sometimes I don't hear from him for several weeks. He likes to fish this time of year. He told me he was going up north to spend some time looking for bass."

To Philadelphians, "the Shore" is the strip of beaches that stretch from Long Beach Island to Cape May. Come Memorial Day, families would decamp to the beach, fathers coming down only on weekends, leaving women and children to stroll through barefoot summers.

Once hot-weather resorts with ramshackle Victorians and shingled cottages, tiny strips of beach now hold $3 million mansions, marked more by chrome and glass than by charm and class.

Longport, the tiny town at the tip of Absecon Island—Atlantic City and its casinos loomed large at the other end—had the grace and small-town atmosphere of the fifties Shore, even if Cher could be found exercising in a rented castle on the beach. Only a few blocks separated beach from bay. The streets America knew from Monopoly ended here—Atlantic, Pacific, Ventnor.

It had been at R. M.'s insistence that we kept the already scheduled fund-raiser at the Shield home. The worst preparation for a debate, he said, was overpreparation. And I knew that was too true.

Carver had driven down with me, more to keep me cool than to review the security for the debate the next day. He'd been thrilled when we went over the marshlands at the smell of the fish and the salt, tiny boats chugging under the curvature of the Margate drawbridge, which connected the land to the island. I knew that Carver's grandfather had lived his whole life on a tiny island in southern Maryland, making his living as a fisherman and a handyman. And Carver had told me that his happiest childhood times were spent with his grandfather, "just piddling around."

But I wasn't ready for Carver's reaction to the Longport beachfront or to Larry Shields's house. Directly across the street was another mansion, only this time the gray-shingled sides and the rococo eves made it somewhat more appropriate to the beach.

"I'm glad these people are on your side, Senator," he said, coming around to open my door after making a few quick quips about the blinding stainless-steel front doors. "Because this kind of an aesthetic is a real worry. It causes terminal ugliness."

Carver stopped his architectural tirade just as

George bounded out the front door to greet us and bring us into the house. The structure may have been garish, but the crowd gathered inside were restrained and refined. I'd never seen so many strands of real pearls in one room—worn with simple cotton pantsuits or dangling over perfectly pressed T-shirts.

This was a casual event, but I realized that when we asked for contributions, if every couple popped in a piece of jewelry, my money-raising problems would be over.

And they were all couples. It only hits me once in a while, now, maybe because most events have couples and singles, maybe because I'm now experienced at going places by myself and coming home the same way. But this was definitely a husband-and-wife crowd.

"Larry, our host," George said with a stretched-out smile while he positioned me in front of an attractive brunette and a much shorter man, "and Sheila, his wife."

"Senator," Sheila said, grabbing my hand, "before you meet your fans, could we ask you for a couple of photos. Maria!"

Four adorable children were instantly produced by an Hispanic woman in a white uniform. The kids, whose ages probably ranged from ten down to two, were interchangeable towheads, their sun-bleached hair bobbing above blue eyes.

The kids smiled and held my hands.

"Are you famous like being on TV?" one of them asked.

"We've had our pictures taken with at least thirty-two celebrities," the oldest announced. "And four of them were senators."

"The rest," Larry said with a grin, "were aging rock 'n' roll stars or lounge acts."

Laughing, we left the kids and moved into the crowd. George and Larry knew everyone—names, a funny anecdote, something about their kids. George and Larry made it an easy event, George taking away any talk of poll numbers by telling people they were "betting on a winner."

And the guests seemed to try very hard to make pleasant conversation and not push issues. The photographer followed us around, from introduction to introduction. Sheila had stayed back with the children, smiling and gracious, stopping a few times as she crossed the room to give a quick hug or an obviously warm word.

I knew her from somewhere and it was driving me crazy.

"So, how about our view, Senator," she said, skillfully turning me slightly so that what seemed like the entire Atlantic Ocean was directly in my face.

"It's a great work of art," I offered. "And this is very nice of you and your husband . . ."

"Anything for George. And for you."

"Now when would you like me to speak?"

"No, not necessary. We wanted this to be a group of

your real friends and supporters, just coming together to show you our support. We're constituents, you know." She made the pronouncement as if telling me she'd just moved in next door to my mother. "We're in Ardmore. It's very easy, with the kids. Safe and good Catholic schools nearby."

"Are you from Philadelphia?" I asked.

"Yes, yes. In fact, Senator, you know me."

Of course I did. But who was she?

"I'm sorry, but with the campaigning and everything, I just am losing about seventeen gray cells a second," I said, trying to cover my discomfort. "From politics? From public health?"

"No, no. Norie, I went to high school with you. To the Academy of Notre Dame on Rittenhouse Square."

"Not with me. I'm much older."

"I was two years behind. Lois Reilly."

"No. Of course. Lois, how wonderful! And you look wonderful, too."

No wonder I didn't recognize her. Lois Reilly was a pudgy girl with braces, not the model-type who stood in front of me, wearing the most perfect linen shirt and pants—a sleeveless shirt and her upper arms looked great! What did she have, I thought, a painting aging in the garage? She looked at least ten years younger than me, and I thought I was holding up pretty well. And after four children. Wow!

"I try. It's very important to Larry that I always look my best. And, now that we have all these kids . . ."

"They're wonderful. So cute with their blond hair."

"I wanted blonds. I specified that. Blonds. And from Catholic backgrounds. Very important, I thought. Because even if their hair gets darker, they still are blondish in the summer and then, again, only the second from the oldest seems to be getting more brown in her hair."

I was confused and it must have shown.

"Sorry, Norie, I'm just so used to everyone knowing. Larry and I couldn't have kids. I met him when I was at Trinity and he was at Georgetown. We got married right after graduation. We wanted kids. We tried and tried. So when I turned thirty-five, we adopted. And adopted and adopted. Although I think we're going to call it a day with four."

"Is my wonderful wife telling you about our wonderful family, Senator?" Larry startled me, giving me a bear hug from behind. "We're worried about the future. That's one reason we're supporting you."

"And the environment," George said, appearing at my other shoulder.

"This," Larry declared, waving his arm around in an all-inclusive circle, "is a group of people concerned about the health of the beaches and the ocean. The purity of the air, the safety of our food. Although, Senator, some of them do it a little more for professional reasons than others."

"That's great, although I'm not sure what you mean," I said.

"A few folks here are from New Jersey," Larry explained. "They're involved in some casino-related businesses. Restaurants. Linen supply places. Electronic entertainment."

"That translates as jukeboxes, Norie," George said.

"But whatever we do," Larry said, "we know how precious natural resources are. We're involved in two big issues here, Senator. The use of the wetlands and the necessity of preventing beach erosion. Both are important for people—and for the economy of the Shore."

"The Shore is important to Larry, Norie," Sheila added. "Because of our children and the way they love the beach. The air, you know, is so key to children's health."

"I also love it, honey, because it's flat. No mountains. No countryside. Flat. Gotta have it."

It was obviously an in joke, because George and several people standing nearby laughed. I shrugged unknowingly.

"I've got vertigo, Senator. I won't look out of a third-floor window. I won't go up any higher than I could climb on a step stool."

I turned to George.

"Sheila said no speech. But I was only planning to talk for like ten minutes," I told him. "Why not have me do just a couple minutes, and then people still get some time to relax."

"No speech," Larry intervened before George could respond. "No pitch needed, Senator. George asks. We do. Here we are." He motioned to a preppy-looking man standing by the door to the patio. "What's coming at you is sixty-three thousand dollars on the hoof. Wrapped up as a thank you from all your loyal fans."

My head was boggled. I'd raised $63,000 and I hadn't even had to get on a plane. I took the stack of checks as gracefully as I could, but when you're talking about $63,000, it's hard not to grab.

I stood clutching George's arm, standing at the bulkhead, trying to steal a few minutes of summer before I headed back to Philadelphia.

"This was wonderful, George," I managed, feeling quite touched by the success of the event and the way he was supported by his friends.

"You're wonderful, Norie, and I really feel like a rat for the pressure I've put on you this past couple of months. You'll raise the money. *We'll* raise it—and you'll win," he said. For a moment I thought he was going to say something else, something more personal, but the moment fled when Sheila called us from the driveway.

Almost all the contributors left before we did, with a lot of good-byes all around and many promises to watch the debate the next night on television. There was an endless buffet, which people kept comparing favorably to the one Merv Griffin offered at his casino, and Sheila insisted on packing us a picnic lunch for the drive back.

We climbed into the car and would have driven out of sight, except Carver was hunting in the glove compartment for a map to see if there was an easy way back on the expressway. We turned the corner at Atlantic Avenue and pulled over to the curb. He was digging around in the glove compartment, all the while quizzing me about the event and the amount of money raised.

I decided to get out and have two more minutes of the Shore. Straining to see what blue I could catch sight of beyond the bulkhead, I watched a couple come down the driveway from the house I just left.

In the fading light, I could just make out Larry and Sheila, walking hand in hand, and looking, as we used to say, like they were going to make out themselves. I got one of those teenager chills when I saw him pat her on her rump, then pull her close and push his face into her hair.

She folded into him, and the delightful feeling of the moment made me both happy for them and wistful for the moments I'd never have—times of growing older and still acting like kids. Perhaps the intimacy was too much. I took the few steps back to the corner, and turned for one last moment.

The woman was just stepping into the arc of the streetlamp so I was able to tell, without a doubt, that the figure was perfect, the slacks were white, the shirt was sleeveless—but it was not Sheila.

The debate was three hours away—and I still had no punch line.

My mother's house was as crowded as it had been the day I was married, with many of the same people milling around—my mother, my dad's friend Stash, who was driving me and who danced with me at the reception, Jeanne Callaghan, and her daughter, who was giving me what I said must be a "natural" wash and blow-dry.

"Just a little height, Norie," Mary Ann begged. "Just let me back-comb it a little bit on the top."

"If I wind up looking like a cactus, you've had it, Mary Ann. Natural. That's the word of the day," I said, and leaned over to grab my iced tea.

"If natural were natural, none of those people in the movies would have a job," Jeanne said, and she and my mother launched into a long discussion of which TV stars wore wigs and when they first lost their hair. How did people all across America know things like that? And, more important, why were they frequently right on target?

"So are you really prepared, Norie," Jeanne asked me, bringing on a large shushing sound from my mother. "Marie, I'm just asking her a logical question."

Logical wasn't that I should think I would have some quiet time before the debate if I got dressed at my mother's, but I always got more nervous if I were left alone to worry and fret. I still had no punch line.

"Tell me the truth, Norie," Jeanne asked. "Do you really want to be a senator again?"

"That's a crazy question, Mom. You think she'd rather be a hairdresser?" Mary Ann leaned over and hugged me. Of the Callaghan's five children, she and

I were the closest. We'd been in the same grade, walked to school from first through eighth. But when I got my scholarship to Notre Dame Academy, Mary Ann went on to Mercy Tech, a technical high school run by nuns. She got both her high school degree and fine training as a hairdresser. At last count, she owned four shops, all in busy suburban malls.

"It's been so long since I did a comb-out," she said, laughing, "that I'm afraid I'll give you some waves right over your face."

"So answer my question, Norie, about the Senate," Jeanne insisted.

"I like it. I think I'm doing good work. I think I can do a lot more good."

Mary Ann fiddled with my hair a few more minutes, then I went upstairs to put on my best St. John knit suit. I think I look ten pounds lighter when I wear it, but it's ten pounds I've put on in my forties. That's why Kathleen kids me about the color, saying it's "menopause blue." I told her it was "more hot stuff than hot flashes."

I laughed when I thought of the line and wondered if Dugdale would be able to handle it if I started bringing up hot flashes. From there my mind did a stretchy leap and suddenly I was thinking about Sheila Shields, with her tight body and her graceful linen outfit and four perfect children and a husband who did all those sweet and touching things with somebody else just steps from her front door.

I knew I was halfway home when I saw Linda Vespucci in the crowd outside University of Pennsylvania's Annenberg Center Theater.

"Mrs. Norie. Senator. We're here with you," she screamed, waving a massive poster that proclaimed, GORZACK. DON'T ABUSE HER—P.A. CAN'T LOSE HER.

"How about the sign, huh?" she bellowed, somehow mushing herself between police sawhorses and winding up behind Carver as we walked into the hall. A policeman tried to grab her and pull her back, but I shook my head no and held on to her arm.

"I been reading the Internet like crazy, Senator Norie, and I'll tell you, there are some bastards out there who don't deserve to be Americans," Linda said, waving her sign up and down.

"She's got to hand over her placard if she's going into the hall," a police captain told me. Carver nodded his agreement.

"Look, I'll catch it on C-SPAN late tonight. What else do I have to do but watch the reruns? I'll keep my sign, thank you," she told the officer, then leaned over and gave me a hug. "You'll get him. He's a thug."

Carver and I went into the hall but quickly turned to the right, heading around the back of the auditorium and going toward backstage. There was still an hour until the opening salvo, but R. M. had wanted me in the building and in my holding room.

"Dugdale is crazy. He could bring in one hundred people wearing bloodstained hospital coats and say you're a murderer. I don't want you in any confrontation with members of the audience," he'd warned.

The audience had been a big question mark. Marco had taken on the selection of the one hundred supporters we had tickets for. Dugdale had a similar number and then some one hundred tickets went to the press. The balcony was reserved for TV camera crews and still photographers.

R. M. was stretched out on the sofa in my dressing room, sipping Diet Coke and looking rather calm.

"So we don't have a punchy line. I'm not worried. Use the slogans. Talk about 'a minimum wage being a family value.' Stay on message," he wound up, "and you'll win."

Now I needed a few minutes alone. As I sat there, my head darted from face to face, issue to issue. Jack, my mother, Bercolini, Kathleen, Milton, the Jericho syndrome, fund-raising, Dugdale, Linda Vespucci.

What was her line? "Don't Abuse Her. P.A. Can't Lose Her."

I almost had it figured out, my punch line, when I heard a roar from the auditorium. The audience had been let in.

Just at that moment, Kathleen threw open the door.

"You won't believe it. Marco is a genius," she said, waving me to follow her.

Peeking from behind the heavy velvet curtain, I could see about half the audience. It took a minute for Marco's machinations to hit home.

"Brilliant. He's over the top," I said.

A few minutes later, I was behind my podium—and, in the audience, I could identify my hundred supporters.

Marco had done his job well. On many of the supporters were union buttons and badges of all kinds. Here went people who knew the value and values of a decent living. Here were honorable women who had devoted their lives to serving social justice.

And how did I know which members of the audience were my supporters? Pretty easy, since they were all wearing habits.

Marco had combed the parochial schools of Philadelphia and enlisted the services of one hundred sisters.

Moral values, indeed. Top this one, Dugdale!

The debate flew by. I followed my script. I answered every charge with a turnaround phrase. I used my slogans and I waited. I had my line.

Dugdale was masterful. As R. M. had warned me, every question of his was a statement. This was push polling on a massive level.

R. M. had even been right about the titles.

"He'll never give you the benefit of calling you senator, so we have to strategize as to what you'll call him," he'd said in one of our practices.

I'd suggested and we agreed on "Mister Hank Dugdale," which we all believed made him sound like something out of a Saturday morning TV show. The title even seemed to throw him off the first time I used it, which made me careful to use it every chance I could.

I was well prepared, but Dugdale was a natural at television and the years he'd spent either selling his book or his crime expertise had given him the kind of practice a campaign couldn't provide.

"Isn't it true, Mrs. Gorzack . . ." was the opening phrase of every question and, time and time again, I said a simple "no," then presented my position.

I waited.

It was his last question. He was going for the jugular.

"Isn't it true, Mrs. Gorzack, that you have repeatedly gone soft on lawbreakers, that you've changed laws to protect criminals not citizens? Isn't it true, Mrs. Gorzack, that you are indeed helping criminals to prey on people? And isn't it true, Mrs. Gorzack, that you have hoped to gain votes through sympathy over the loss of your husband?"

Maybe I had a punch line worked out in my head. Maybe he just hit me so hard that it was my instinct to fight back. Whatever, I came out swinging.

"Mister Hank Dugdale, I've had enough," I said. "You talk about values. Isn't telling the truth a value? You've lied about my record and who I am. And I've had enough of it.

"I am tired of your lies and I am tired of your abusive tactics. I *am* a U.S. senator. That is my title. You might not like a woman being a senator, but I am there and I am doing the job.

"I have given you every courtesy throughout this campaign. And, in the name of partisanship, you have corrupted what patriotism means for me and for my supporters and yes, for all the people in Pennsylvania.

"I've given my life to my state in public health work and I gave my husband to my country. You have twisted my record and you have tried to beat down my husband's sacrifice.

"You are a thug, and all your fancy words and slick manner don't change who and what you really are.

"You don't fool me, and you won't fool the voters of Pennsylvania.

"You talk about crime. Mugging in this state *is* a

crime, even if the victim is a U.S. senator. No more. That's it. It's all over. The abuse stops here."

The audience, my supporters, and, I was convinced, some of Dugdale's, stood up and cheered.

I won. That's what the papers said the next morning. That's what my supporters told me. That's what the look in my mother's eyes said.

But the way I really knew I won was when I looked at myself in the mirror, late that night at my mother's.

We had gone out after the debate—R. M., George, Marco, Kathleen, my mother, Milton, Nancy. Heck, I was so excited I almost invited Mrs. Vespucci. I kept myself under control, though, and asked her to meet me for lunch the following week.

The Vesper Club was almost empty. It was August and everybody was still at the Shore. But we made up for our size with our noise.

We ordered champagne. We toasted each other. We cheered the waiter and the bus boy and every line from the debate. It was one of life's best moments.

Gone were the minor disagreements. Forgotten were the arguments about message or media or me. It was all one big happy political entity. And it was swell.

By the time I was in my nightgown, it was well after midnight.

I looked in the mirror, my mouth edged with a little toothpaste white, and I shot myself a big smile.

"I *am* the U.S. senator. No kidding. It's me. Senator Gorzack."

* * *

Like every bully, Dugdale had folded as soon as I stood up to him. And, like most cheaters who lose in a fair fight, he was crying "foul" as soon as the victory was posted. How dare Mrs. Gorzack accuse him of shout-them-down tactics. How dare I? Huh!

Tuesday morning, the lines were burning up between Dugdale supporters and my Capitol Hill office.

"These people could save themselves some money if they would just fax these complaints to the state office or to the campaign office." I was speaking to Milton on the cell phone when he gave me the numbers. The Senate had started its summer recess, and I was on the campaign trail full-time.

"Surprise!" Milton said. "We're getting flooded with faxes in both those places, too."

"If there's nothing else hanging . . ."

"I hate to bring this up because I think it will get you off message," Milton started. "You put a call in to a guy named Jake Singer. He was the Teamster who was talking to people, claimed to know about midnight dumping. You got his name from the building trades rep."

"Sure. Did he call back?"

"Not exactly. We've got a message here from his niece and I've called the Teamsters business agent in Philly to check this out." Milton paused and I knew bad news was coming. "The guy's had a hunting accident. It's actually a fishing accident."

"And he's dead?"

"Yep."

We were *this* close. That's what kept happening. Bercolini was ready to tell me whatever he knew—and he was murdered. Joe Hauser was ready to testify—and he was killed. Mary Devine—where was Mary going when she was run off the road? I'd have to check. And now this Singer guy. Something clicked.

"Can we get a picture of Singer?" I asked.

"I guess. From the union or the niece."

"Get the photo. Give copies of it to Bercolini's staff, to the FBI, to the state troopers. Bercolini met with someone from the Teamsters the week before he was killed. Somebody had to see them or know them. Or maybe even the niece knew about a meeting."

"Whether it's the same person is a real stretch, Senator," Milton warned. "There's a lot of Teamsters out there."

"Yes, Milton. But if this guy *was* the guy Bercolini met with, then we know that Bercolini's death might have a lot more to do with companies dumping trash than with the militia trashing the government."

Suddenly, the campaign was turning around.

The debate, exactly as R. M. had said, had everyone taking a second look at the race.

Over Labor Day weekend, the crowds seemed bigger, the applause seemed stronger, the campaign went better. Kathleen Burns had been the right choice as campaign manager.

Every morning when we started out in Philadelphia,

Stash showed up at my mother's house with a carefully constructed schedule for the day. The same thing happened if I was overnighting in Pittsburgh, only there it was Dale Baum. Contact names; a good description of the event; the people who would be at each event who I might have met before; the names of any volunteers expected at any event.

Dugdale and I met six more times during the month of September for face-offs, following the debate procedure we had agreed to at the beginning. I held my own. A few times, I thought he edged me out, while a few times I snuck ahead of him, and a couple debates were a true draw.

But the damage had been done. He'd been painted as a bully—and it stuck. It wasn't just that I was playing what might have been seen as a woman's issue and standing up to an overbearing and abusive personality. No, it was a real "people's issue," since good people of all sexes were against abuse.

I felt I'd hit a brick wall with the Jericho syndrome. I'd mobilized as many RiverWatch volunteers as George and I could scare up, but we still had no lead as to *who* was dumping and *what* kind of trash could turn itself toxic enough to cause leukemia.

The *what* was a slightly different prospect, since some of the plastic containers and bags did carry bar codes or expiration dates. In every case, though, there was the tedious sifting through of rubbish, the careful preservation of a piece of trash that might contain a date-specific tag, and the final data compilation of the total pieces salvaged.

In three weeks of what Milton referred to as "systematic trash collection," more than seven hundred dated or bar-coded pieces had been identified. Not one piece carried the bright red tag that would have designated radioactive materials. That, at least, was a relief.

Now came the truly tedious process of tracking down just what they were, where they came from, and who possibly used the material *before* it was dumped.

There were some glitches in my Senate scenario and my campaign script. A key piece of legislation that my campaign and my constituents were counting on—it would have brought some seven thousand jobs to the Lake Erie area—just didn't get out of committee. George, for all his good intentions, was more caught up in his business than he had foreseen, and Marco was forced to take over some of the fund-raising efforts. More than a hundred thousand letters asking for support were ready to be mailed to schoolteachers when Mrs. V. noticed there was no union bug, meaning they had been printed by a nonunion shop.

Mrs. V. was herself a sometimes glitch, but I was very fond of her. My mother, who was working most days as a volunteer, had lunch frequently with Mrs. V. and explained that her flamboyant personality hid a sincere and kind human being.

If I was liking being the candidate, Marie Kurek was loving being the candidate's mom.

R. M. had worked out a little sample script for her, and she spent her days phone-banking. She called lists of women involved in senior citizen activities. She called lists of women involved in food banks. And she called lists of women who had lost a relative in Vietnam.

But where Marie was at her best was calling men.

It turned out that you put my mother on the phone with any man—eighteen to eighty—and she could convince him to vote for me. On her call cards, when she marked favorable and another volunteer called back in several days just to see how accurate the assessment was, the potential voter was firmly and completely in my column.

"I don't know what she says," Kathleen told me, "and I don't want to know. I only know that if we had clones of your mother, we could all go on vacation and just show up to vote."

Mrs. V., on the other hand, could not be allowed on the phone. Her conspiratorial paranoia came on strong when she got the chance to influence a potential new ally.

"Just imagine this," R. M. heard her say one day before she was denied phone privileges, "that you are taking poison into your body every day. That you're paying for it. That in the end it will kill you. And the federal government is saying, 'Hey, have some more!' That's what these food additives are all about. And what are you going to do about it, huh?"

What we did about it was revoke her phone privileges.

Now she brought massive amounts of computer printout with her every day to the campaign office and, when I would stop by a few times a week, press me to take these matters under advisement.

As I said, it was all turning around.

25

Carver continued to float around the campaign. He'd become such a constant that I had to frequently remind myself why he had come. And more frequently, to question him on why he was still with us.

"Don't you think it's time you went back to the job the taxpayers think you're doing," I asked him one morning on our way from the airport into Erie. We'd had what passed in this campaign as a quiet several weeks.

The official law-enforcement agencies continued to pursue investigations into the deaths of Joe Hauser and Congressman Bercolini, as well as the road-warrior tactics used against Mary Devine. Seeing Carver hovering over my campaign, like a cranky mother hen, just kept reminding me of the tragedies—past, and I hoped, not to be repeated. But he wasn't budging.

"No. I'm here for the duration," he answered, and I could tell from that one line that there was no discussion.

The day-to-day operation of the campaign was considerably less crisis-ridden. First off, I wasn't being pushed and shoved by protesters everywhere I went. My able campaign manager had pulled off that little piece of diplomacy.

In her first days running the operation, Kathleen had approached Dugdale's handlers and told them that the constant picketing and protesting had to stop. "Or," she warned, "I will have gray-haired grandmothers lying down in front of your limos."

The Dugdale people tried to pawn off responsibility for the protests on the Values Coalition and on its leader, Vic Stample. Kathleen wasn't buying.

"You can call it the Values Coalition," she told Dugdale's campaign, "or you can call it chocolate milk. It has the same flavor. And if you don't call off these dogs, I'll unleash mine."

She related this message to me, and I was a little taken aback.

"I never knew you to be so aggressive," I said.

"I played girls basketball," she replied. And I knew she was tough.

So Carver just kept floating around.

That day in Erie, he seemed a little more focused

than usual. When most people are nervous, they get jumpy. Carver was just the opposite. He was sitting in the front seat of the car, doing the left and right look-around. I'd seen the Secret Service agents do it when they were covering the President, and it didn't make me more comfortable that Carver felt the need to employ such actions.

"Do you mind if I ask you what's on your mind," I tried from the backseat.

"Nothing. Just looking around. Never spent much time in Erie."

"It's a great little town," the volunteer driver offered. He was a grad student, and had been promoted from phone-banking to candidate transportation, if that was an advancement. "I come from Beaver Falls myself, so the traffic took a little getting used to."

This conversation was going nowhere.

When we got out of the car for the luncheon meeting of the Erie Chamber of Commerce, Dale Baum was waiting. In campaigns, people go up very quickly. Up—and sometimes out. Since our visit to the Bucks County Arts and Crafts Fair early in the summer, Dale had blossomed and was now assistant press secretary for the campaign. There was, however, no full-time press secretary, so he was having one great time.

"I've got three camera crews inside, Senator, and one is set to do a network feed. ABC," he said, escorting me through the lobby and briefing as we moved. "It turns out the chamber president, Craig DuVal, is really a big Dugdale booster, so watch out for his intro."

I looked around to find Carver, but it wasn't until I'd finished my open turkey sandwich with gravy, my ice cream with chocolate sauce, my speech, and my Q&A that I was alone with Carver.

We were in a hotel suite, sitting in the living room while Dale made phone calls from the bedroom. No matter how many times a day we stopped, no matter what was happening, Dale would need to be on the phone with someone, somewhere. I hated to think what his phone card bill was like. Excuse me, *my campaign's* phone card.

"Something is bothering you. Spill it," I told Carver.

"The Keystone Militia," he said, mumbling the words. "They don't like you."

"That I know. That you know. Tell me something new."

"They don't like you a whole lot more than any of us realized."

"I'll bite. How much don't they like me," I asked.

"They don't like you enough to want you dead," Carver answered. "And that's a good bit of not liking."

He gave me the details then and there.

The Keystone Militia had put out a "Wanted" poster on their Web page—and it accused me of treason, "a capital crime."

I was scared. No doubt. This was a lot tougher, a

lot more threatening than anything that had gone before.

I had a television interview in the next ten minutes. I had three more stops before I could head back to Philadelphia. I wanted tomorrow to be the election and for it all to be over, not because I wouldn't be under such a threat but because I could crawl under the covers and go to sleep.

I was bone tired. I rallied for the interview, but I thought I was pretty inept during my visit to an auto-parts factory where three women were the night supervisors. My final stop in Erie was at a massive central kitchen where Meals on Wheels were prepared and more than three hundred seniors, from close-by homes, ate on the premises each night.

"You didn't have to tell me," I told Carver as we were driving back to the airport. He'd climbed into the backseat and was going over the schedule for the next day. "I didn't have to know that these crazies want me dead."

"Yes, you do. You have to be on your guard. And this is the time to start. I was going to wait until tomorrow, when you're home, but I decided that we were going to see a lot of people today, and I wanted both of us to be ready if there were any problems."

"Do you think we need extra security? I don't want to campaign from inside a bubble."

"Senator, you've had extra security all day long. And you will continue to have extra security," Carver said. "Of course, when you see what's got us all worried, maybe you'll want something more."

"Right. Maybe I could borrow that tank from Michael Dukakis."

Carver had his handy-dandy little laptop and he punched up the unofficial Norie Gorzack Web page.

"I like the new picture," I told him. "It's so attractive with the mouth hanging open and that one chunk of hair making me look like I'm wearing an eye patch."

I stared at it for a minute.

"Where do you think they took this picture," I finally managed. "It just makes me deranged that these people are creeping and crawling around me."

"I don't think *they* took the picture. I think they bought it from a newspaper or from a free-lance photographer. The Keystone Militia is not going to bother sending out one of its valuable superpatriots on reconnaissance with a Kodak." Carver put his face up close to the screen. "I will tell you, though, Senator, whoever took this picture of you was no friend."

"Okay, so punch up my real Website. Go ahead," I insisted. "Just punch in my name without any of the stuff you had to do to get that other stuff up on the screen."

Carver did just that and, zap, I was on the screen again, this time looking perky yet professional, large type balancing across the top of my head, proclaiming "Jobs Are a Family Value, Too."

"It's terrific," Carver admitted.

"Mary Devine said she could get it up in a few days. We have some young women from the University of Maryland who are volunteering in my Capitol office, and they really put it all together." I watched as Carver scrolled down the several pages that followed, outlining bills that I supported, statements I made. There was a good bit on the Jericho syndrome, although I was feeling a little guilty this week that I hadn't been more on the case.

"Very impressive," Carver said. "Too bad I'm not a resident of Pennsylvania. You'd get my vote."

"Carver, if you spend any more time trailing me around the state, you can vote twice."

Milton called up late the next night with a lot of "mea culpas," although he had them phrased in all that lawyer language that basically said the world changed and that's why he wasn't wrong.

"So I took the photos of Mr. Singer into Bercolini's office and showed them around," he was explaining.

"Wait. Just one minute. *You* took them *personally*. You went from our office—on the Senate side—to the office on the House side," I managed.

"It's not like I went by dogsled or anything. Jeez, Norie, sometimes you act like I'm some sort of an uptight cliché lawyer. Okay, so I went to Bercolini's old office and, what do you know—one of the staffers recognized Singer. She had been traveling with the congressman to some dam sight north of Jericho and Singer came up and started talking to Bercolini."

"When, Milton, when did all this happen?"

"She checked her calendar and figured it was like two weeks before his death," he said. "Also, Norie, I had like an hysterical phone call from Carver yesterday. He's sending some security team over here to check out the office."

"He's just overreacting," I said. "Bercolini was right. This Keystone Militia is a bunch of guys running around the woods, playing with guns. I think we're onto the real stuff with this Teamsters guy."

The scenario seemed simple, now that I had some facts. Bercolini meets with Singer two weeks before he's murdered. It was safe to assume that Singer told Bercolini about the midnight dumping. That's what he apparently was always ragging about, according to the union rep at Marco's meeting.

Marco! He'd know some other people who would know Singer. Or would know how to track down his friends.

Only problem was, I couldn't find Marco. I tried his beeper. I rang his car phone. No Marco. There was no use trying to call him at home. Marco didn't believe in residential service. He had a beeper and a cellular, and, as he had told me, that was that.

I called his office back and left a long message on his machine—details about Singer, about how I thought that Bercolini and Hauser might have had the same pieces of information. I called George and hit his machine. I certainly hoped my good friends were out campaigning for me. I left a message asking George to have Marco call me if he happened to talk to him. Also, could he please get me somebody who knows about tracing toxins.

Then, and only then, did I go and get my beauty sleep. It was crucial, since, the next day, I was off to meet the scourge of daytime television, Miss Birdie Pew and "Watch the Birdie."

CHAPTER
26

The few times I'd caught her show, she seemed perfectly lovely, but R. M. and Hilda both warned me about her. Their cautions were mild compared to those of my mother and Mrs. V.

"Like, I'm watching her a lot. More before the campaign, of course. And she's got a little tricky thing. With her glasses. She like pulls them down, to get a better once-over of you, because she can't believe what she's seeing. And then it's all over," Mrs. V. said.

My mother had a slightly different angle.

"Don't tell her anything that's too perfect. About loving Jack. Or your job. Or even me. What she does is pick it apart. 'Oh,' she'll say, 'so I guess that spoils you for anyone else.' And then she'll announce after the next commercial that it's thrilling that you made this announcement never to get married again, right here, with Birdie."

"If she's so awful, Mom, why are you always watching her," I asked, thinking the question might put her on the spot but dying to know the rationale.

"Norie, I'm home alone," my mother replied, pursing up her mouth the way she did when she was thinking something out. "You think it's more interesting to watch some out-of-work comic sing famous musical numbers? That's okay for the young moms. I need a little boost to get myself going. Birdie is exciting. She gets people to say things they wished they hadn't said."

"I'll watch myself. I'll watch what I say."

"Don't talk too much."

Which was the direct opposite of the advice I got from R. M.—after he finished complaining about Kathleen and Milton scheduling me on the show.

"She's a barracuda. Take control. Take over. Keep her from asking questions. Nobody is safe. Not just politicians. She's done in nighttime talk-show hosts, retired generals, lifesaving surgeons, and her own sister," R. M. insisted.

"You're the consultant. What should I do? And anyway, her sister?"

"Little known but true. When Birdie started out, twenty years ago up in Cleveland, she was a duo. 'Birdie and Babs.' It was a soft, coffee-and-rolls kind of show. 'Here's a man to tell you how to get grubs out of your lawn,' or 'Here's the most famous divorce lawyer in Shaker Heights and he'll tell you how not to get ruined.' "

"And then? What did she do?" I asked. This would be great to talk about, if I weren't the next thing in her sights.

"And then, one day, when they had a plastic surgeon on, old Birdie asked Babs to fess up. Babs denied having work done. Then, in the interests of modern journalism and making everybody as uncomfortable as they can be, Birdie showed photos of Babs—before and after. Once the pictures were shown, Babs was both redone—and done. Nobody wants a talk-show host who doesn't tell the truth."

The best advice on dealing with Birdie came from Hilda.

"Talk about cooking. You cook, right?"

"Yes, I'm good, but not great."

"Talk about it. Talk about buying cheese or how to tell if asparagus is good or what to cook if you only have chicken wings and grape jelly and barbeque sauce."

"Hilda, you obviously don't cook. That's gross."

"It makes sweet and sour wings. Or it did when I first got married. Anyway, just take old Birdie over and chat her up," Hilda advised.

"How have you handled her?" I asked.

"Me? I wouldn't go on that show for a million dollars," Hilda snapped back. "And Birdie's from Cleveland."

I thought navy blue. Like a schoolgirl. And hair not too fluffy. Birdie could be one of those famous TV personalities who teased and back-combed and colored a little too much and now has thick-hair envy. Oh, I was nervous about that if I was making jokes for the bathroom mirror, like I was back in grammar school. I could wear the large Miraculous Medal that I got in the fifth grade for writing the best composition. Or maybe carry an eight-by-ten photo of my mom, Birdie's fan.

Or, better yet, my mom herself.

"I'm not coming out on the stage with you," Marie insisted, coming down the stairs. "And if I'd known I was going to be on display, I would have had Mary Ann Callaghan come by for a quick comb-out."

"You look cute," I told her.

"That's what younger women always say to older women when the older woman looks like an old lady," Marie countered.

I leaned down and hugged her. She was getting smaller and smaller and I made a mental note to have the doctor double-check her weight.

Carver was sitting in the kitchen, having his second cup of coffee. He was driving us to the station where we'd be met by Birdie. Although her show was usually filmed in L.A., Philadelphia was one of the stops on her "Colonial America" tour. I hoped I wasn't another monument by the time she was done with me.

"After the show, I'm going to peel off for about an hour," Carver told me as he tucked my mother into the LeSabre. "I've got a man to see."

"Carver," I razzed him, "with you guys it's always a guy to see or a man to meet or a fellow who wants to tell me something. Guy stuff."

"No, really. Stash will pick you up and take you to your next stop and I'll catch up with you there."

"And you're not going into the lion's cage with me?" I asked, not really kidding. "I need your moral support."

"Where I'm off to, there'll be TVs. I'll catch you on the tube," Carver countered, keeping his eyes too squarely on the road. He really had something bothering him—and I hoped it wasn't something that was going to bother me.

"I hate to be a bother, Senator," one of a seemingly endless supply of Birdie's assistants said, touching my arm, "but have you brought a scarf or another change of clothes with you?"

"No. Isn't what I have on okay for TV? I know I've worn this blue on the air . . ."

"No, no. It's fine. It's just that sometimes Birdie and a guest really strike a rich chord and then we try to continue the conversation for play the next day. But so it won't look like it was shot the same day. . . ."

I said nothing, just stared at "Missy," as her brass

name tag read, waiting until she had talked herself into the corner. Perfect Birdie makes everyone tell the truth in front of the nationwide audience, but isn't above pretending that a guest has made a return trip on another day. Sure, for a second shot at the guillotine. I'd file that away.

"Just a little TV ploy to keep everything fresh and lively," the assistant finally managed.

"Is a ploy like a trick?" I asked, and flashed my best campaigning smile. I was ready as I would ever be for Birdie.

The set was supposed to be Birdie's living room, with the two hundred members of the audience seated just about where the big-screen TV should be.

"We're thrilled to have as our guest today Senator Eleanor Gorzack. You might remember that the senator was the wife of a navy pilot, a war hero, who was missing in action for decades. Then the senator, in a great piece of luck, was in North Vietnam—what we used to call North Vietnam. And there she met a doctor who had worked in prison camps. Another one of those he-used-to-be-our-enemy people. The United States seems to be getting a lot of them as new friends these days. Anyway, in North Vietnam, the doctor so admired the senator that he gave her access to the dog tags and graves of almost two dozen American heroes. Now isn't that some story."

Birdie grinned and took us to a commercial break. She grabbed a clipboard from the back of the sofa and furiously began to thumb through pages crammed with charts and graphs.

I was furious. Birdie had talked as if she had been there in North Vietnam with me. She seemed to be implying that I was some sort of a communist sympathizer, that I was friendly with the Vietcong or something like that. She was out of her gourd if she thought I was going to let that go unchallenged.

I could take her on, I thought, sitting there on a flouncy sofa in a pretend living room, keeping that darn smile stuck on my face. I would tell her that she had no right to question my patriotism, that she had no right to relate the details of my life with so little regard for the truth.

My explosion was ready to rip—when I looked off-stage and caught sight of my mother. One of the people running around with clipboards had offered my mother the best seat in the house, assuming she'd want to be in the front row of the audience and thus get her face known to millions. My mother instead requested a stool backstage to "watch how it really works."

Which was how my eyes caught hers and how I caught the wink and her little wave. My mother's wink and wave were one of God's great creations. When I was young, that wink and wave were part of learning about life. After every minor go-round—a fight with my best friend in the third grade or a bad report card or not being able to go to Willow Grove Park—that wink would slip out and I would know that everything was A-OK. Or when I gave the American Legion speech at eighth-grade graduation, that wave sent me encouragement and kisses and success.

The wink and the wave were also a sign to stay cool, don't lose your temper.

So I caught the wink and wave and my explosion never came. Instead, I found myself looking into Birdie's eyes and asking just how the Vietnam War affected her family. Then I swung around to the audience and asked them how the war affected them. Hey, we were all part of the same happy breakfast group, right? Several women and one man told stories that were every bit as personal and tragic as my and Jack's tale.

Just as a third woman finished speaking, Birdie tried to go to a commercial. But I stopped her, right there on television, just by reaching out my hand, grabbing her arm, and asking her to hold on, "for just a sec." We were in the living room, right?

"I lost my husband and I waited a long time to know for sure that he was gone forever. I don't know if it hurt more then or hurt more now.

"I know that all of you who lost loved ones in the war have to learn to give up the hate and the revenge. I'll tell you how I did. When that doctor in Vietnam— that once enemy—when he led me to my Jack and those other men, he became my friend forever.

"I hope one day we can all learn that lesson, not just abroad, but here at home, and turn enemies into friends."

The audience clapped and cheered. It wasn't my "Jobs" speech, but I felt it was true to who I was—and who Jack was.

Birdie got her way with the commercial break. One of Birdie's little aides had told me not to talk to her during these breaks, that she was holding on to her concentration so she could give it her all when the camera turned on.

I waited for the clipboard to swing up from behind the sofa, but instead she leaned over and whispered something in the vicinity of my right ear. I shook my head, and mouthed, "I didn't get it."

"I said, 'You are a smart little number for someone who looks like she just came off the farm.' That's what I said," Birdie hissed.

Marie was still on her stool and I glanced up and got that little wave, that special exhortation to hold it together. Or, as Bobby Kennedy was reported to have said, "Don't get mad. Get even."

The lights went on and a voice warned, "ten seconds." Now's the time, I realized.

"Birdie," I said, in a stage whisper, just as the red light flashed over the camera. "I'm thrilled to be here, on this show. Just as happy as a pig in mud. I only wish Babs could be here, right along with us."

I felt like the million dollars George kept telling me I still had to raise.

After the show, Birdie was as sweet and pleasant as

she could be. She told me she'd have me back on over her dead body.

People in the audience kept wanting to shake my hand and tell me their names. The four other people with special ties to Vietnam all came up and hugged me and I hugged them and it was an emotional and special time.

"*You* did it," I told my mother as we walked down the back corridor and out to the talent entrance where Stash would meet us with his car. "I saw your little wave and I knew what to do."

"Norie, you did beautifully. The way you just took over," Marie said, squeezing my hand, "reminds me of the time you were supposed to be a guardian angel in the May Procession. Do you remember that?"

The young aide with the "Missy" pin was leading the way.

"Thanks so much, Missy. You were very helpful," I told her.

"Oh, no, Senator," she said, "I'm Rachel. Birdie likes us all to wear 'Missy' pins because she has trouble remembering our names and this way, she looks to the guests like she's really close to her staff."

"Well, Rachel, thanks for that very interesting piece of information."

"That's okay, Senator. I'm going to New York and do *Rosie* starting next week."

I turned and followed my mother down the steps. The alley was narrow, cobblestones and green plastic bags setting up mixed cultural signals.

"Senator, do you want to go back and go out the front door?" Rachel asked.

"No, I see my driver. It's fine."

Stash was near the bottom of the long flight of concrete steps.

"Norie, Marie," he shouted over his shoulder as he turned and walked down the alley. "I'm going to get the car and bring it right to the end of the alley. Take your time."

My mother waited at the bottom of the steps for me and took my arm. We watched Stash turn the corner and disappear from sight. It was the last time we saw him alive.

When it happened, it made a noise like a car crash. Not a big car crash. Just a car crash.

Marie grabbed my arm a little tighter and said something about hoping Stash hadn't had a fender bender.

One woman screamed. And screamed. I told my mother to stay where she was and I ran the last feet to the end of the alley.

Stash's car was there, a little to the left, where he had parked it. He could have left it there, could have waited until my mother and I got in, and then turned on the motor.

But he was always trying to make things easier for me and for my mother, so he had gone ahead and started the engine. Just turned the key, the cops told me later.

One turn of the key and the bomb went off. It had

been attached to the ignition switch when Stash had stopped for gas earlier that morning. That's what the cops managed to put together in a couple of hours.

It was a professional bomb, they told me. It was a singular example of a conventional killing machine perfected by gangsters and revolutionaries. The nail bomb was a real work of art.

Some seventy-five nails were stuck in the upholstery of the car, like rough needles pushed into a pincushion. Several had pierced Stash's chest, instantly killing him. One spike nailed his hand to the steering wheel.

My mother had followed me down the alley and staggered with shock to the car. I tried to hold her back but she grabbed Stash's hand through the window and held on to it, much as she had held mine a few moments before.

The tears fell down her face and she looked very old, and if the man or men who had done this were within my reach, I would have killed them.

This anger would take a long time to go away.

CHAPTER 27

The notice from Stash's family had requested only Mass cards, no flowers, but the floral tributes at the McCaffey-Dinan Funeral Home stretched from the casket around the two parlors into the reception room and out into the hallway.

One large cross, fashioned out of carnations and roses, held a simple banner, GRANDPOP. Another arrangement, with violets and lillies, lay at the foot of the open casket. The gold letters on its ribbon spelled out DAD.

Stash would be waked two nights, with a Mass at St. Timothy's on Saturday morning. People came by to pay respects to the family and to visit with old friends. His three daughters stood near the casket, receiving, the place where their mother would have stood if she had still been alive.

My mother and I had come early, for the rosary, then I took her home. Or rather Carver and I took her home, since he wouldn't get more than three inches from me since the explosion.

He blamed himself. He had been watching the Keystone Militia Web page and was sure something big was coming down. He had left us at the studio to stop by the division of the Philadelphia police that kept its investigative eye on "groups."

"You name it," he told me, driving back to the funeral home from my mother's. "Black Panthers. Ku Klux Klan. American Patriot League. Young Communists. They're watching them all. But I shouldn't have been there. I should have been with you and your mother."

"So you could have gotten killed? I don't think so, Carver." I looked out the window at the rowhouses sliding by and realized that until I went to high school, I didn't know people in Philadelphia could live in a single house.

"I'm going to go in here by myself," I told him when we pulled into the side driveway. "There are enough off-duty cops inside to populate—"

"A donut chain," Carver finished up.

"If you say so, chief."

I sat for a few minutes with Jeanne Callaghan, who assured me that my mother was shaken up but perfectly all right.

"She's lost her husband and, before that, watched you lose yours. So if she's a little shaken up, it's nothing compared to what she's already been through. She'll be fine," Jeanne insisted.

I stood at the side of the casket at exactly 8:30 for the arrival of the mayor and several members of the city council. Then, in a manner I learned from my family when I wasn't even a teenager, I made my way through the wake, starting once again at the front door. I would stay until nine o'clock when the family left for home, as a mark of respect.

I stood on the front steps, pretending that I needed a little fresh air. A half-dozen men stood to one side, a few of them smoking. One man, Bill Kaiser, had a terrible cough and kept hacking as he tried to say hello.

As long as I could remember, I had known these men. They were members of the Holy Name Society, with my father. They played cards and darts with him, and stood each other for drinks on Friday night before they came home. These men worked in factories and on the waterfront, as firemen or cops. They mostly had bad feet, from standing outside in cold weather. Their kids mostly spent their careers sitting down, thanks to their fathers.

Many of these men still called me Norie, and with many of them, I still used "Mister" in front of their names.

"Norie," Kaiser said, finally catching his breath, "I just want you to know the whole city is furious about what happened to you and your mother. And Stash, jeez, he was a great guy."

"Thanks, Bill. But I'm a little worried about your cough. Are you off the smokes?"

"Has to be thirty years. Just allergies, I guess," Bill said. "Where's your security, hon. Don't you need some bodyguards or something. I hear this militia has you marked."

There was one thing about wakes—faced with the existential crisis of life versus death, a lot of people managed to get ginned up and say things they would never try in a regular setting.

"The Keystone Militia announced today that I am not marked. They keep insisting they've got nothing to do with any of the violence."

"You think that's true?" Bill asked. "I always got antsy going up in that part of the state. It's like south Jersey. Only no Jersey Devil."

One had to have grown up in Philadelphia to recognize the older generation's antipathy toward the rural parts of the state. Pennsylvania was like a little country unto itself, with centuries of wars going on among geographic parts of the state.

"They're people, just like us, up there," I tried, and was turning to talk to another man who was a friend of my dad's.

"Yeah, but maybe it was all that poison that got dumped up there, has to be six, seven years ago. It had to affect these people's brains. Maybe . . ."

"What poison? Bill, what are you talking about?"

"I used to drive over the road, maybe twenty-five years ago. When long hauls were really hard. No place would take a trucker. No pulloffs to catch a couple hours sleep. Schedules that meant you were always ten or fifteen miles over the limit. Then I went into business with my brother-in-law. Aluminum storm windows and doors. We put the windows on your mother's house." Bill stopped and took a cigarette out of a pack in his jacket pocket. I kept a poker face.

"But Jericho. 'Poison.' What about that?" I asked. Older people have a rule: They're going to tell you what they're going to tell you at the pace they decide on. Clearly Bill didn't go over the speed limit in conversation.

"I still know a lot of truckers. One guy, he came to me. Yes, seven years back. Said I could pick up some big money taking what he calls 'hot waste' up around Jericho and dumping it. I said it was illegal. Immoral, too. He said it didn't matter. It was just a one-time thing. But I said no."

"And what was the 'hot' waste?" I asked.

"Who knows? At the time I thought maybe it was like stuff from a holdup. You know, 'hot' stuff. But that couldn't have been it. Then I was reading all this stuff in the papers about the junk that's showing up in those lakes in the Poconos. And I figured out that maybe the 'hot waste' was really poison. Like radioactive stuff or something like that. I almost called you on it, Norie, but I didn't want to bother you, being a senator and all that."

It took me several hours, but by midnight I had Jake Singer's niece on the phone. She lived close to Harrisburg, but didn't seem to know much about government or news stories about the Jericho syndrome, or remember that I was running for the Senate. They say that at any time two percent of the people eligible to vote cannot name the president of the United States. I now knew I had met one of them.

"Mrs. Gates, I just want you to try and think if your uncle ever said anything to you about what he was talking to Congressman Bercolini about. Anything," I said, clearly enunciating each word, as if I were speaking in a foreign language.

"Nope. He didn't talk too much. He liked baseball and fishing. Mostly fishing. He'd worked hard all his life. His second wife wiped him out. She was a number. With the divorce. He had a lousy lawyer," Opal Gates revealed.

She was not a proactive talker, but she would answer questions and I couldn't hang up. I was back in public health mode and I kept pushing the envelope, positive that one question could lead to another and then to some kind of an answer. We'd covered his work record, his marriage record, and his fight with Social Security before we got to sports.

"Fishing? By himself or with some buddies?" I asked.

"Oh, by himself. He was a loner."

"What kind of fishing? Ocean or freshwater?" I asked.

"Mostly lake. That's not ocean, right?" Opal asked me.

"Right. Lake. And did he fish nearby?"

"Yes. But not as near as he used to."

"Is that right? Do you remember where he used to fish?"

"Sure. Ten, twelve years ago he used to go right over near Jericho. Couple lakes there, ponds really, that he thought were swell. People used them in the summer, but that was it."

Another pause. Push, push!

"And now? Recently, I mean."

"Oh, he would head north, up over the state line. He just didn't want to mess around Jericho."

"And do you know why?" I asked.

"Not really," Opal said, then paused as if for the first time filtering a piece of information, wondering if she could tell me. "Now I don't want to be disrespectful, Senator. But I can tell you what my Uncle Jake used to say. He had a great sense of humor."

"Of course he did," I managed, almost going through the phone to shake the information out of Opal. "And he said . . . ?"

"He used to say that what was dumped in those lakes could make the walls of Jericho fall down."

I got Milton on the phone at home.

"I want people who can test for radioactive traces

all over that area. I don't care if they're from the state or from the feds. I want a lot of people and I want every one of those ponds or lakes tested now," I told him.

"Norie, it's the middle of the night. You have three weeks of campaigning to go. Dugdale would have a field day with this, if he finds out," Milton mumbled into the receiver.

"I don't care. I think we've been dancing around these deaths for months. If there is radioactive material in any of those bodies of water, we've got to track it down. And I mean now."

"Norie, you can't just dump radioactive stuff. Drivers have to sign manifests, documents, papers. Check with Marco. Get him to have the union guys explain what they go through. Check with George. One division of Taylor Technology certifies these kinds of removals. They both can tell you that it's impossible," Milton concluded.

"That's all correct, Milton. But the dumping took place. So why don't you set your alarm for six a.m. and get on this. Thank you very much."

I hung up the phone.

I called Marco on his cell phone and got no answer. I called George both at home and at the Shore and got the machine both places. Somebody out there was having a bigger personal life than I was, that was for sure. I went upstairs and went to bed.

I plowed through the next three weeks. I know there are people out there who love campaigning, elected officials who will tell you they like government but mostly they like politics. It's not me.

Mary Devine and I spent an hour every night on the phone, reviewing what new information she'd managed to ferret out during the preceding twenty-four hours. If I wasn't sleeping much, Mary wasn't sleeping at all. We were slowly closing in.

Several of the smaller lakes, all ringed by small manufacturing plants and all close to Jericho, were showing slightly higher levels of radioactivity. The tests, of course, could only show the current level—not what the waters had registered when the "hot waste" might have been dumped, seven years before.

Mary was currently searching down what was manufactured around the lakes, as well as what might have been made during the assumed time of the dumping. It wasn't easy. She was also trying, using scientists at a couple of Pennsylvania hospitals and universities, to figure out exactly what chemicals were in the water.

As for the last weeks of fund-raising, the public polls, in the newspapers, showed me up—slightly. A three-point lead, all within the margin of error, did not bring about a flood of checks from people who wanted to be with the winner.

Hilda Mendelssohn had me on the phone several times during those last weeks, giving me specific names and phone numbers to call.

"These are all people who want more women in office, especially in the Senate," she'd tell me. "You've got to make every phone call work, so we're targeting only almost sure things."

Then the brilliant Milton Gant finally cashed in on his weeks of research and figured out that we could challenge the Dugdale campaign on its use of Values Coalition funds.

"It's against federal law," Milton yelled into the phone during our conference call with Kathleen, Marco, R. M., and George. "He can't use a nonprofit organization's funds interchangeably with his campaign money."

"And are you sure, Milton, that's what he's doing?"

"Yes. Yes. First, we know he's been on the Values Coalition shows on cable consistently over the past six months. That's one violation. Then I've followed his boys at major stations in Philly and in Pittsburgh. The media buying company Dugdale uses has received money from different bank accounts."

"That doesn't necessarily mean a violation, Milton," George said. "We have money wired from different accounts. We send money from Gorzack for Senate. And the DSCC wires money from Washington."

"I'm not talking about party money, George. Just listen for a change. Sometimes the money is drawn from the Dugdale for Senate Campaign account. Other instances, it's the Values Coalition account that's drawn on."

"Whoops! Sorry, Milton, you're right," George declared. It was hard to get George to admit he was wrong about anything, but Milton had really bitten his head off. Campaign tension was getting to everybody.

"So what do we do?" Kathleen asked.

"Norie, you do nothing," R. M. said. "The national party has to look into this immediately. We'll get several election lawyers working on it tomorrow morning. In Washington and in the state. See if we can get some hard facts in the next couple days."

"I'll bet you we'll blow Dugdale out of the water," George said, clearly delighted at the discovery.

"Maybe we won't sink his ship," Milton said. "But we could put a heck of a hole in the side."

We did.

Not that Dugdale would go down without a fight.

By the weekend before the election, he was flailing around, blaming the federal election-law violations on poor management of the campaign and a lack of sophistication on the part of his supporters in the Values Coalition.

"What could be better," Hilda told me on the phone after reading me an article in the *Washington Post*. "He says he doesn't know how to run things and that his supporters don't know what they're doing. Great. Now the state should elect him senator? No way."

She was back in Ohio, campaigning in congressional elections. She'd be making a few stops for me in Pittsburgh the next day.

"Hilda," I told her, "before the election, before the

results, I just want to make it clear that if I win, you are the keystone, the responsible party. If you hadn't stepped in, organized my campaign, helped me raise the money, been my friend—I don't know what would have happened."

"You would have lost, Norie. That's it," she said, then laughed. "Probably. But that's not what is going to happen. You, knock wood, will win on Tuesday."

"Vote early and often," Linda V. yelled at me as I came out of the voting booth at the Cara Mia Senior Citizen Casa, a few blocks from my mother's home.

"Linda, I did just vote," I insisted, waving my hand at the half-dozen photographers and video camera-men who had recorded this pseudo-historic moment. "What are you doing here, at seven a.m.? Don't you ever sleep?"

"I sleep here, Senator Norie. Your mother was worried about me being in the house by myself, so she got me in here. In your neighborhood."

I turned to my mother, who gave me a quick shrug and mumbled something about Linda's volunteering for the Sunshine Club.

It was a fitting start to my seventeen-stop election day tour.

"Not that election day campaigning does very much," R. M. had said. "But we need to keep you out of everyone's hair."

Since he had two other Senate races and several House races, R. M. would be spending the night in

D.C. Josh Kaplan, though, with only my race, was locked up with a phone bank in Marco's office—polling, identifying districts that should be getting polled, while comparing numbers with his pollster friends who worked for the various TV networks.

By 5 P.M., Josh got the word to me—as I was heading for the Warwick Hotel from the airport—that I had won.

"But Josh, the polls don't close for three hours," I insisted.

"Doesn't matter. The key precincts are all in your column. I'd say you've got it by a comfortable five point margin." I didn't believe him, of course.

I went down to the ballroom about 8:20 to thank all my workers, just as two networks called the race in my favor.

The actual numbers—54–46.

I waited until 10:30 to declare victory. All the networks had declared me the winner. The raw vote tally—with more than 80 percent of the votes counted—showed me far in front. Still, Dugdale hadn't called me to concede.

"Just go out and declare yourself the winner. Dugdale is just trying to spoil it," R. M. insisted from D.C. "You want to make the network wrap-ups. You won it, fair and square."

"With a lot of help from my friends," I said, and that's how I began my thank yous in my speech. "And with a real sacrifice by one person, who believed in my candidacy."

My mother started to cry. I didn't know if it was the mention of Stash, the cheers from the crowd, or my victory. I thanked my volunteers, my friends, and the people of Pennsylvania who believed that, "a minimum wage was a family value."

The cheers kept coming although I did hear my mother yell to Marco, "What about the forty-six percent who voted for Dugdale? Why didn't we get them?"

"That's okay, Marie," I heard Marco shout, as he stood behind me, holding his arms aloft in a victory salute. "Whatever the numbers are, it adds up to a victory for our girl."

Maybe I had seen a hundred election night parties on TV. Maybe I'd been at a dozen. Maybe I knew that at one point, the balloons would drop down from the ceiling, that the polka music would play when I took the stage, that the governor would tell the audience that everyone knew all along that I was a winner.

Maybe. But that didn't change how I felt. Election, by my state. An elected woman Senator. There weren't more than a literal handful of women elected to the United States Senate—and I was one of them.

So the balloons looked magical, the polka was perfect, the governor sounded sincere, and I knew that I was truly a United States Senator.

CHAPTER 28

The Senate was in recess, but it was the Senate, not this senator, that was on vacation. I wasn't complaining, especially when I read the paper each morning and watched the disintegrating, unfolding drama of Dugdale and Co.

Our finger-pointing at the Values Coalition had done more than call into question their political checks. Seemed like there were a lot more iffy expenditures than just the way they bought time for commercials.

Political reporters, with little to do now that the election was over, were in a feeding frenzy with a lot of questions for Values Coalition director Vic Stample.

The first was, "Where are you?"

Stample, along with approximately $500,000 of the Values Coalition's cash, had fled the country. Dugdale took to the airwaves to repudiate Stample. And also to take a swipe at me, whom he still kept referring to as "my opponent."

Hey, I won. It's over.

So, starting at dawn, I was all over Philadelphia thanking the voters—at diners, the fish market, the courthouse. Afterwards, it was time to digest our win.

"Why do these people always make it 'us versus them'?" I asked Kathleen during our celebration lunch at the Four Seasons in downtown Philadelphia. "In some ways, many of the people in the Values Coalition are just like the people in RiverWatch. They're concerned about what's happening in their world, and they want to change it, to fix it."

"That's a fine analysis, Senator," Kathleen announced, holding her glass of white wine up in a mock toast. "But the Values Coalition people shoved you off a step, tried to keep you from speaking, and were a generally undemocratic bunch of creeps."

"I want to be fair, Kathleen. I want to be an honorable and good winner," I answered, toasting her back. "These people just want their ideas to prevail. By any means necessary."

"Well, they were sure incompetent about it."

The waiter came up and we ordered the special, which was some sort of crab cakes with two different sauces. Kathleen looked bothered, though.

"You don't want the crab cakes?" I asked.

"No. We have some loose ends to clean up and we should go back to your office for an hour or so after lunch. Janet Fisher called me from D.C. There are some checks that just don't have the right kind of ID, and she can't get George on the phone no matter what kind of a message she leaves."

At the office I had several urgent phone calls from Mary Devine waiting for me, but Kathleen was standing there and, back in Washington, Janet Fisher was trying to get her books straightened out.

"It's all to do with that seashore party," she told us on the speakerphone. "Mr. Shields wrote a five-thousand-dollar check to the DSCC. So did his wife. Then we had forty one-thousand-dollar checks. And the rest was in five-hundred-dollar contributions."

"What do we need, Janet?" Kathleen queried, sounding a little cranky for someone who had just managed a winning campaign *and* had a very lovely lunch at the Four Seasons.

"We need everything, really. I don't have a Social Security number on either of the Shields checks. I don't have a Social Security number on at least twenty of the other checks. And Sheila Shields's check has to be reissued, since it was written on a company account."

"And George?"

"Senator, I've been calling George Taylor since the week after the event. He just will not return my calls. I leave messages at his office. I leave messages at his home. He doesn't want to talk to me," Janet complained.

When the call ended, Kathleen and I sat scrutinizing each other, as if one would be able to tell the other what was going on.

"I think he's in trouble," Kathleen started. "It's weird, but it's money trouble. We went for lunch about three weeks ago, right after Stash's funeral. It wasn't a big check. We were at some place on Roosevelt Boulevard. You know George, he always picks up the check. And he did. But then the waitress came back and said his credit card had been rejected."

"Maybe he forgot to pay a bill. I've had that happen. It just slips your mind," I said, racing for a better answer. "Maybe with the pressure of the campaign—he has been under stress—he just isn't keeping up."

"Maybe," Kathleen said, drawing out the syllables. "But then, after he paid the check with cash, he started in on me about how I wasn't managing the campaign accounts correctly. How he had put in for maybe ten thousand dollars in expenses, and that none of it had come back."

"Ten thousand dollars? What did he do, rent a tank?"

"For all I know, that or a ship. When I got back to the office, I spent like an hour pulling together all the expenses that George had submitted. Not just ten thousand. No, he'd already collected eight thousand. He had billed the campaign for a total eighteen." Kathleen sat back in her chair and puckered her lips. I thought she might cry. "It was all crazy stuff. Like receipts from gas stations. God, Norie, it was every lunch George had eaten since July first. It didn't matter whom he took out to lunch, it was all on the campaign tab billed to us. He even put in a couple of Vesper Club bills, when the Gang of Four ate dinner together."

"This isn't George. He's obviously in some kind of trouble," I agreed. "But why wouldn't he come to us, let us help him?"

"I don't know," Kathleen said. "But you better track him down and you better find out. Because I'm not writing him a check and he obviously needs to get the money from somewhere."

Kathleen sat there while I put in a call to George, and she stayed around while I tried him three more times. Each time the machine answered and I heard its self-satisfied little beep. Each time I left a message, saying how important it was for him to call me back.

Kathleen had to head over to her United Way office. She was taking a few days off before heading back to her *real* job, "Although it won't seem so real after this."

"You could decide to do campaigns all the time. Hilda says a woman campaign manager, especially with all the women running for office, would clean up," I tried.

"I'll do it again," she finally countered, "when I get a candidate I really like and really want to give my all to. That'll be the next time you run."

As soon as she had left, I tackled the pile of messages on my desk, beginning with Mary Devine.

"I've got it," she yelled into the phone. "I know what and I know a whole bunch of whos. But I can't figure out why."

I stopped her from going any further.

"Have you told anyone what you've uncovered," I asked.

"No, Senator, I just put the call through to you."

"Get out of your office. Go get Milton. Go back to my office and call me here, on my private line."

"Senator, is this necessary?"

"Mary," I warned, "you know some very important information. Other people have known some of this same information. They are now dead. I want you to do exactly as I say. and I want you to call me back in exactly ten minutes."

I hung up and beeped Carver. He'd gone back to Washington for a few days, saying he would start back on his private security with me when I returned to D.C. the following Monday. In the meanwhile, I had an off-duty Philadelphia cop who went everywhere with me. She was thirty years old and the best shot in her division. I felt okay.

When Carver called me back, I filled him in on what Mary had uncovered and asked him to go immediately to my office.

"I've got no details. But she's a careful researcher and I'm sure she's onto something," I told him.

"So much for getting my garden ready for winter,"

Carver complained. "I'll be with her in less than an hour."

Mary was on the phone, along with Milton. I sat by myself in my Philadelphia office. Mary laid out her research in the clear and careful way I knew she would. As she talked, I kept looking at a photograph I kept on my desk, a photograph that meant a great deal to me.

It was us—the Gang of Four—minutes after I had been sworn in as a U.S. senator. Marco and Kathleen on one side of me, George on the other. Our friendship was a keystone to my life, and, after the campaign I put them all through, I knew I meant a lot to them.

"So I had these two researchers, from Penn. Grad students, really. We had their names from Ramona Sanchez in the state Department of Health. They had volunteered when the first garbage was discovered."

"Right. And they went up to Jericho?"

"I had three sites. All pretty commercial. I asked them to evaluate the water. They did. We got them water samples, and, after several days of doing whatever scientists do, they could tell us that the waste was from a nuclear reactor. One of them thought it was probably waste from one or many of the small reactors that kind of populate universities and research centers," Mary said. "The other one thought it could even be waste from Three Mile Island. But then she backed off on that theory."

"Mary, that was some twenty years ago," I interjected.

"Yes, but both the scientists said that when they flooded Three Mile Island, they produced a lot of low-level radioactive water. It was temporarily stored in places up and down the eastern seaboard—a lot of it in massive warehouses in south Jersey. Then it was supposed to be trucked off to Idaho or to that new nuclear dump that they're building somewhere out west. Nevada or Utah?"

"*How* can we be producing this much nuclear waste? I thought we weren't into nuclear power in this country," Milton asserted.

"We produce high-level radioactive waste—that's the stuff you hear about, like the rods used in nuclear power plants. But, all over, in hospitals, universities, and power plants, we're turning out tons of *low-level* waste—the clothes technicians wear, the water used to cool down the reactors, even the IV bags from chemotherapy—it all has to be put into safe containers and buried or hauled or something."

"But the disposal of all these materials must be covered by regulations? Manifests are mandated for so many materials," I said, "that there should be records of every single item. Have you located the people authorized to dispose of secondary nuclear waste?"

"Yep," Mary said. "Hold on."

As excited as I was about Mary's discovery, I wished that I could get off the phone that instant and try to track down George. I stared at my photograph. He had to be in enormous pain to be doing these insane things around money.

"I've got a list, Senator, of the companies who monitor such disposal in the Pennsylvania area. It's not very long, just five names, since it's pretty complicated stuff," she said.

"Anything familiar?" Milton asked.

"Oh, yes, sure. Here's one. Taylor Technologies. Isn't that your friend's company, Senator? It's at the top of the list."

George called me at nine, at home, sounding a little rushed, but not very different from his usual self. He chatted a few minutes about some of the news coverage of the election, said we needed to have lunch next week, and then asked me what was so urgent.

"Urgent isn't the word, George," I told him. "I've got a lot of questions for you. And I want to see you face-to-face. Tomorrow. Alone."

"Can't do it," he said. "Just can't take the time. We can do this on the phone, can't we, Norie?"

"No. I want to see you tomorrow. I'll meet you at the Country Club Diner, over on Bustleton. Early. Like eleven, before the crowd."

"Norie . . ."

"George, don't mess around with me. I think there's been enough messing around. Now let's try to fix it, okay?"

He mumbled something and hung up the phone.

C H A P T E R
29

Remarkably, George was already in a booth waiting for me when I showed up at the diner.

"It doesn't look good, George," I said, pointing to the gadgets laid out in front of him on the Formica table. "Two cellular phones and a beeper are not a nutritious breakfast."

George fiddled with his sunglasses, but didn't remove them. For a minute, I thought maybe this was all a terrible misunderstanding. Mary Devine had read the wrong list of companies; Kathleen had looked at the wrong envelope of receipts; Janet Fisher had the wrong pile of checks.

But the smile on George's face twisted into a grimace, and I felt my palms get sweaty. I almost felt lightheaded as I sat down and slid into the booth, directly across from him.

"Take off those glasses so I can look into your steely blues," I told him. He was a handsome man, my friend George, although the days since the election had taken their toll. He looked maybe fifteen pounds thinner, his face drawn, and when he removed his sunglasses, I saw a shockingly vivid blue and purple smear across his left eye.

"Hey, Norie, not too pretty, huh. I bet it's one of the best of its kind. It did startle me when I saw myself in the bathroom mirror this morning. 'George,' I asked myself, 'what have you done to yourself?' And I had no answer."

"Do you have one now? Do you want to tell it to me?"

"I know some people who get a little angry when you don't do exactly as they ask."

"George!"

The waitress interrupted us. I ordered a toasted bagel and coffee. George said he'd have a cheese omelette, "since cholesterol is not a worry anymore."

"I'm worried," I said as she walked away. "I've got a lot of worries. One worry is that you are somehow mixed up in this toxic dumping that's ravaged all these people's lives. I can't believe it, but that's where all the research is pointing. At you."

"Norie, you remember when Shoeless Joe Jackson was involved in the Black Sox scandal? Big betting go-round back in the teens. When Shoeless Joe got fingered, there were crowds outside the stadium or the clubhouse or something. And one little boy is supposed to have said, 'Say it ain't so, Joe.' "

George shrugged. That simple movement broke my heart. My friend!

One cellular started to ring. George didn't answer it and, after several rings, it stopped. He punched in a series of numbers and watched as a phone number appeared on the miniscreen. He didn't write the number down, but simply pressed his "clear" button.

"What's Shoeless Joe got to do with it, George?" I tried, not knowing where the conversation should go—and surely not clear about what I was going to do when it got there.

"Shoeless? He's got nothing to do with us, Norie. You and me. Friends. We've been friends for maybe a dozen years now, right? And I've really enjoyed it."

"Then come back, George, and answer me. What have you to do with the toxic dumping near Jericho?"

"Nothing. Everything. Nothing and everything. I swear to you that no one involved with Taylor Technologies has dumped anything. Nothing. None of our leased trucks. None of my employees. They're clean. Good, clean people."

I was getting answers and no answer. I was also getting mad. This wasn't some ideological debate about trees or rivers or how much science to teach in grammar schools. Three people were dead and I was now very sure that George had something, if not everything, to do with it.

"What *could* Taylor Technologies do to help in the illegal dumping of toxic waste, George?"

"We could phony up a manifest. We could show that a couple tons of radioactive-tinged water was sealed, was contained, was cleaned up, good as new—and instead of putting that water through the costly process of decontamination, we could just grind out the paperwork and let somebody get rid of it. We could dump a little other low-level waste along with the water."

Our breakfast came. I watched while George carefully salted his omelette and spread butter on his toast.

"Don't you feel some regret, George, some remorse, that you did this terrible thing? People are sick and people are dead and . . ."

"And I could have been dead. Very dead. And I didn't want to die. And they told me, they assured me, that the water would be taken out to sea and dumped there."

"Would that have been so much better?" I asked.

"Yes. Of course. For God's sake, Norie, every other country is shoveling crap into the ocean, hand over fist. We've got all these wacko laws that prevent us from doing what the rest of the world thinks is just fine," George insisted, somehow lecturing me like I was the criminal.

"These 'wacko' laws made you a whole lot of money, George. You were Mister Environment. You were the one who wanted tighter regulations, better air and water, a safer world," I insisted. I could hear my voice getting louder, and I saw one of the waitresses give me a quizzical look, like did I want more coffee. I shook my head to keep her from coming over.

"A safer world. That's right, Norie, and then suddenly, the world wasn't very safe for me. And unlike heroes—your late husband, for example—I chose survival. Not of the planet, but of me." George paused, and took a large bite of omelette and a gulp of coffee. "I chose me over them. I chose the one person I knew from a lot of people I didn't know. And, honestly, I didn't think anybody would be exposed, or be hurt."

"But a lot of people got hurt. All that's followed, George, is it really all tied in, the way I think it must be?"

"I don't know. And that's the truth."

"How can I trust you, George?"

"You can't. But you have to. Give me a week . . ."

The other cellular was ringing and this time George answered it.

"Yes, she's here." He paused. "I'm leaving." Another pause, while something was said to him. "No, not yet."

George turned off the phone, grabbed his other gadgets, and started to slide out of the booth.

"Norie, I'm asking you—hold off for a week. Just a week. Thanksgiving. Give me that. You owe it to me."

"I owe you a lot but . . ."

"And this time, you have to pick up the check."

I tried to say something, but he literally sprinted out

346

of the diner and I was left with two cups of cold coffee and a lot of questions.

The next day in my Washington office I was faced with a wide variety of opinions about the next steps to take.

I didn't like any of them.

Milton wanted me to immediately turn over the information I had to the Department of Justice, the Nuclear Regulatory Commission, and the FBI.

Carver wanted me to sit tight, but to talk on a need-to-know basis with the FBI.

Marco, who'd come down from Philadelphia with me on the train that morning and who had known George twice as long as he knew me, wanted me to do nothing—now or in the future. "Whatever happens, you play in mud, you get it on your shoes," he said, and I knew he had cleaned up his adage for my benefit. "Leave it alone. Let the authorities deal with it."

As far as hard information about George, Marco knew more than all of us—although he had assumed that it was all old news to me.

"George got into a little money squeeze in the late eighties. He had done the flashy office downtown. He had gone through the first divorce and was well on his way into the second. He made several bad investments."

"Did he tell you this casually?" I asked. "He never told me. We spent all that time together. Gosh, Marco, you and Kathleen and George and I must have had dinner together a couple times a month. And on the phone . . ."

"No. Not casual, Norie. He had to. He came to me because his company was devalued after he was forced to start mortgaging properties. He needed cash. He wanted to get a pretty big loan from a union pension fund. But when I told him there was a lengthy investigation of both the business and personal finances, he stopped pursuing it."

We kept talking about George, but we couldn't talk to George. And that's what I wanted. How did he get involved, who threatened to kill him, and why had he knuckled under to the pressure?

We knew nothing. The meeting lasted almost two hours, and nothing was accomplished. We agreed to get back together late in the afternoon.

I had a fairly full schedule, considering that the Senate was out on recess. I'd pushed off a lot of decisions, a lot of work, to concentrate on the campaign, and I'd promised myself that, come December, I'd take a vacation. Once I got caught up.

One afternoon appointment was with Janet Fisher. She'd had no luck in reaching the Shields family, nor had she any luck in reaching anyone at the Whitegate Trucking Co., the name on the check from Sheila.

It rang a bell with me, though.

And with Mary Devine, who had it in her records as one of the trucking companies that carried radioactive waste. I sent Mary back to her computer, and, finishing up my campaign business with Janet, I waited.

The crazed pace of my first year in the Senate had left little time to wait. Or to think. Or to imagine what life would be like when I knew I really belonged in the place—or at least had been sent there by voters who believed I belonged.

Mary interrupted my reverie.

"Whitegate is a biggie. Lots of waste disposal. Hospital. Research labs. You name it, they haul it. Or"—she looked at her papers—"they did until a few months ago. Then they shut down."

"You mean they went out of business?" I asked.

"Not clear. They just stopped. No contracts. No working phone number. But all the trucks are still registered in the company name."

"How do you know this?" I asked.

"I can find out just about anything if I have a corporate tax number or a Social Security number. I found Larry Shields's. And I found Sheila's, or rather, Lois Reilly's."

"She didn't take her married name?" I almost yelled.

"She's not Shields. She's not married. She has no children. She couldn't give you a check on her personal account because she has no personal account with more than a hundred dollars. She is a dealer in one of the smaller casinos. I've checked. She doesn't declare any dependents. Lives alone, in a place called Egg Harbor Township, near Atlantic City."

"And the children? What happened to the children?" I was frantic.

"Who knows?" Carver said, following Mary into the room. "They probably rented them for the day."

All we could figure out, when faced with the facts, was that Larry Shields had set me up. And set George up.

Only a few checks from the event came with the information necessary to cash them. The others carried no information—because they were never meant to be cashed.

"There was no question," I told Kathleen on the speakerphone set up on a coffee table, "that Larry had this idea to give us phony checks. What he thought was going to happen I don't know. But George, when he set up the fund-raiser, didn't understand that the place would be filled with ringers."

Marco, Milton, and Carver were gathered around the speakerphone, all of us still telling each other that we couldn't believe what happened.

"God knows who was with you in all those photographs," Carver warned me. "All those people in their lovely outfits and their happy faces and it was all fake. You've probably met more second-story men than most cops meet in a lifetime."

"But George would know the checks weren't good, once he saw the crowd and realized he didn't know anybody," I said.

"So it had to be Larry's little deal. What a total creep!" Marco said. "But then, once he gets you there and George there, he really has George over a barrel, right? He tells George to do just what he wants him to do. And that's that."

"Marco, are you so sure that George wasn't part of this? We know he was part of something," Milton chided him. "We know he had something to do with the dumping that caused all these vets to have leukemia. We know he had something to do with the people who were murdered to keep them quiet."

"I'm not so sure, Milton," Carver said, "of every single one of those potent facts. You're just jumping from one little conclusion to several big ones."

"He *told* Norie that he covered up the dumping. He said that, didn't he," Milton charged, looking at me. I nodded in agreement, but then I shrugged.

"Well," I said, "George told me that manifests could be faked. And I guess he said Taylor Technologies—"

"But he didn't tell you definitely, is that what you're saying?" Marco shouted, standing up and beginning to pace back and forth like a defense attorney. "So we really don't know that George did anything, do we? We really don't know that he committed any crime at all."

"We know some things, Marco," I answered. "We know something has gone very wrong with our friend. And we know that he's in some kind of real trouble. And we know he's not in touch. And none of that is very good."

* * *

The plan we decided on was a modified version of Carver's strategy. We wouldn't go to any of the federal agencies—yet.

"You're covered for a week or so because you're talking to me about all of this. And I am, ex officio, a direct arm of the White House," Carver told me.

"Pretty ex officio," I replied. "One presidential phone call and all the other rules are forgotten? I don't think so. And I don't want you putting yourself on the line for somebody you hardly know."

"I know you. I'm charged with taking care of you. It's clear that old George is also trying to take care of you, someway or another," Carver said, nodding his head as his own chorus of agreement. "So I say let's give George a chance. Anyway, just to be on the safe side, I'm going to make a few inquiries myself."

Which was, it turned out, pretty fruitful.

Carver decided to check up on old Larry Shields with the people who might know him best—the local police authorities in south Jersey.

Larry, it turned out, was a lot better known in the Atlantic City casinos than in the beachfront estates in Longport. He was also a familiar name and face to the gambling commission. Seems like Larry was a real fund-raising friend to a lot of people—only none of his other beneficiaries were running for public office.

"This man is a loan shark of the worst kind," Carver said. "A clever one. Modern. Running everything on computer. You can pay back your debt by having your bank account debited."

"No way," I said.

"It's true. He's got all these phony mortgage companies and, according to the gambling commission, the poor sucker who takes Larry's money pays it back like a regular loan. Only problem is, the interest rate is a lot higher."

"And George?"

"You know it before I tell you, don't you, Senator? You have figured this out, the money thing."

"George loved sports. Loved to gamble. Always telling me 'I'll bet you this, I'll bet you that.' He was tense, wired, for a long time. But it would get better and then worse, better and then worse. I was sure it wasn't alcohol or drugs. So it was another addictive substance, gambling!"

"Did you ever see him gamble? Place a bet or tell you about a bet?" Carver asked.

"No, but I saw him lose. Last summer at the ball game, he was almost deranged at the Phillies blowing a sure thing."

"So George had money troubles . . ."

"Not just from the business. It's a chicken-egg thing, isn't it, Lieutenant? What came first? Business problems? Or the gambling? He needed money for both and he had less and less," I said, adding up the facts we had. "And he kept picking up the checks. Always treating."

"This time," Carver said, "somebody has left him holding the check. And I think it's one that he can't cover."

* * *

I'd broken a vow that I'd taken when I first went into public service. The campaign made me do it. I now had a fax in my home.

My mother loved it and checked it several times a day, to see if any "important documents," as she called them, had been wired through.

I'd made a quick mall stop on my way home—really a thirty-minute detour—and picked up the bits and pieces of life that had gone by the wayside during the campaign: pantyhose, moisturizer, a new white shell, and the cutest little black flats I'd ever seen.

My mother had taken the onset of cold weather as her cue to head to see my brother and his family in San Jose, so the loneliness of the fax's beep-beep startled me as I came in with my packages.

Mary Devine must have worked twenty-four hours a day, I concluded, envying the energy of the young. Now she'd put together a list of the small manufacturing plants around the three "hot" small lakes—and, since the dumping was assumed to be seven to ten years ago, she had gone back and listed the businesses that previously were on that land.

One caught my eye. "Church's Drywood and Paneling." They'd gone out of business, according to Mary's list, some five years ago.

It might tie in. My guys up in Jericho were mostly construction workers—and, in my head, I made the connection between their leukemia and the allergic reaction of Jeanne Callaghan's grandson, all those months ago, when his parents used drywall.

Wow! If radioactive water had been used in the drywall, then I was close to a solution. That was my brilliant idea.

Boy, was I wrong, as I found out when I rang up an old friend, Bob Pollard, who had a construction business in Virginia.

"Nope," he said. "No water in drywall. That's not the way it works. Drywall is made up of gypsum and glues. You want to keep it as dry as possible. No water there."

Good theory, Norie, I told myself. Too bad it was totally off base.

We talked for a few minutes about other things and I was ready to hang up when I thought I'd ask one more question.

"Is there anything made, a product used in construction, that would require large amounts of water?" I asked.

"Well, sure. Not 'made' but 'fabricated,' using large amounts of water. Take any operation where stone or marble are cut, where they fabricate pavers or tiles or stones for installation. There's tons of water running through that plant, enormous amounts every day."

"Explain it, please."

"So you have a big piece of some stone. Let's call it limestone. From Indiana," Bob began, working right at the basement level where he knew my knowledge of construction lay. "The limestone is shipped to the fabricating factory in big chunks. Has to be cut up, fabricated. Stone and marble operations have big saws to do the work. But the saw must be constantly sprayed with water. That's why such factories are always situated next to a river or a lake or a pond. That's so they can just pump the water in. Usually with some big hose."

"So then the water sprays on the saws and the marble . . ."

"Norie, the water sprays on everything. The guys who work in such plants wear waders. The mist is everywhere. It's like working in a rain forest."

I ran my finger down Mary Devine's list. "Old World Marble and Stone" jumped out at me. I had it.

I thanked Bob profusely, then called my nurse friend Frannie up in Jericho.

"Hello, I'm working the early shift," she mumbled into the phone, obviously a victim of her many grown children's late-night calls.

"Frannie, it's Norie Gorzack. I have a quick question. I know all your guys with the leukemia worked in construction. What exactly did they do?"

"Oh, ah, well, most of them are carpenters, and that's what they were doing when they got sick. Yes, carpenters, now that the economy is back on track. A couple plumbers. God knows, in this area, nobody in construction had construction work for a couple of years. It just all closed down."

"When the economy was bad, what did they do then?"

"Jeez, Norie, I have to go get my notebooks. Hold on."

In a minute she was back and I could hear her rustling through her notebook.

"Here's one. Okay, and another. Gee, I got a whole bunch of guys who all worked in one place for a couple years. Isn't that a coincidence? All in the same place."

"And do you have the name of the place they worked?" I asked her, praying that this would be the link.

"Yeah, it's here. Old World Marble and Stone. Over on Ellerbby Pond. That's it."

I told Frannie what I was zeroing in on, and she said she'd call me back with any further information when she got to the hospital early in the morning. I hung up and just sat in my darkened bedroom.

In my mind I could see those men I knew, up at Northeast Hospital, hooked up to IVs and tubes—and I could see them years before, probably thrilled to get regular work when the construction work petered out. I knew how these things happened. One guy got a job in Old World, and he called up his buddies, knowing they were all hard up for money.

So there they were, all strong and vibrant, working in that mist—that deadly mist—as the big saws cut the limestone and the marble.

And there was Joe Hauser, their union guy, finally

figuring out that their critical illness came not from their trade but from the unlucky happenstance of a bad time for construction guys out of work and a waste-removal company that didn't care how they did the work.

CHAPTER 30

Thanksgiving. That was the day George had set for a deadline, when he'd be back to me. Thanksgiving was here, but George wasn't.

His absence put a nasty autumn chill on a holiday I always loved. The crisis with George had left me deeply saddened, the stale air of crime and deceit somehow smothering me.

An early morning in Fairmount Park followed by the parade would be wonderful. I resolved to pick myself up and enjoy it.

When I got to the park, along the chilly Schuylkill River, young men and women were warming up to participate in the annual Turkey Trot—healthy young and old things running through the crisp air. Although the running craze was not around when I was young, the Turkey Trot was. Boys only then. No girls, as we called them.

People all over America have seen the park, but they don't usually know what it is, only some background trees. When Rocky runs to the top of the steps of the Philadelphia Art Institute, he's right on the edge of Fairmount Park. It goes on for miles—picnic areas and fields, the river always providing the best scenery in the city. Large flocks of gray and black geese are recent arrivals, showing up several years back—and deciding that all the Florida–Canada commuting was just too hectic, they stayed.

When the first wave of immigrants came from Europe they walked in the park and lunched in the park—while the already established Main Line gentry took their skulls out from the clubhouses on Boathouse Row and rowed the river. The faces of the runners this Thanksgiving Day were the essence of the many waves of migration that had washed on Philadelphia's shore. Or at least that's what I told them in the three-minute speech that set the stage for the starting gun.

One thousand of them, their numbers pinned onto sweats and tank tops, started to jog off, up the hill. I stood near the coffee table with Marco and Kathleen and counted the number of gray heads, and we told each other how we all planned to do more exercise this coming year.

What we really wanted to talk about we all plainly were ignoring, and that was the whereabouts of the fourth member of our little cabal. Strange, the election over and my winning and Kathleen having such a success and Marco feeling great about the union support. And George, who should have been part of all this, missing.

He said he would get back to me. And I believed him. So did Carver, who kept telling me to hold on, that friendship was, as he said, "thicker than mistakes."

I heard a shrill voice yelling my name and turned to greet Linda Vespucci, who, in honor of Thanksgiving, was wearing a feather turban that might have come directly off the tail of some turkey. I didn't have to introduce her to Kathleen, who had channeled Mrs. V.'s energies through five months of campaigning.

"So you're the union honcho," she said by way of introduction to Marco. "I didn't see you around the campaign office, doing any of the hard work. Now you show up, after she's won!"

Before he could answer her accusation, Mrs. V. turned to me.

"You wanna know what? I was on the Net this morning, which is what us computer types call the Internet. And I was looking for the Keystone Militia Web page and it was gone. Totally wiped out. Like it blew up or something," she finished up. "So, what do you think about that, huh?"

We just shook our collective heads in wonder, because I knew, Kathleen had learned, and Marco had obviously caught on to the fact that to argue with Mrs. V. was not a sensible thing to do.

"And you know what else is gone? The Values Coalition page. Which I only occasionally look at, but I figure I'm getting enough values at church, where I also do every single novena that's offered. But it's gone," she almost wailed, "and I don't know what happened to it."

We offered Mrs. V. a cup of coffee but she declined, saying she was heading to the parade and we could catch her there.

"How did we ever keep her under control?" Kathleen asked, but none of us laughed. There was something sincere and good about Mrs. V. And, this time, something quite fascinating in the information she brought.

"So *both* the Web pages—the Keystone Militia and the Values Coalition—shut down at the same time. What a remarkable coincidence!" I said with mock shock. "Maybe everything on the Internet was Vic Stample's baby," I offered.

"Now Stample's gone. With the cash. It would be ironic that it wasn't Dugdale using the Values Coalition, but Stample using both the organization and the candidate," Kathleen said.

"It's hard to tell—since I never met him. But, wait, Kathleen—you met him. When you negotiated their pickets away from my appearances. What was he like?"

She whipped her head around, like she was doing a double take, and burst out laughing.

"I never told you. There wasn't time at first, and then I guess I just forgot. He was very weird." Kathleen started to giggle. "He was very young. Like twenty-five years old. And he had an English accent that sounded put on. Somebody from south Philly playing Henry Higgins in the school play. But the strangest thing was that we had to pray before we had any discussion. So God could be part of our conversation."

"That's something," Marco muttered. "Especially since Stample was all the time taking up the collection."

"That's not the only thing, though," Kathleen insisted. "About the Web pages, he kept wanting to talk to me about the Internet and how God had designed the computer to write out his message."

"And all the time, young Vic was waiting to write himself a check. Very nice," Marco commented. "An answer to a prayer."

The reviewing stand sat squarely on the north side of City Hall, which could be my favorite building in the entire world, including St. Peter's and the Eiffel Tower.

I was not alone. Philadelphians were crazy for their City Hall, erected in the late nineteenth century along the lines of *hotel de ville*, the typical municipal building found in almost every French city—and I held myself to be a bit of a buff on its history. The center of city government and the courts, it was constructed in the crossroads of William Penn's colonial town, on one of the squares he set aside for public buildings and public spaces. Ranked as the country's largest municipal building—its city council chamber is larger than the House of Lords—it was hard to miss, as if Rockefeller Center rose up in the middle of Fifth Avenue.

With four eight-storied sides—that an architectural trick makes look like only four—its tower rose to just a few feet short of that of the Washington Monument. Of course the tower was augmented by the massive cast-iron statue of William Penn in his Quaker hat, surveying his metropolis below.

The building's location served as an obstacle to an easy traffic flow on ordinary days, but permitted, during parades, the crowd to yell in a time-honored tradition, "They're coming around City Hall," as each new band or float appeared.

This Thanksgiving, the sun shone brightly and my brown St. John's knit suit was enough protection against the rather mild weather. The stand itself was bright in the early-afternoon light. The stand had been built at exactly the height so the women in the reviewing seats could spend the entire parade wondering if their skirts were hiked up around their thighs.

Parades were good, I thought, especially when it was a blown-up squirrel waving at the crowd and not me. I was bone tired, the exuberance of the victory wearing thin, corroded by the stress of unfinished business, of George and the elusive Larry Shields. "Fight, fight, Cahillites" the Roman Catholic High School band shouted out as they passed by in review.

I was straining to see Winnie-the-Pooh coming around the corner when, out of the corner of my eye, I caught sight of George. Not by accident, since he was waving at me with his Phillies cap. He motioned for me to come down off the stand and meet him inside the archway.

I leaned over a municipal judge and told the mayor I'd be back in a moment.

"Don't miss the string bands, Norie," he warned.

Philadelphians were always nuts for string bands, and, although the New Year's Mummers Parade was their home base, a scattering would be found today. Or at the opening of a shopping center. Or when a team won even a division title.

"Mayor, I wouldn't miss it," I said with what I thought was a lot of conviction. I scrambled to the back of the platform and allowed a fire captain to help me down the rough wooden steps.

George had disappeared. I headed for the City Hall archway where I last saw him.

Once inside the arch, I felt the noise of the crowd behind me, almost like heat, while the light of the courtyard in front of me had a feeling of silence. My senses spun around. I was lightheaded and jittery.

George was just to my right, leaning against the large sets of doors.

"Quick. Here, inside. I've got to talk to you."

I ran toward him.

"I've only got a minute. I'm going away. But I couldn't go without seeing you, saying good-bye," George sputtered, hugging me close to him. "Just had to say how much your friendship—"

"George, for God's sake, you can't run away from this. Everyone wants to help. Marco, Kathleen—"

"I'm beyond help, Norie. I'm going to do the only thing I can do. I'm going to clean up as much of this mess as I can," he said, sounding calmer now. "That's very ironic, isn't it? That I'm going to clean up this mess. That's where I got into trouble. Saying Larry Shields and his phony trucking company had cleaned up two loads of radioactive material."

"Whatever happened, George . . ."

He wasn't going to listen to me.

"Whatever happened is that I closed my eyes. I didn't know because I didn't ask questions. And when you began to poke around about the vets and their leukemia, that's when I really started to duck. I stayed out of it. I didn't want to know."

"When did you know, George? When did you know that you were involved in what was happening?"

"When you started with those women, those sisters, their damn lake." He took a deep breath. "I knew Shields was making a fortune with his waste removal, and I assumed he wasn't doing everything by the book. Then I realized that if Shields was using the Pocono lakes as a dump site for his regular hospital waste, why not the 'hot stuff'? So I figured it out."

"And . . ."

"And I finally put a lot more together. Bercolini—well, I didn't realize that anything tied in when that happened. But Hauser—then I knew that something else might be coming. That Shields was crazy. That he had to be stopped. That he was a killer."

"And you were in his power. George, why? You had so much. You were so successful, so smart."

"Too smart, I thought I had the market figured out. The market of the late 1980s, and thank you very much, I wasn't as smart as the guys who sold out and got out. So I needed cash and I was gambling too much and the next thing I knew, here was my friendly neighborhood shark. Only he talked like us, and he went to Georgetown. Only he doesn't tell you that he only lasted one semester. Sick son of a bitch. That whole charade that he put us through. That woman."

"George, I've been trying to track her down. I feel sorry. She was someone who went to school with me. And now she's a dealer and forced to play this part."

"Probably into Shields for money. Or worse. But"—he looked down at me and flashed a smile I remembered—"I'm not one to make judgments. Anyway, I told him I'd phony up a couple of manifests. Once I did it, it was 'in for a nickel, in for a dime.'

And, as I have frequently said, old girl, it was off to the races."

"I can help, George. We can get lawyers," I pleaded, holding on to his arm. "We're real friends, George. We can help you. It's not like you're Larry Shields or anything."

My mother always said, "Say the devil's name and he appears at your shoulder." I'd done just that and I knew, without turning around, that Shields was behind me.

"Well, you've still got friends in high places, George," he said, and I turned to see him edge around to my left. "Me. I'm going to jail for a long time. But not you, right? You've taken care of yourself again, haven't you, George?"

"You took care of me, Larry. You tied me up in a tight little package. Just like you tied up that congressman after you murdered him."

George was shouting and Shields reached out to crack him across the face, I thought with his hand, but then I heard the smack of metal against bone and I realized he was holding a gun.

"You slimy son of a bitch," Shields screamed at George. The gun had smashed open George's face, and his body slumped against the wall and slid slowly down to the marble floors of the hallway.

"I'll kill you right here, you bastard," Shields bellowed.

Shields was blocking my escape, so I ran down the hallway, past dark offices, looking for another way out of the building. I turned a corner and ran to the next set of doors to the next archway up in front of me. But when I reached it the lock was on. I turned in terror to see Shields just yards behind.

I took the stairway. Up one flight, then another. I could hardly breathe, my chest hot and the air cutting into me like a sharp stone.

A little twist and turn. I knew I was in the tower, close to the observation deck at the feet of the Billy Penn statue. I pushed the steel-and-glass doors that opened on the deck. Locked!

I turned and ran up into the narrow stairway that went through the statue itself. My breath was gone, but I kept forcing myself on. For several long minutes, there were only two people in the world—me and my pursuer. I could hear his feet clang against the metal steps and, as I saw the light from the doors, I could also see that a wooden sawhorse cut off access. A large sign warned in English and Spanish that to proceed further would be dangerous.

I threw the sawhorse down, in back of me, and shoved on the doors. They were locked, but the bolts at the top and bottom had been left undone and, as I pushed my body's weight against the doors, the lock cracked and I was on the brim of William Penn's hat.

This was the original observation deck, closed many years ago and unknown to most people. Work was obviously under way, sawhorses and buckets lined up outside the door and orange plastic ribbons tied across the black metal railing.

Shields was behind me and my only hope seemed to be to edge my way around the hat and flee down the stairs ahead of him.

I took a few steps backwards, waiting for him to follow me, but he stood inside the doorway, his one arm braced against the doorframe, his hand waving the gun at me.

"Come here. Now. Come here," he shouted.

I stood back. It seemed an absurd thing to ask me. I might only be a few feet away, but I was half hidden behind the crown on Billy's hat and I wasn't giving up that little bit of protection.

"You heard me. Come here. Now. Or I'll shoot."

Why wasn't he shooting? I asked myself. Why not just rush out after me and start firing that gun?

George was unconscious on the ground floor. Nobody saw me come into the building. And I could hear the sound of string bands making their way up Market Street.

No one would notice the ping of a pistol above the riotous sound of the bands and the parade.

Why not go after me? As the thought raced through my head, I strained to see over the edge of the hat. Its breadth hid the sidewalk around City Hall from me—and hid me from the many police who were standing there.

It hit me. He *couldn't* follow me out on the hat. Larry Shields was afraid, afraid of heights. He had vertigo. He told me that. He couldn't stand heights.

I just had to wait, I thought. Eventually, someone

would realize I wasn't there or would find George in the hall. Unless—and this scared me—unless George managed to stumble away. He would have no idea that Shields pursued me, that I was trapped high on the edge of the hat.

"Trapped on the edge of Billy Penn's hat." It made me giggle. I couldn't stop it. Hysteria, probably, but I let the giggle rise to a laugh and opened my mouth and laughed out loud.

"Don't laugh at me, bitch. I'm coming out there and I'll deal with you," Shields screamed and lurched forward. He held on to the orange plastic that acted as a flimsy banister and started to inch his way toward me.

I slid backward, keeping him in my sights and hoping I wasn't in his.

We did this little dance for maybe a minute, slowly, carefully, each one of us following our prescribed steps.

"Norie, where are you?" The voice came from behind Shields. The crown of Billy's hat blocked my view and I turned and ran, trying to get around to the door to the deck, to the voice that I knew was George's.

Shields had the same idea, and went backwards.

We met, with George, at the entrance to the deck. Shields pointed his pistol at one of us, then the other.

I watched as George lunged toward him.

Shields stopped him with a quick shot that sent George to his knees. George clutched his stomach, red spurting out like some grotesque Gothic fountain.

I heard what I thought was Shields's victory cry, but I turned just in time to see him topple backwards over the side of Billy Penn's hat, to the street below.

I heard the screams from the crowd but rushed to George—pulling off my jacket, using it to try and stop the flood of blood.

And telling George even though he was unconscious, that he was my true friend and that he would be all right. I only believed half of what I said.

It was only moments before Carver and half the city's police force were upon us. The paramedics wrapped George's wound. They placed him on a narrow stretcher and started down the stairs.

Carver held me back—both on top of Billy Penn's hat and, minutes later, when George had been placed in an ambulance, and I had been kept from going with him.

"But why can't I see him, why not?" I cried, leaning on Carver, beating my fists against his chest in frustration and anger.

"Because he's gone. Forever. Dead, as far as we are concerned."

"But I could say good-bye. Just a few words."

"Norie, George is gone. It's all over."

Sometimes, when I'm doing something routine, I think about George Taylor. My friend, and, as it turned out, my protector.

I hope wherever he is, that he's happy.

Carver insists that the Witness Protection Program takes very good care of its participants, placing them in new lives and helping them get on with it.

I'll bet George is doing just fine.

The Philadelphia Daily News

WASHINGTON, D.C. (*Special to the Daily News*)—Eleanor (Norie) Gorzack was sworn in today as a member of the United States Senate representing Pennsylvania.

Senator Gorzack will fill out the four years remaining in the term of the late Senator Michael Gannon.

Political observers, here and in Harrisburg, see Gorzack's win as having real implications for politics in Pennsylvania.

SIGNET (0451)

THE *MURDER, SHE WROTE* MYSTERY SERIES

☐ MARTINIS & MAYHEM
Jessica can't wait for drinks and dinner on Fisherman's Wharf, a ride on the cable cars, and a romantic rendezvous with Scottish policeman George Sutherland in San Francisco. But what she doesn't know is that solving a murder may be penciled into her agenda.
(185129—$5.99)

☐ BRANDY AND BULLETS
A posh retreat in cozy Cabot Cove, Maine, offers struggling artists a European spa, psychiatry, and even hypnotism. No one, however, expected a creative killer. And when an old friend mysteriously disappears, Jessica Fletcher fears a twisted genius is at work writing a scenario for murder—putting Jessica's own life on the line.
(184912—$4.99)

☐ RUM AND RAZORS
From the moment Jessica Fletcher arrives at a four-star inn nestled by a beautiful lagoon, she senses trouble in paradise. She finds hotel owner Walter Marschalk's throat-slit corpse at the edge of the lagoon. It's time for Jessica to unpack her talent for sleuthing and discover if the murderer is a slick business partner, a young travel writer, a rival hotelier, or even the lovely widow Laurie Marschalk.
(183835—$4.99)

☐ MANHATTANS AND MURDER
Promoting her latest book brings bestselling mystery writer Jessica Fletcher to New York for Christmas. Her schedule includes book signings, "Larry King Live," restaurants, department stores...and murder?
(181425—$5.99)

All books written by Jessica Fletcher and Donald Bain